PRAISE FOR SHANNYN SCHROEDER

"Schroeder's latest For Your Love sizzler has everything a romance needs."

— RT BOOK REVIEWS, TOP PICK ON THROUGH YOUR EYES

"If this sweet romance doesn't have you dancing a jig, nothing will!"

— KIRKUS REVIEWS ON THROUGH YOUR EYES

"Schroeder infuses plenty of emotion into this strong love story."

— BOOKLIST ON IN YOUR ARMS

MEETING HIS MATCH

SHANNYN SCHROEDER

ISBN: 978-1-950640-20-1

Mac stormed into his mother's office, yanking at his tie. He pointed at her. "You set me up."

"Stop being melodramatic, Malcolm. What are you talking about?" She barely glanced up from the file in front of her.

Mac closed the door behind him and then saw Paul, his friend since college and recently hired PR consultant, sitting on the couch against the wall. He pinned Paul with a stare. "Did you know about this?"

"About what?"

Paul's face revealed nothing, but Mac knew the guy could bluff.

"I met with the producers, as you requested. They want to change the format." He looked between his mother and Paul, waiting for one of them to crack. The idea for the matchmaking show had been his mother's idea, and when the studio decided to move forward with it, it had been based on Mac being part of the show. They'd liked the spin of having a male matchmaker. Mac had agreed based on Paul's urging that it would help build the business.

His mother sat back in her leather chair and waved a hand as if swatting an imaginary fly. "They mentioned something about making some changes, but they didn't get specific."

Mac sank to the chair across from her. "They want to turn it into some kind of competition. To pit me against some dating expert." He barely managed to say it without using air quotes, but hell, he'd seen the videos of their so-called experts.

"And the problem, Malcolm?" His mother folded her hands on her lap. "Do you think you're not up to the challenge?" One eyebrow arched regally as she spoke. One thing Gail Sterling excelled at was looking superior regardless of what she was doing. She rarely let that image slip.

He wouldn't take her bait. He knew better. She was waiting for him to admit he didn't have the skills to take over Everyday Love. She was fine with him running the office and the books, but she didn't think he could be a matchmaker. "I have every confidence in my abilities. But the people they're looking at…" He pushed out a heavy breath. "Let me show you."

He rose and went behind the desk next to his mother. Paul joined them. Mac wasn't surprised Paul hadn't said anything yet. He'd always enjoyed the way Gail poked at Mac.

Mac stood his tablet up in front of his mom and tapped the screen. He flipped quickly through videos of the three contenders, all of whom were young women.

"They're cute," his mother said.

"They're not dating experts. They're pick-up artists who aren't interested in helping people find true love and commitment. They're looking to get laid."

Paul snickered. "Nothing wrong with that."

Mac shoved his friend's shoulder. "They're not taking the show seriously. They're making it a joke."

"It's only as bad as you allow it to be," said his mom. "If you're the matchmaker you say you are, the only people who matter are your clients. The competition has no effect on how you do your job."

Putting it like that was worse than poking him with a veiled dare. This challenged the core of who he was. And she knew it.

Paul tapped his shoulder. "You can't lose sight of the fact that this show, regardless of the format, will give us great publicity. You'll be poised to be *the* matchmaking company in Chicago. And your mom has a point. This pick-up artist won't have the skills and background you have, the reputation of this company. It'll be an easy win."

Mac absorbed what Paul said. When Mac had convinced his mother to bring Paul on as a public relations consultant to breathe new life into the company, he had never imagined going in this direction. He looked at Paul and Gail. "So we're going forward with this no matter what?"

His mother angled her head as she looked up at him. "Unless you back out. They don't want an old lady like me on camera. It's all about the hot, young studs."

Mac groaned. "Please don't. It makes me a little sick when you talk like that."

She laughed. As much as he resented the fact he'd come home last year to help with the business and she hadn't trusted him with clients, he loved his mom. Hearing her laugh was great. She'd been much too sad since his dad died.

He went back to his seat on the other side of the desk. "So if I go through with this, I'm in charge. You agree to retire and take it easy, leaving Everyday Love in my hands."

There went the eyebrow again. "If you do this *and* succeed."

He'd grown up in these offices, watched his parents build it from the ground up, long before *Millionaire Matchmaker* was a TV hit. He couldn't believe his mom was even entertaining the idea of selling the company.

"Define succeed. I can't control votes to win the contest."

"We'll figure it out."

"I want it in writing."

Her jaw dropped. "Don't you trust me? I'm your mother."

He smiled. "And because you're my mother, I know how you like to change the terms of an agreement."

"Paul is our witness." She swiveled in her chair to look at Paul. "He'll decide if you succeed, based on new clients brought in because of the show."

They weren't the best terms, but Mac could live with them. He nodded to his mom and shook Paul's hand. He knew how to read people and he knew he could be one hell of a matchmaker. In addition to his degree in psychology and years of working as a counselor, he'd spent most of his life watching his mom in action.

Yeah, this was a lock.

$\sim$

Natalie shoved through the door of her apartment and her roommate Jillian greeted her by taking the pathetic banker's box from her arms.

"How are you, sweetie?" she asked.

The question made things worse. Nat didn't know why she was still so upset. They'd given her notice her position was being cut. She'd known for weeks. But actually cleaning out her desk and walking out of the library that had been her home for the last two years was damn hard.

"I feel like crap. At least when people retire or quit because they're having a baby, they get a party." She tossed her purse on the chair and flopped onto the couch. "All I got was a bunch of 'I'm sorrys' and pitiful looks." She slowly tipped to the side until her face was in the purple pillows Jillian had bought to brighten up the place. "What am I gonna do?" she moaned into the soft cotton.

Jillian nudged her leg. "First, you're gonna sit up and have ice cream with me."

Natalie shoved up and accepted the pint and spoon. She scooped the first bite of chocolate peanut butter bliss into her mouth. She didn't think even her favorite ice cream could remove the pain of this day.

Jillian sat with her own, peanut butter-free ice cream. Natalie didn't know how she'd lucked out finding such an excellent roommate. They'd started out as strangers while both still in graduate school—library science for Natalie and law school for Jillian. In those early days, they hadn't seen much of each other, but over time they became best friends. Natalie couldn't think of anyone she'd rather have at her side right now.

Natalie stuck the spoon in the container and reached up with her free hand to let her hair down. Jillian smiled. "Maybe you should go out tonight. Gem could always use a new video," she offered, referring to Natalie's onscreen alter ego.

"Both Natalie and Gem are off the market for tonight. We want to wallow. Even Gem could appreciate that." For a moment it struck Natalie as strange that she spoke about both herself and her alter ego in the third person. But then, everything about this day felt strange. She wasn't a librarian anymore.

"You're wrong. Gem always wants to go out."

Nat rested her head on the back of the couch and closed her eyes. "Really, Jillian. I can't dress up and be bubbly and flirty. Not in a bar and not in front of the camera."

"I'll go with you, even if you don't go as Gem. Be Natalie. No video. We can still have fun."

Nat huffed. She'd discovered after her failed marriage that no, Natalie Hale was not fun. After that discovery, she'd done what she did best: research. She read everything she could get her hands on to learn how to attract men. Then she dated.

Gem was born because she needed an outlet for what she learned about herself and dating, but she wanted to keep that part of her life separate from her life as a librarian. It started as a blog and then she tried videos, recounting her dates. She'd never expected any of them to gain traction.

"Speaking of Gem," Jillian said. "I looked into that email you told me about."

Natalie opened her eyes and looked at her roommate. "And?"

Jillian smiled. "I don't know. I looked them up. Klein Studios is a real production company."

"What do they produce? Porn?"

Jillian laughed and Natalie felt a little better. "They do talk shows and a few local reality TV things. Might be legit."

"Why the hell are they emailing me? Sounds like a scam."

"It can't hurt to check it out. You're unemployed. If you do an appearance, it would be a paycheck."

Natalie sighed. Was her life really reduced to doing whatever possible just for a paycheck? "I don't know if I'm good enough to be Gem in front of other people."

Jillian licked her spoon. "Sure you are. I've seen it hundreds of times."

"I never thought something like this would happen." Things had gotten weird since a couple of her videos went semi-viral. The upside was that the monetization was kicking in, so she'd made enough money last month to treat herself to a mani-pedi. The downside was that the trolls came out in force so she had to be vigilant about monitoring comments.

"Well, it's not like either of us thought you'd become so popular with your blog and videos. I mean, *I* always knew you were special. I just wasn't aware the rest of the world would realize it." Jillian tapped Natalie's thigh. "No more moping. You've had weeks to moan about losing your job. Time to move on."

"I don't wanna," Natalie whined.

"Think of the example you're setting for all of your followers. You're the first to tell them to get back up, dust off their butts, and get in the game."

Natalie hated it when Jillian threw her own words back in her face. But she had a point. Pity parties wouldn't fix anything. While finding a date wouldn't fix her job situation, it would at least take her mind off it for the night. "Okay, let's go. You pick the place."

Jillian stood, still holding her ice cream. "Crap. I didn't think you'd agree. Now I have to get dressed again."

As Natalie marched toward her room to change, she called over her shoulder, "No lawyer clothes."

WHEN NATALIE AND JILLIAN RETURNED HOME HOURS LATER, Nat felt somewhat better. She still questioned if she should've gone home with Doug to take the remaining edge off. Jilly probably wouldn't have minded—not too much anyway. But it wasn't cool to leave a friend unless that was the plan.

As they kicked off their heels in the living room, she looked at Jillian. "Thanks for making me go out. It was worth it."

"Really?" Jillian asked. "If the guy was all that, why are you here with me?"

"I didn't say he was perfection. Probably not worth abandoning my friend in a bar." She sighed. "He was a pretty good kisser though."

"Then what was the problem?"

"His personality. He was boring. Very pretty to look at, though. I kissed him to shut him up."

Jillian laughed. "You're terrible. I'm going to bed. See you tomorrow."

"Uh-huh." Natalie went to her laptop and booted it up. She hadn't done a video for Gem in a while. She'd thought about tabling the videos and maybe even her blog for now, but without a job, what else did she have to look forward to? Recalling her night with Doug, she'd considered what to talk about.

Tonight, it was all about the touch. After freshening her make up, she opened her video program and started.

"Hi, everyone. I know it's been much too long since we've had a chat and I apologize. Sometimes silly things like life get in the way of my dating habits, but I'm baaaack." She smiled and winked at the camera.

"So here's today's Dating Gem. You know how I always say no matter how bad things are, you need to move forward? Today I needed that reminder and I'm glad my bestie was here to give it to me. I had a horrible day and after she plied me with ice cream, she dragged me out to a club."

She laughed a little. "I know, can you believe it? She had to drag *me*? Anyway, she got me dancing and drinking which loosened me up a bit. I felt myself open to possibilities. My body language immediately adapted and within minutes, I met a guy."

Natalie smiled again and licked her lips. "I saw him at the bar and he was good looking, cute in his sweater and Dockers. As a side note, let me just say I can't wait for summer to get here so guys will go back to wearing short sleeves to show off some arm. Anyway, I introduced myself and we started to chat. That's where he almost lost me.

"Something pick-up artists pay close attention to, besides the obvious body language, is touch. Now ladies, I'll tell you, guys who've studied the art of pick up have a whole routine about how and where and when to touch you. If they're doing it right, it won't make your skin crawl, but it'll lead you where they want to go. But regular guys? They kind of suck at it. The ones who are good touch everyone all the time, so it's a little more natural for them. But most guys are afraid. They don't want to turn you off or scare you away."

Natalie leaned forward like she was ready to spill a secret. "So it's up to you, ladies. You need to give them permission to touch you appropriately without saying anything. If you come right out and say, 'Touch me,' it's gonna get messy. Wrong kind of invitation. However, if you touch his arm lightly when he tells you a joke, you're closing the distance and letting him know it's okay to be in your space.

"Maybe reach around him to grab something instead of asking him to pass it. Let your arm, your shoulder—hell, your boob if he's cute enough—brush against him to show you're open to his touch. Unless he's a total dolt, he'll get the hint and make his move."

She settled back in her chair again. "As for Doug? He definitely took the hint. I almost went home with him. But at this point, I think you all know my rules. If you go out with a girlfriend, unless you're both out to pick up guys, you go home with your girlfriend."

Natalie firmly believed you shouldn't dump your friends for a guy. She'd learned her lesson about that long ago. "Doug didn't turn out to be much of a conversationalist, but he was one hell of a kisser. We exchanged numbers, so options are open. And next time, he'll be comfortable enough to start touching right away. Like fore-foreplay. Until next time."

Natalie clicked off and then spent a while editing and adding in her opening with logo. What had started as a personal experiment had developed into quite the little venture. Gem had a following. People actually listened to her advice. Natalie felt better knowing she spread some good in the world.

MAC SAT ON HIS COUCH AND SIPPED HIS WHISKY. PAUL CAME from the kitchen with a beer. Mac had missed hanging out with his friend for the years Mac and his wife had been living in New York. The divorce—and coming back to Chicago—had righted Mac's life. He'd become a man he didn't particularly like and being at home made him feel like himself again.

"I don't know why I'm drinking with you," he said to Paul. "I can't believe you let my mother do this shit."

Mac stretched his legs out and set his feet on the coffee table. As soon as he'd gotten home, he changed out of his suit and into jeans and a sweatshirt. Paul mirrored his movements, but he still wore a suit. Mac couldn't remember the last time he'd seen Paul in anything other than a suit.

"I didn't let your mom do anything. Gail does whatever she wants. We brainstormed options and ideas. The TV show was her idea, but it's not a bad one."

"I know. I was okay with doing it when it was just me helping people find love. That's what we do. But what the producers are doing now is pretty bad. It's gonna be a joke." He glanced at Paul from the corner of his eye. "But as my friend, you'll declare me a winner, right? No matter what."

Paul's face turned to stone. "You're my friend, man, but

Everyday Love is my client. I'll help your mom decide what's in the best interest for the company."

"You're fucking kidding, right?"

Paul took a slug of beer. "Nope. The company comes first."

Mac brought his feet back to the floor and braced his elbows on his knees. "This is my family's company and she's thinking about selling it." Gripping his glass, he swirled the amber liquid. "It's my legacy. I belong here."

Paul hadn't moved, so Mac looked over his shoulder. Paul shrugged. "Then don't fuck it up. Are you sure this is what you want?"

"Yeah."

"I know you think you do. But I remember in college how you talked about your mom's business. It was a joke. An embarrassment."

"I was twenty and love was nothing more than having a naked woman in bed. I am capable of learning from my mistakes." An image of Ariel, his ex-wife, swam in his head.

Paul pointed a finger at him. "And that right there is what I'm talking about. Your whole face changes when you think about Ariel."

Was he that transparent?

"I'm asking if it's Everyday Love that you want, or are you using it to rebuild your life after Ariel?"

"Both. I came back because my mom said she was thinking about retiring and selling the company." He finished his whisky. "Even after the divorce, I wasn't happy in New York. Coming back to Chicago, working at Everyday Love, it feels like home. I've learned everything my mom always tried to teach me about matchmaking. I can do this."

"Why do you want to?"

"Would you ask me that if I were a woman?"

"If you were a woman, I'd probably be trying to get you into bed."

Mac cringed. "My point is, I believe in true love. Even after—no, especially after—Ariel. I know what true love isn't. I should've listened to my mother when she told me Ariel wasn't for me." He pinned Paul with a look. "Don't you dare tell her I admitted that. She saw something I was blind to. But I can see it in other people. If I can't find it for myself, I can help other people find it."

He set his empty glass on the table. "For the last year of our marriage, I drove Ariel crazy because I kept setting up all of our single friends. Every date we had ended up being a double date. She thought I was too much like my mother. Maybe I am. I was good at it."

"Okay, man. If you're sure. It's one hell of a story. When the show hits, you're going to have offers. Magazines, interviews, probably a line of eligible women looking to hook up with a man who professes his belief in true love." He took another swig of his beer. "It's like a friggin' chick movie waiting to happen."

Mac hadn't considered those repercussions when he'd thought about the show. He'd only thought about it being a way for him to prove his skills as a matchmaker and businessman. "I only need that line of women to pay for my services." When Paul chuckled, he added, "As a matchmaker."

"So what's your worry about how the show goes down, then? Why does it matter who they have working against you?"

"Because they're all women. And the clients will all be women." Mac reached for his tablet. "The one that's in the lead—this Gem woman—there's something about her."

"Why is she in the lead? You didn't say anything at the office about her."

"Nothing's a done deal, but she's local so they save on

getting her here and the last couple of videos she's done have garnered a shitload of views." He pulled up "Dating Gem" on the tablet.

The screen filled with a beautiful woman with long, dark hair and wide bright blue eyes. They were almost enough to distract a viewer from the lush pink lips curved in a seductive smile. Gem began speaking about her latest excursion to a bar and how many guys she'd managed to meet. Twenty seconds in, Mac hit pause. Her face froze and if he kept looking at her eyes, he could get lost.

"That right there is the problem," Mac said. "She's cute and bubbly and entertaining. The camera loves her. The clients will love her. She's fun."

Paul laughed. "If fun is the goal, she'll have you beat hands down. But the producers want romance. Viewers looking for fun are going to MTV or something. If they want a catfight, they're watching some Real Housewives show. You have the chance to be better than *The Bachelor*."

Mac knew he could do this job. Maybe not as well as his mother had, but she'd been doing it for almost thirty years. He didn't know if he could do it in front of a camera. He stared at Gem and wondered why she'd become a pick-up artist.

"Look at it this way," Paul continued, breaking Mac's concentration on Gem. "She's looking to hook up, but the clients arc looking for the happy ever after. You can provide that. She—" he pointed at the screen, "—can only offer happy for the night."

"It seems unfair, though. You think she knows what she's getting into?"

Paul tapped Mac's thigh and then stood. "Not our problem. You do your job and win. I'm out of here. Early day tomorrow. Let me know if you hear anything from the producers."

"Will do."

Paul let himself out of the condo and Mac continued to stare at Gem's face. He didn't like the dishonest feel of the show's setup. He supposed once they hired Gem, or someone like her, he'd give her a friendly warning. Then it would be up to her to decide how to proceed. He was all for fairness in love and war.

CHAPTER 2

"Knock, knock," Jillian called as she pushed Natalie's bedroom door open, carrying two cups of coffee.

As soon as Natalie heard Jillian, she closed her eyes and pretended to be asleep.

"I know you're faking it. You never sleep past six and it's seven thirty." She sat on the edge of the bed and set the extra cup on the nightstand.

"I don't have a reason to be awake."

"Yes, you do. I called that studio. After talking with Bradley Winford, and informing him that I'm your lawyer, he assured me his offer is legitimate. You have an appointment in two hours. Go find out what the offer is, but don't sign anything until I look at it."

Natalie sat up in bed. "What?"

"Get dressed and get downtown."

She flipped off her blanket and got out of bed. "How could you do that? I don't know if I want any part of this."

"If I didn't do something, you'd still be sitting here wondering. This way, you find out what they're offering and then decide if you want to do it. Besides, your video from the other night already has over a hundred thousand hits. You're a star." Jillian handed her the cup of coffee.

Natalie accepted it and took a gulp. The hot liquid sloshed in her stomach. How could Jillian do this to her? A TV show. She didn't belong on TV. She belonged in the stacks. The thought made her stomach turn again. She didn't have a job. If this TV thing was paying, she should consider it.

Jillian stood. "I have to get to work. Do I have to be late in order to make sure you go to the meeting?"

"No. I can be an adult." The statement might've been more convincing if she'd said it without a pout.

"It's just a meeting. Get the information. See how it sounds. We'll discuss it tonight."

Jillian left and Natalie stared at her closet. For the last couple of days, she'd lounged around the apartment in her pajamas, not seeing the point of getting dressed. She knew Jillian had her best interest at heart by making this appointment. Natalie would feel better getting dressed like a professional.

She pulled her interview suit from the hanger. It was the one she'd worn to get her last job. It would be good practice for future librarian interviews. Jillian had a point. Natalie had spent enough time wallowing. She needed to update her résumé and get back out there. After tying her hair back, she applied a bit of makeup. She glanced at her contact lens case and debated.

Forget it. This was a business meeting, not a date. In just under an hour, she was out the door and on her way to her first interview that wasn't an interview.

She made good time getting downtown to the studio. Once at the office, she gave the receptionist her name and took a seat. She looked around at posters lining the walls.

There wasn't one show she knew. She sighed. This wasn't where she belonged.

"Ms. Hale?"

Natalie turned.

The receptionist nodded at her. "They're ready for you. This way."

She led the way back to a conference room. Inside, five people looked up. A middle aged good-looking guy stepped forward, his eyes slightly narrow as he took her in. "Ms. Hale, I'm Bradley Winford. I spoke with your lawyer."

Natalie shook his hand. "It's nice to meet you."

He gestured to a chair and Natalie sat. He proceeded to introduce the other people sitting around the huge oval table, but she felt so out of place, she wasn't paying attention. She folded her hands over her crossed legs and waited for Mr. Winford to get to the point.

Unfortunately, he simply sat and stared at her. After a few minutes, she was ready to squirm in her seat. "I'm sorry, Mr. Winford. Is there a problem?"

"To tell you the truth, I'm not sure. You're not what we were expecting."

She tilted her head and considered what he meant.

"We've only seen you online and this—" he pointed awkwardly at her, "—is different. You're obviously the same woman we saw online, but not exactly."

"Oh," she said, realization dawning. "You expected me to look like Gem."

"Well, actually, yes, we didn't know that…"

He didn't seem to know how to finish without sounding like an ass, so Natalie put him out of his misery. "Mr. Winford, Gem is an alter ego. I'm a librarian by day, so I didn't want to be myself while putting my dating life online. I've carefully separated the two areas of my life. In the real world, I'm Natalie Hale. Online, I'm simply Gem."

He stared, looking almost like he didn't believe her.

"Seriously?" she asked, arching an eyebrow. "Excuse me one minute," she said and turned her back to the group.

Her interview suit was definitely the wrong outfit to pull this off, but she'd have to make do. She let her hair down and fluffed it, knowing it wouldn't look as good as it would if she were heading to a bar, but it would get her point across. She dug through her purse and found her favorite red lipstick and swiped it on. Then she added some glitter eye shadow for emphasis. Lastly, she flicked open a couple buttons on her blouse.

When she spun back around, she pulled her glasses off, winked at Mr. Winford and held her arms close to her body as she leaned forward because it would increase the appearance of her cleavage. You could never go wrong with more cleavage.

He barked out a laugh. "Oh my. That's who we're looking for."

Natalie slid her glasses back on her face so she could see what everyone was doing.

"I'm sorry for the misunderstanding, Ms. Hale, but when you came in you definitely looked more librarian than dating siren."

Dating siren. That was a new one.

"Now that I've proven who I am, can we get down to business? I'd like to know more about what this show is you spoke with my lawyer about. It seems odd for you to reach out to me. Like I said, I'm a librarian, not an actress."

Mr. Winford settled back in his chair. "We're not looking for an actress. We need a fresh face. We're going to be producing a reality dating show. You would be competing against a professional matchmaker. Over the course of six weeks, you will each meet with the same three clients. You help the clients find true love."

Natalie listened. She didn't know what she'd expected, but it wasn't this. "What's the point of the competition? If you already have a matchmaker on board, why do you want me?"

"We believe you, or someone like you, will keep things interesting for viewers. Your approach to dating is different than how a matchmaker works. We want you to teach others what you've learned about dating."

"You still haven't explained the point of the competition. What would I get out of this?"

Winford smiled again, a slick smile this time. "You'd get paid for doing the show, of course. Then we plan to offer ten thousand dollars to the winner of the competition."

Ten thousand dollars? Natalie gulped and did her best not to let them see how much that would mean to her. She inhaled slowly. "And how exactly is the winner determined?"

"Since this is our first run, the show will be a web series, online, streaming only. The market is ripe for this kind of show with the right social media exposure. We'll film everything and air the first episodes. A week later, we'll air the other half of the season. After they've all aired, we'll tape one final episode as a wrap up. During that time, the clients will each vote for which of the two of you they felt offered better advice. In addition, we'll host an online voting platform which will remain open between the airing of the last episode and the finale."

It was a lot to take in. She still had no idea why her. "When do you need an answer?"

"By the end of the week. We'd like to start filming within the next two weeks." He slid a folder across the table toward her. "Here's our boilerplate contract. Have your lawyer look it over and let us know if you have any questions."

Natalie nodded and reached for the folder. Then a very important thought hit her. "Since you're obviously looking for Gem to star on this show, does that mean no one will know my real name?"

"What do you mean?"

"I mean, I can choose to be Gem and no one will even know Natalie Hale exists?"

"You can work under whatever name you prefer, Ms. Hale." He stood. "We look forward to hearing from you."

Natalie left the office in a daze. In her car, she glanced at the contract and the words jumped and blurred. They hadn't just talked about a show; they'd offered her a job. She couldn't deny she was a little excited about the prospect of doing something—something she loved—and getting paid for it. She'd been giving advice on her blog and in videos for free to a mostly anonymous audience.

She blew out a breath and took a moment to tie her hair back. Six weeks. That's what Winford had said. Six weeks of work on a show and she could still look for a library job. And if she won the competition, she wouldn't have to panic or dip into her savings to survive.

Tossing the folder on the passenger seat, she wouldn't decide until Jillian scoured the contract. Even Natalie knew that boilerplate meant there was room to negotiate. What to negotiate for was a different story.

On the way home, she stopped and bought a bottle of wine to share with Jillian. It was part bribe, part celebration.

At least her life was moving forward. It might not be the exact direction she'd hoped, but it was movement.

Natalie spent the next few days revising her résumé and looking for a new job while Jillian handled negotiating the TV contract. Jillian had consulted an entertainment attorney and thankfully thought of things Natalie hadn't considered.

Like having cameras in her face all the time. Jillian made them limit that to studio work and in the field with the clients, like on dates, but they wouldn't be allowed to follow her home.

What a laugh everyone would have. Gem, dating expert at home. Wouldn't they all be surprised to learn how quiet her real life was? It would probably ruin her chances of winning if the audience learned she was a fraud.

In between stressing over her résumé and combing through job listings, Natalie read up on Everyday Love, the matchmaking company that would be her competition. That was another piece of information Jillian had gotten for her.

Everyday Love's web site was woefully out of date. Actually, it was dated. The information was current, including services and what a client could expect, but the site itself wasn't very fresh or welcoming. She found Gail Sterling, however, to be a fascinating woman. On the web site, she appeared distant and almost snooty, as if everyone was beneath her. Natalie had no idea how a headshot could convey that, but hers did.

But when Natalie Googled her to read more, she found troves of articles on the woman. The journalists and bloggers did her justice in a way her own web site hadn't. After reading about Gail and her experience, Natalie knew she didn't have a chance at winning the competition. Natalie didn't have anywhere near the experience Gail had. The woman had been matchmaking for almost as long as Natalie had been alive.

Jillian came through the front door looking beat. Sad that was the norm for her friend, but at least she was employed. She plopped on the chair across from where Natalie worked on the laptop.

"What's up?" Natalie asked.

Jillian dropped a pile of papers in front of her. "Your

contract is done. Look it over and if it's good, sign both copies. They want to meet later this week to get things moving."

"Wow. That happened fast."

"Well, there wasn't much to negotiate. I asked for more money, but since you have no experience, that argument didn't really have legs. They gave me your name and your privacy, so I figure that's a win. There's also a non-compete and NDA, so no writing or vlogging about this until it's over."

"I'm supposed to abandon my blog and YouTube channel?"

"No. You can do what you normally do and promote the show. You just can't talk about specifics. You know, you can't give away what hasn't aired."

Natalie picked up the contract and flipped through it. "Is it good?"

"You have to decide, Nat. If you want to do the show, this is probably as good as it's gonna get." Jillian kicked off her heels and wiggled her toes.

"Okay, then. I guess I'm doing TV." She looked at her exhausted friend. "If by some miracle I win this, I'm taking you on vacation."

Jillian laughed. "As if I have time for a vacation. I'd settle for a weekend in bed."

"I'm going to be a matchmaker soon, so I bet I can arrange that."

They laughed and Natalie got up to get the wine. As she poured a glass for each of them, they talked about Everyday Love and what Natalie had learned.

"I still don't get why they want me," she said. "Is their goal to show young versus old? Expert versus newbie?"

Jillian sipped her wine. "Whatever their expectation, they're not going to say. It would ruin the *reality* feel of the show. But watch your back. You know they're going to set up drama."

"How? We're setting women up on dates, teaching them techniques, helping them find love."

"What if they put the same guy in the path of all the clients? Drama."

Natalie froze with her wine at her lips. She hadn't thought about such a possibility. "You think they'd do that?"

"And have the chance to catch a catfight on TV? Hell, yeah, they would." Jillian drank again and closed her eyes.

Natalie had never been a fan of reality TV, so she never thought about how real or scripted anything was. "Okay. I'm going to sign this and then you're going to help me develop a list of possible things to look for and avoid. You've watched a gazillion episodes of reality TV. I bet you have it all catalogued in your head."

Jillian laughed again. "Not much to figure out. Imagine the worst possible scenario and they'll try to make it happen. Every. Week."

Natalie's stomach sank a little. She wanted this. She hadn't realized how much until talking with Jillian right now. She bit her lip.

Jillian patted her hand. "You'll be fine. You're not a drama queen and you're not rattled easily. You're a smart girl. It works to your advantage that they've totally underestimated you."

Natalie gulped her wine and prayed Jillian was right.

~

MAC PACED THROUGH THE RECEPTION AREA WAITING FOR Bradley Winford and this Gem person. He'd yet to get a last name on the woman. He tried sitting on one of the armchairs but was too restless. He'd asked Paul to come to the meeting, but he'd had other clients to deal with. As Mac made another circuit through the room, cursing himself for his need to arrive everywhere early, the front door opened and Gem strode through, looking a little harried.

Once inside, she smoothed a hand over her hair and down her dress, which was blue, a shade darker than her eyes. The front dipped low, but not immodestly so. She rolled her lips together and trekked on crazy high heels to the receptionist's desk. She was told to have a seat, the same way he'd been.

She sat on a chair, her back stiff and hands folded in her lap. Briefly closing her eyes, she inhaled deeply and when she reopened them, her gaze met his. Her left eyebrow quirked but didn't make it to a full arch. Her lips moved incrementally into a smile. Then she shot her gaze downward.

Shifting on the chair, she angled her body and crossed her legs. She knew exactly how to draw a man's eye, he'd give her that. Eyelids lowered slowly and then she glanced up at him again, barely making eye contact.

Was she seriously hitting on him?

When she brushed her hair off her shoulder—not quite a flip—he confirmed it. She was flirting. He stayed rooted to his spot, afraid to continue his pacing because then he might miss something good. Slipping his hands in his pants pockets, he rocked back on his heels waiting for her next move.

Really, if this was the best she had, he truly had no worries about competing against her.

When he didn't respond to another smile or a too-obvious bend at the waist to reveal cleavage, she stood. She strode with a slow, hip-swaying swagger to where he stood and pointed at the poster behind him. "Have you ever seen this show?"

Her voice was low and slightly husky. In the right room at the right time, it was the kind of sound that would've had an effect on him. He ran his tongue over his teeth and looked at the poster.

"No, I've never seen it."

"Too bad. I was hoping you could tell me if it's worth binging." She reached in her purse and pulled out a pack of gum, offering him a piece.

He shook his head but continued to watch her. She slowly folded the stick of gum on her pink tongue and when she reached around him to toss the wrapper in the trashcan, she not too subtly brushed against his arm.

"Excuse me," she whispered. When she straightened, she extended her hand. "Hi, I'm—"

"Good, you're here." Bradley Winford's voice boomed through the room.

Gem turned, smile bright. "Mr. Winford, good to see you again."

Winford shook her hand a little too vigorously. "I see you've met Malcolm."

What Mac wouldn't have given to see her face.

"Who?" she asked.

Brad pointed to him. "Malcolm Sterling, your competition for the show."

Slowly, she turned and the look on her face was even more priceless than he'd imagined.

Mac stepped forward. "Malcolm Sterling from Everyday Love."

A flash of something came across her face, her mask slipping. It wasn't just surprise. There was something else there. Quickly, she schooled her features back into the flirt. It seemed to be the only thing she did quickly. She shook his hand and offered a brief smile.

"Nice to meet you, Malcolm. Gem."

Brad clapped his hands. "Let's get this started, shall we?"

Gem turned and followed Brad. Mac fell into step beside her.

"My friends call me Mac."

"Excuse me?"

"Only my mother calls me Malcolm."

"That would've been useful information to have, oh, say, ten minutes ago. You obviously knew who I was the minute I walked in." Her voice came out a sharp whisper so Brad couldn't hear.

"I did," he admitted.

"Any reason you didn't introduce yourself?"

"I was enjoying your flirting techniques."

She shook her head and stepped into the conference room. She waited until Brad took a seat and took the one directly across from him. Mac chose the seat beside her.

She shot him a look of irritation.

Suddenly Mac decided this adventure might not be so boring after all.

A slim redhead with her hair in a tight bun came up behind them and set black folders on the table in front of each of them. She handed one to Brad with a smile before settling in a chair behind Brad.

Gem scooted her chair closer to the table. "I feel like I'm at a disadvantage here, Mr. Winford."

"First, call me Brad. Why a disadvantage?"

"Before arriving today, all I knew was that Everyday Love would be on the show. No one mentioned Malcolm here at all. I thought I'd be working with Gail Sterling."

Mac wasn't sure if he imagined it, but she might've put a little extra emphasis on his name. "Don't you mean working against?"

She waved her hand. "Semantics. I'd hoped to work with her. Even learn from her. Everything I've read about Mrs.

Sterling tells me she has an amazing track record for helping get people together."

"Malcolm is her son. We think pairing the two of you on the show will draw viewers across demographics."

Gem slid Mac an assessing look.

"Checking out the competition for real this time?" he murmured.

She opened her mouth and then closed it without a word.

"I have a question," Mac said. "You know who I am. Who are you?"

Her eyes remained locked on his. "Gem."

"Gem? That's it? No last name?"

"Just Gem. Like Madonna or Cher."

Brad cleared his throat. "Gem prefers to work under her pseudonym. Under contract, we won't reveal her legal name. If she chooses to share it, it would be up to her."

"I'm good with Gem," she said, breaking eye contact and turning back to Brad.

Mac wondered why she needed to continue with a fake name even in the privacy of the office, no cameras.

"As you know," Brad started, "we plan to have cameras on the two of you throughout the entire process. Today will be the only day we meet without cameras in the room."

Gem's swallow was nearly a gulp. Mac nodded.

"In addition to filming you coaching the clients, we'll also get one-on-one time with each of you to critique what's happening with the clients."

"So you expect us to bash each other when the other isn't around," Gem said.

Interesting take on what Brad said.

Brad chuckled. "I'm sure a little criticism wouldn't hurt."

NATALIE WAS HAVING A HARD TIME KEEPING UP HER GEM persona. After rushing to the studio, flirting with Malcolm had seemed a natural way to play her part. Too bad he wasn't just some sexy stranger for her to hit on. But now, listening to Brad talk about the expectations for the show, she began to think Jillian had been right.

The fire in her belly wouldn't settle, but she hoped to keep it contained. "So you want us to fabricate criticism to liven up your show?"

Malcolm shifted next to her. "I didn't sign on to have someone make fun of my company or my methods. I thought this was about helping people find love."

Like he was the one with something to worry about. Malcolm's gaze swung to her as if she'd said it out loud. She hadn't, had she?

Brad held up a hand. "It is. However, I think we all know if everything goes smoothly, no one will watch. Viewers want drama. Our hope is that because your approaches are so different, there will be disagreements. That's the reason cameras will be with you as well as with the clients. Your up-front shots will be like a video diary of the process. You can discuss the clients or each other. Whatever works."

"No, not whatever works," Natalie said. "My…" she searched for the right word, "colleague here, obviously knew who I was before my arrival. If he spent any time on the Internet, he'd know how I operate, what I do. I know nothing about him. In addition, this competition is hardly fair given that Malcolm has a company behind him with thirty years' experience."

"She didn't know what she was getting into?" Malcolm asked Brad.

How she *hated* when people talked about her as if she didn't exist, sitting right in front of them. "In my original meeting I was told there would be a professional matchmaker, which as I'm sure you're aware, could mean any number of things. I just found out about Everyday Love a couple of days ago."

"She's right, Brad. It's not a fair competition. She doesn't have a chance." Malcolm leaned back in his chair and crossed an ankle over a knee.

Natalie's hackles rose again, so she clamped her jaw tight.

Brad looked at them.

Before he could say anything, Malcolm spoke up again. "To even things out, you can have access to my mother. Gail Sterling founded Everyday Love. She's been a matchmaker for almost thirty years. I'll set up a meeting right now." He pulled his phone from his suit coat.

"Why the hell would your mother help me?"

His steely blue eyes met hers with a smile. "Oh, don't get me wrong. She won't help you win. But she can answer any questions you have about matchmaking, her process, whatever you think I know that would give me an unfair advantage."

"Why would you attempt to even the field?" Her suspicions multiplied.

Malcolm leaned over, putting his face within touching distance. It was a mighty fine face: his blue eyes had the slightest lines fanning out from them, his mouth surrounded by a trim mustache and beard—one that begged to be touched, lips curved between a friendly smile and a taunting smirk.

"Because when I beat you—and make no mistake, I will win—I won't have you cry foul. I play fairly."

Natalie opened her mouth with no clue what she planned to say.

Brad pounded on the table. "This. This is it exactly. I wish I had a camera in here right now."

Both Natalie and Malcolm swung to face Brad. Natalie

had almost forgotten he was there. Where the hell was her head? Her argument with Malcolm had taken on a life of its own. In that brief conversation, she learned one very clear lesson. She needed to keep her wits about her. Malcolm was every bit the worthy adversary.

She settled back in her chair, pulling away from Malcolm's orbit. "I'll take the meeting with your mother." She turned back to Brad. "What's next?"

Brad pointed to the folders. "Here's the schedule."

They all flipped open the folders and took a few minutes to scan the calendar. Natalie was surprised to see they planned to start filming within the week. In two days, they were to meet again to go over the selected clients. Then two days later, she and Malcolm would meet with the first woman.

"We get to meet the clients alone, right?"

"Cameras will accompany you, as I said."

Natalie shook her head. "No, I mean, I meet with them and then he meets with them separately."

"For the initial meeting, yes. The rest, we're playing by ear."

She nodded and waited for Malcolm's input. Nothing. Maybe none of it mattered to him. He was so cocksure he'd win. Well, she'd show him. Although she'd started this for the paycheck, now she wanted to do well. She didn't know if she could win, but she would definitely try.

The one thing she had going for her was that as much as Malcolm thought he knew about her, he didn't know Natalie. The librarian, the researcher, the student in her would suss out every bit of information about Malcolm Sterling, the matchmaker.

CHAPTER 3

*M*ac left the meeting with Brad and Gem filled with a new purpose: find out who Gem really was. He'd come to the studio today as a formality. It didn't matter to him what Brad had planned. Mac knew he'd win the competition. He'd prove to his mother he was more than ready to take over Everyday Love. Gem had been nothing more than a pretty face on the Internet.

When he'd seen her mask slip at their introduction, he'd been intrigued. He immediately knew there was more to her than the brief bit he'd watched online. He didn't believe for a moment she worried about a level playing field. She had to know she was out of her league.

Yet she pushed.

Whatever happened during that moment when he'd offered a meeting with his mom caused a spark. He felt what Brad had seen. Mac knew himself well enough to know that if Gem truly was nothing more than an Internet confection, that wouldn't have happened. She asked smart questions, held some safe suspicions.

Outside the studio, she nodded at him and rushed off to

her car. He tried not to watch the muscles of her calves lengthen or the sway of her ass in her dress. He failed. Pulling his phone out again, he called Paul.

"What's up?"

"I need you to dig into this Gem person."

"You do know I work for your mom, not you, right?"

"Trust me. This is information we all need. Gem is a pseudonym. I just left our first meeting, and even with no cameras involved, she insisted on using Gem. No last name. Nothing."

"So?"

"There's more to her. That's all I'm saying." Mac unlocked his car and climbed in.

"I'll see what I can find out. Call you later."

They disconnected and Mac went to the office. His mother was meeting with clients, so he had some time. At his desk, he booted up his computer and Googled "Dating Gem." In addition to the videos, she had a blog. He scrolled through the pages of posts to get to the first one. He knew he'd find the most personal information there. Before she'd honed her craft and her online persona, she would've been closest to her real self at the beginning.

Her first post was relatively short, explaining the title of the site. Growing up, her grandmother had told her if a guy didn't treat her like a precious gem, he didn't deserve her. Gem had decided she would explore the world of dating and share her own dating gems with her audience.

Mac wondered at what point Gem had become her name. It didn't seem like that had been her intention at the beginning. He read a few posts and gleaned a bit about her, just as he'd thought. She was divorced and from what he could tell, the guy did a number on her. If he had to guess, her ex had cheated.

After a few months of online dating, she'd given up. Too many liars. No shit.

Then she had a slew of posts that were book and video reviews of pick-up artists and dating experts. This was the beginning of her change. Her dating posts after that point were reports of her attempts at implementing what she'd learned from her self-education.

She appeared to have great success. Not all that surprising. He'd seen a couple of her videos and now he'd met her. She was beautiful and engaging. In her videos, she tended to disguise her intelligence, leaning towards bubbly frothiness, but in person, she failed at hiding it.

The more he learned, the more he wanted to know. The problem was, he wasn't wholly convinced it was all about the TV show and competition.

Paul called and said he'd had no luck getting Gem's real name. Confidentiality and all that. Mac decided his mother was his best chance to get anything. He strode down the hall to his mom's office and knocked.

"Come in."

He pushed through the door. Upon entering, he was reminded why he preferred to meet in his office. Hers was too frilly and fussy. His mom believed the best way to get people to open up was to make them feel at home. Mac didn't disagree, but this space was just a bit too comfortable.

"Mom." He took a seat across from the desk.

"What can I do for you?"

"Did your assistant tell you about the meeting with Gem tomorrow?"

"Who?"

"Gem. From the TV show?"

"I haven't looked at tomorrow's schedule yet."

"We had our first meeting today. Long story short, she feels at a disadvantage because I have a successful matchmaking company behind me. I told her she could talk to you, get whatever insight she thinks she needs."

"Oh, Malcolm. How silly are you? You're going to give away all of your knowledge and training? Your edge? How do you expect to win?"

He sighed. "I'll win by being better at helping people find love. I have faith in myself. Wish you did too."

He leaned forward and braced his elbows on his knees. "I want this to be fair. I want the show to showcase the fact that I'm honest. Trustworthy."

"So what exactly do you need from me?"

"Answer her questions." He shifted back in the seat. "I also want your take on her."

The corner of his mom's mouth inched up. "Now that sounds interesting."

"After meeting her today and digging into her blog a little more, I can't get a read on her. Nothing matches."

"And?"

"And I want to understand who she is so I know how to best beat her."

"Is that all?"

"Of course. What else would there be?"

She shook her head as if he missed the point of the conversation. He knew that head shake better than any other movement his mother made. Right now, he didn't want to know the reason behind it.

Natalie hadn't been sure how to dress for her meeting with Gail Sterling. Sure, this was all part of preparation for the show, but Natalie didn't like being Gem all the time. She'd begun to question if she had it in her to maintain it.

She settled on Gem's hair and makeup, but Natalie's wardrobe.

Thinking about her wardrobe made her realize she'd have to invest in more outfits for Gem. Her selection was enough for clubbing and dates, especially since she rarely went on more than four dates with any guy. Beyond four, it started to feel like a relationship. If she had to be working with clients and going out with them, she needed more options. She tabled the idea for later and left for her meeting.

She parked on the street near the Everyday Love office. She'd prepared a notebook with some questions just in case she needed them. Inside the building, Natalie rode the elevator up to the fourth floor. The building was located in Chicago's Gold Coast, so the business must've been doing well enough to afford these rent prices. The location had Natalie questioning her expectations.

According to the web site, Everyday Love had been created with the idea that everyone, regardless of the size of his or her bank account, deserved help to find love. Having offices in this part of the city created an image of people with money. Much like Malcolm Sterling himself.

His suit had been bespoke, fitting him perfectly. Definitely not off the rack. Natalie had always loved a man in a good suit.

She shook her head as the elevator doors opened. She absolutely did not need to think about how good Malcolm looked in a suit. Or what he might look like out of it. Heat crawled up her neck with that thought.

Natalie bit the inside of her cheek and walked to the reception desk. "Hi, I'm Gem. I have a meeting with Gail Sterling."

The receptionist nodded and stood. "Right this way."

Natalie followed her down a hall, passing two other offices with closed doors. She briefly wondered if Malcolm was behind one of them. Would he be part of her meeting with his mom?

At the end of the hall, the receptionist swung the door open and waited until Natalie walked through. Then she left.

Gail Sterling stood behind her desk looking as exquisite as she did online. In a classy suit that probably cost more than one of Natalie's librarian paychecks, she came forward with a smile.

"You must be Gem."

Natalie halted for a minute. Yeah, answering to Gem all the time would take some getting used to. "Hi, Mrs. Sterling. It's nice to meet you."

"Gail, please." She pointed to a leather couch against the back wall. "Have a seat and let me know how I can help you."

They sat and Natalie pulled her notebook from her bag. "I'm not quite sure how, or even if, you can help me. As I'm sure you're aware, I'm not a matchmaker, yet the producers of this show expect me to compete against your son. It seems a little unfair for him to have all of your expertise at his back while I've got nothing but my own experiences."

Gail laughed quietly. "Well, your personal experiences might count for more than you'd expect. While it's true Malcolm grew up being surrounded by this business, I won't be helping him during the show. He needs to do this on his own."

Hmm…Natalie found that interesting. She hadn't gotten a hint of tension from Malcolm when he brought up his mother. If they didn't get along, why would he do this show?

"Oh, I think I'm going to like you," Gail said. "I can see your wheels turning as I speak. Just out with it. What do you want to know?"

Natalie cleared her throat. She hadn't expected Gail to be so upfront. "I was wondering why you aren't willing to help

Malcolm. I mean, obviously, if he succeeds, your company benefits."

"You're right. However, I need to see how Malcolm will do on his own. He wants to take over when I retire, which will be soon. I love my son dearly, but he's always been too business-oriented for my liking. Not everything can be boiled down to a transaction. I need to know he has the heart for the job."

This interview was far more interesting than Natalie had imagined and she'd only been in the office for five minutes. "Can you explain what you mean by having the heart? This is a business for you. You can't ignore that."

"I never ignore it. But it's only part of the equation for success. You have to believe in true love. You have to believe in the magic of falling for the right person." Gail winked. "I'm not sure my son does. Do you?"

Natalie's heart raced. Did she? Part of her longed for the passion of falling in love, but she wasn't so sure about the true love and soul mate stuff. Once upon a time she had. "I believe it's possible to find the right person to love, yes. If Malcolm doesn't believe in that—in love—why would he surround himself by it every day?"

"Good question. I'm not sure of the answer." She sighed. "I'm afraid we've gotten off course. I think you were supposed to ask me about matchmaking."

"Yes." Natalie fumbled with the notebook. "What's your process? How do you start?"

"These days, it's a lot more complicated than it was when we began."

"We?"

"My husband and I founded Everyday Love together. We were married for thirty happy years. Throughout that time, we helped forge hundreds of successful relationships."

Natalie envied the look of happiness on the older woman's face.

"My process, back when we started was simple enough, and it's still the first step today. I talk with the client. I listen to what he or she wants. Sometimes I get someone who I don't believe is looking for love and commitment. It's evident in that first conversation, so I suggest he or she comes back when truly ready."

"I bet that doesn't go over real well."

"Not usually. But given time, they discover I'm right. And when they return, they're glad I turned them away the first time."

"What about those you don't turn away? How do you know they're ready?"

"That's the question, isn't it?" Gail crossed her legs and leaned against the arm of the couch, studying Natalie. "It's mostly a feeling. I ask them questions about past relationships to discover their current mindset. It's not enough for them to say they're ready for love."

"Unless you can teach me to know the feeling, this doesn't help much."

"If you'd like, you can spend a day here in the office. See how we interact with clients."

"We?"

"My staff."

"How many matchmakers do you have on staff?"

"Just me."

She didn't count Malcolm. Curious.

"But I have others who do some of the beginning interviews and they help decide who we pair up. They work on generating information for our database, and they help with all of the networking."

The more Natalie heard, the more complicated it appeared.

"Tell me about yourself, Gem."

Natalie started at the demand. She hadn't considered Gail wanting to know about her. She should've expected it. As much as Natalie wanted to learn about Gail and Malcolm, of course Malcolm would want to know who he was up against. "What do you want to know?"

"I suppose I'd like to know who you really are because Gem isn't your real name, but I won't invade your privacy. Why don't you tell me about why you've agreed to do this show with my son."

"In all honesty, I could use the money. I was recently laid off from my day job, and I'm using this to fill in until I find something else."

That earned another laugh.

"What's so funny?"

"I'm imagining the look on Malcolm's face when he loses to someone who has no desire to make this her living."

"What makes you think I'll win?"

"I see it in your eyes. You like to help people and you believe in love." Gail shifted forward and stared into Natalie's eyes. "Even if you don't believe in it for yourself. For now."

"What?"

This sent off another round of laughter, and Natalie began to question if Gail was retiring because she was losing her mind. "Don't mind me, Gem. Sometimes I can't help but say what I see when I read people. You're a beautiful, unattached woman and I immediately want to help."

"No offense, but what makes you think I need or want your help?"

"Because sometimes we can't do it alone. We can be wonderful at helping others but be completely terrible at understanding what we need for ourselves." She patted Natalie's hand and then stood. "You'll see."

Natalie watched speechlessly as Gail moved across the room.

Gail spun. "Come on, then. I'll introduce you to the staff. You can talk to whomever you'd like."

Natalie stood and tucked her notebook away. She realized taking notes wasn't the best way to learn here. She just needed to open her ears and her mind and see what she discovered.

MAC WALKED INTO BRAD WINFORD'S OFFICE FOR THE SECOND time this week. Today, they were meeting in a conference room to accommodate having the cameras and director in attendance. Before they started, makeup people came through and applied a thick layer to his face, and he caught sight of Gem sitting through the same torture. She appeared about as happy over the process.

"Hey," he called to her, garnering a grunt from the makeup person. "Did you have a nice visit with my mother?"

Gem smiled widely. "I did. She's a fascinating person."

He wished his mother had used some of her fascinating personality to learn more about Gem, but all he'd gotten from his mother was that Gem was a lovely girl.

Brad sat in the corner of the room whispering with the director. After a few moments, Gem and Mac were shoved together in side-by-side chairs. He flashed her another smile. "Did you learn everything you needed from my mother?"

"And then some," she said with a wink.

"What was that?"

"Your mother was amazingly open. And she likes to talk. I didn't even have to ask too many questions."

Shit. His own mother sabotaged him. He couldn't help

but feel she'd given Gem something to use against him. "Want to share what you learned?"

"Not really."

Brad sat across from them. "Okay, today I'm going to introduce you to the clients we've selected. I want your honest reactions, but try to keep it PG. Of course there will be editing later, but this is the first time viewers will get to know you and how you're going to approach this competition."

Mac and Gem both nodded. Mac noticed Gem's smirk had disappeared.

The director, Mike, stepped up to the table. "The most important thing to remember is to forget the cameras."

"Easier said than done," Gem said looking around the room at the setup.

Mike smiled. "What I mean is, talk to each other, never to the cameras unless we're doing your solos."

She nodded stiffly. Her demeanor changed but Mac couldn't quite put a finger on what it was, so he chalked it up to her nerves.

Mike stepped back. "We're going to add the intro later, so for now, we're going to dive right in. Brad, you're up."

Brad slid folders across the table at them. "Here is the first client you'll be working with. Her name is Melissa."

Mac and Gem opened the folders and read the profile. As they did, a video was cued up on a flat screen on the wall. Melissa's audition tape.

Hi, I'm Melissa and I want to participate in Love Match because I'm in a place in my life where I feel like I need help finding my soul mate. I've had two long-term relationships in my life, one of which resulted in an engagement, but I never made it to the altar. I want to fall in love and get married. I haven't had a relationship in years. I've given up on dating. I really need help.

Mac tuned out much of the rest of what Melissa said and

simply watched her mannerisms and body language. She was open and expressive. Her career as a teacher meant she was a natural nurturer. He wanted to know why she hadn't married.

Mac glanced at Gem. She scribbled notes furiously in the folder.

He found himself drawn to this version of Gem. So intent. Focused. Unlike the bubbly Gem.

The video played out and Brad slid the next folder over. "Our next client is Jennifer."

Again, Mac and Gem opened the folder and Gem sniffed at something she read. Glancing over the profile, Mac saw nothing that should upset or surprise her.

The next video started. The woman on camera was stiff and calm. Not a smile in sight. Mac looked at her occupation. Accountant. She would approach things analytically, logically.

Hi, I'm Jennifer. I need help from professionals. After my divorce, I threw myself into work. I've been busy building my business and I'm quite successful. I waded back into the dating waters briefly and found far too many men intimidated by my success.

Mac stopped listening. She was scared. She opted to believe men were intimidated instead of thinking about how she presented herself. Her guard was up and that was more likely her issue, not the size of her paycheck.

As the second video ended, Brad plowed on. "This is Lisa."

Gem flipped the folder open with much more force than necessary and then tossed it back at Brad.

"I've seen enough."

"Excuse me?" Brad asked. Obviously, when he'd told them to be honest and real, he hadn't expected Gem to get pissed off. And she was clearly pissed.

Mac leaned back in his chair and watched.

"You think I can't see what you're doing? You're completely stacking the deck against me and in his favor." She flicked a thumb at Mac. "You've intentionally chosen three desperate women who have zero dating experience."

Mac leaned forward. He wanted to know where she was going with this.

She spun to look at Mac. "You said you play fair. You think this is fair?"

"This is pretty representative of the clients we normally see."

"Are you telling me that most of your clients are women who haven't dated in years? Come on." She turned back to Brad. "You're billing me as a pick-up artist, right? Do you even understand what that means? I pick up men. I go on a lot of dates. These women don't even know what a date is, much less how to get one. If I have to teach them everything, there won't be time left to find love. Finding love is a numbers game."

It was the first bit of Gem's views that clicked with Mac. She didn't think it was about finding the right people to pair, just that given enough time, they would find each other.

Suddenly, Gem stood and yanked out her mic pack. "I'm done. Find someone who's willing to be a doormat."

Another telling comment. Then she stormed out the door. No way was Mac letting her leave. She was the most interesting thing about *Love Match* so far. He shot out of his chair and called, "Wait."

She flicked her hand over her head in what he thought was a wave, but it could've just as easily been her flipping him off. He ran down the hall to catch her. The woman sure could move fast in heels. "Gem."

Suddenly, she stopped and spun to face him. He almost crashed into her. Then he realized the cameras had followed him. Her gaze flicked over his shoulder at the cameras. He shrugged. Not much he could do about them. Her eyes widened at him.

"No one was stacking the deck. These women were chosen before you came on board."

She crossed her arms letting him know how little she believed him. He stepped closer. "You can't walk out like this."

"I think I can."

"What if you get to pick the third client?"

"What?" She dropped her arms.

Mac knew his mouth was running away from him and he sincerely hoped it wouldn't bite him in the ass. "We'll dump one of the chosen clients and you can replace her with a person of your choosing. I'm sure Brad has a wide selection of women who auditioned."

Gem's eyes narrowed. "Why would you offer that? It'd be easier for you to find someone else to lose to you."

He tucked his hands in his pockets and leaned close to her face. "Because I like a challenge."

CHAPTER 4

atalie left the studio with a thumb drive filled with information on potential clients. Malcolm thought she wasn't up to the challenge of playing match-maker? He had no idea what her abilities were. As she climbed into her car, she texted Jillian to let her know how the meeting went. They made plans to order dinner in and watch audition videos over a bottle of wine.

Brad made it clear she needed to make a decision quickly so they wouldn't lose valuable time. She still didn't know what the hurry was, but with Jillian in her corner, she knew they would make light work of the files. No one could beat Hale and Preston in the field of research.

Although she hadn't said much more to Malcolm after he'd made the offer to let her choose the last client, she appreciated his effort. He sold Brad on the idea. In fact, after her outburst, she hadn't needed to say anything. Malcolm took the lead and before she knew it, Brad's assistant handed her a thumb drive.

She drove home and ordered from her favorite Italian place around the corner. She itched to start looking at videos before Jillian came home, but she resisted. Instead, Natalie scrubbed her face and changed into her sweatpants and T-shirt. Sliding her feet into her comfy gym shoes, she grabbed her keys to walk to the restaurant for her food.

Jillian had offered to pick it up, but Nat knew Jilly didn't need another task. Natalie figured that by the time she got back, Jillian should be home and changed and pouring herself a glass of wine.

Warm spring air greeted her outside and Natalie inhaled deeply. She loved the smell of spring. Unfortunately, in Chicago, spring tended to last about a week. From frigid winter to scorching summer, but that brief moment in between was Nat's favorite. So she took her time walking to Tucci's.

On the way back to her apartment, her mind focused equally on food and matchmaking. In her gut, she feared she could do nothing for Jennifer and Melissa, the first two women chosen for the show. Maybe if she did a makeover and a crash course in dating. Hmmm… it was an idea. Brad never said what they had to do with their time with the clients.

One more thing to talk with Jillian about. Jillian would know if the contract limited what Nat could do.

Inside the apartment, she called, "Jilly? You home?"

Jillian came around the corner dressed similarly to Natalie in sweats. "Your timing is perfect. I'm starving."

Nat set the bag of food on the table. "Dig in. Let me grab the laptop."

"Explain exactly what you need my help with? I got your text, but I'm not sure what we're doing tonight." She sipped her wine.

"Brad, the producer, is letting me pick the final client who will appear on the show with us." She left out that it was at Malcolm's urging. "So I have a thumb drive with audition videos and files on each woman interested in being on the show. You're gonna help me pick."

Jillian unpacked their dinner while she listened. "This should be interesting."

"Maybe." Although Nat had little hope given the videos she'd watched at the studio.

Jillian served up a heaping helping of pasta, and Natalie cued up the videos. The first was every bit as bad as she feared.

Bad probably wasn't the best descriptor. It was more of the same, which was exactly what Malcolm had warned her about. They watched the first few in their entirety while they ate. Even the wine didn't make them go down easier. Then they watched just the first minute or two. Natalie was certain she would know her client when she saw her.

She cleared the dinner mess while Jillian refilled their glasses. They relocated to the couch to get comfortable. With the laptop on the coffee table, they curled up with their wine.

Jillian stared at the screen. "These are depressing me. I didn't think my life was so bad, but listening to these women is making me reconsider."

Nat shook her head. "You're fine. You're not looking for Mr. Right. At least not at the moment. There's nothing wrong with focusing on your career."

While the next video played, Natalie opened her email on her phone. Might as well multitask while waiting for lightning to strike. Still no job interview requests, which was far more depressing than the lack of dating experience she witnessed on the computer. One email caught her eye because Malcolm's name jumped out at her.

She opened the email whose subject line was simply *Any luck?* A quick note from Malcolm asking if she'd chosen the new client yet. How fast did he think she could get through everything the studio had given her? Then again, neither of them had known what was on the thumb drive. She hit reply.

I have possibilities. So anxious you can't wait until our next meeting?

She hit send and returned her attention to the screen. Jillian ruthlessly skipped ahead to the next client. Natalie didn't even think they were watching the first full minute anymore.

A new email popped up on her phone. From Malcolm.

Just looking for a little professional courtesy. I fought for you to be able to choose the client.

She bit her lip while deciding how to answer. *This was a quid pro quo thing?*

No. I told you I play fair. Expecting quid pro quo after the fact would be underhanded.

She could almost see him shaking his head at her. She sighed. She wasn't being fair to the guy. In truth, she was mostly still embarrassed she'd flirted with him and he'd shot her down. Things could've gotten messy if he hadn't. So her pride took a hit. She had to suck it up and deal with him for the next couple of months. So she answered simply, *I'll send you the video when I've decided.*

I look forward to it.

As she closed her email program, she felt Jillian's eyes on her. "What?"

She waved with her wine glass. "I'm wondering what is taking your attention away from these videos you're supposed to be watching. Something so interesting that you look alternately perplexed and intrigued."

"I do not." She tucked the phone next to her. "Malcolm emailed to see if I'd made a choice yet."

"Mmm-hm."

"What's that supposed to mean?"

"It means you already told me he's yummy. He appears to

be more than fair in this ridiculous competition. And now you're chatting via email. When will it graduate to texts?"

"Whatever. We're colleagues trying to get this show up and running."

Just then, a voice on the laptop caught Natalie's attention. As the woman told her story of a bad break-up and horrendous online dates, Nat felt like she was hearing her own story.

Then the woman said, "I've been a catch-and-release girl for a long time now. I think I'm ready to settle down and bring in the big game."

Jillian's face wrinkled, but Natalie hit pause. "That's her. That's my girl."

"Why?"

"She's using terminology from a dating book. I read it years ago. That means that even if she wasn't successful, she has some experience. From the sound of her, she was successful. Otherwise, why point out she was a catch-and-release girl?"

"What is she talking about?"

"The book compared hunting for a guy to hunting animals. Before you go out on a hunt, you have to have your objective clear: If you're looking for a temporary thing, it's catch-and-release. You know, like when you catch a fish and throw it back in the water?"

Jillian nodded with understanding if not total acceptance.

Natalie sighed and tried for patience. She had to remember that Jillian never needed gimmicks or tricks to land a guy. Not for the night or for the long-term. She was a natural. "What this video tells me is that what's-her-name," Nat pointed at the screen and felt a little bad she hadn't even been paying close enough attention to catch a name, "is ready. She's tested the waters. Did you hear the beginning of her story? She could be me."

"Does that mean you're ready?"

Nat rolled her eyes. She knew Jillian was poking her for fun. Nat only did catch-and-release. Anything longer never ended well for her. She couldn't be Gem forever, but she was fabulous for a night. "Other than the terminology she used, do you see any reason not to choose her?"

Jillian lifted a shoulder. "Let's watch it from the top and then decide."

Natalie did as Jillian requested, but in her gut she knew this was the client for her.

~

MAC DIDN'T KNOW WHAT HE'D BEEN THINKING EMAILING GEM. He wasn't even sure she'd respond, but when she did, it was fun, almost flirtatious. He knew better than to flirt with her and open that window, but she intrigued him.

And he was a little nervous about who she'd pick as the final client. He hadn't seen all of the videos; therefore, he had no idea what was lurking in the files. It wasn't long before his email lit with a new message.

Here's my girl, Ashley. I think she's the perfect addition.

Mac heard Gem's bubbly voice make the declaration and it sent a ripple of unease through him. He opened the video file and watched. Oh, hell. Ashley was a party girl, young, and Mac didn't believe she was looking for a real relationship. But he wouldn't give Gem the satisfaction of knowing he was worried.

He simply answered with a quick thanks and sent the file to Paul. Within ten minutes, Paul called.

"Hi."

"Why are you sending me a video of a woman looking to settle down? Trying to give me a message? I already told your mom I don't need her services."

Mac smiled. His mom had always tried to work her magic on everyone she cared about. "No. That's the client Gem chose."

Paul laughed. "She sounds like Gem."

That hadn't been lost on Mac, either. "Did I screw myself by giving her this?"

"I don't see why. You can work with the first two. The voting for the contest is two-fold. The clients each get a vote and then the online audience votes. If you get two-thirds of the clients, you're golden."

"What about the audience? She has a huge online following. That gives her an advantage."

Paul chuckled again. "Who do you think is going to watch this show?" He didn't wait for Mac to answer. "Women. While Gem might have a following and will get votes from her fan base, there will be many women who will vote for you because you're you."

Mac withheld the groan.

"Whatever works, man."

He hung up with Paul and emailed Gem. It took three tries for him to get the wording correct. *Interesting choice. Go ahead and send to Brad so he can get everything lined up.*

A moment later his email pinged. *Already sent. Wasn't waiting for your approval.* Followed by a winking emoji.

Mac liked this setup less and less. He dug into the information he had on each client. He needed to prep for his first meeting with them. Part of him wanted to call his mom and get her take on them, but he couldn't. It would feel like cheating. He knew how she approached clients, how she questioned them, how she decided with whom to pair them.

While it wasn't magic, it wasn't a simple numbers game like Gem thought either. It was about knowing the client, her wants and needs, and why she hadn't been able to find a successful relationship on her own. Something held her back. Mac needed to know what that was.

The thought brought him back to Gem, who was clearly *not* one of his clients. He couldn't afford to waste headspace trying to figure her out, but she kept jumping in his brain. He wondered if she saw herself in Ashley and that was why she'd chosen her. Or was she oblivious to the similarities? No, Gem was sharp enough that she'd seen it.

What made her think she could find Mr. Right for Ashley if she couldn't do it for herself?

The question itself was dumb and Mac recognized it as soon as he had the thought. Maybe Gem wasn't looking for Mr. Right anymore than he was looking for Ms. Right. He didn't believe his own lack of a perfect relationship would hold him back from helping others.

Refocusing on the clients, he prepared to prove to his mother what a successful matchmaker he could be.

~

NATALIE HAD SPENT THE NEXT FEW DAYS PLOTTING AND planning. She knew what she was up against with Malcolm. He had a database of men who were looking for relationships. Nat knew she'd have to get creative if she wanted to help these women. She brainstormed with Jillian and every other woman she knew about the best places to find single men and where to go for a great date.

She'd narrow her selections after she met with the clients. Coming to the meeting fully armed was how Natalie liked to run things. Of course, no one would expect that from Gem. With her notes in her bag, she dressed in one of Gem's favorite outfits. The short black skirt, pencil-thin heels, and a fuchsia silk tank top that tied in the front showcased her best assets. The heels made her look taller. The pop of color drew attention to her great cleavage. And the tie in the front always allowed men to imagine unwrapping her.

As she headed for the studio, Natalie hoped they had a better space set up than the conference room. No way would that make for good TV. She was surprisingly calm given that this would be her first time in front of a camera as a faux matchmaker with her clients. Her nerves didn't jangle even a little. Odd.

But then she remembered that since she'd given Malcolm access to the clients first, she wouldn't have to see him today. Her week had been relatively quiet since their brief email exchange. She didn't know what it as about that man, but something pushed every button she had.

The thing was, she knew he was attempting to be decent, but her gut wanted to rebel against it every time.

With any luck, she would have a simple meeting with the clients to gauge how she should plan teaching them the art of finding the right guy. She snorted. As if she knew how.

The little seed of doubt struck, and she swallowed it down.

She *did* know how to find a guy. It would be up to each woman to assess how right a man was for her.

As soon as she walked in, she was ushered into a studio. It looked professional enough to her. The three women were all waiting and from across the room, Nat watched their body language. Jennifer sat stock still, only her eyes shifted around the room. Melissa chatted with the guy who fitted her with a mic and Ashley paced slowly around, checking out the people setting up.

Nat swallowed hard. Showtime. She walked forward with a smile on her face. Before she could open her mouth to introduce herself, a guy stepped up and pinned a mic to her blouse. Then he faded away like a ninja.

"Hi, everyone, I'm Gem."

Ashley and Melissa came closer and stood on either side of Jennifer's chair. None of them said anything.

"How are you all doing? Excited?"

Ashley smiled and Melissa nodded, but Jennifer just continued to stare at her. She'd definitely be a tough nut to crack.

"I'm not a TV person, so I can't give you direction about how to sit or stand or where to look. My plan is to simply talk with you, get to know you, and then talk about my plans and philosophy for dating."

"Excellent," Ashley said.

Jennifer tilted her head and pushed her long ponytail over her shoulder. "What makes you different from Malcolm?" She pointed up and down at Nat's outfit. "Other than the obvious."

Nat bit down her initial response. "He's a matchmaker. I have no idea how he works. I'm a dating expert, a pick-up artist. I can help you attract men, a lot of them, so you have your pick of who to date. I don't think it's my job to find a guy and tell you he's the right one for you. I want to teach you to be comfortable finding your own guy."

Jennifer eased back and nodded. Nat hoped that worked. She clapped her hands. "Ready to get started?"

From the corner of her eye, she saw a cameraman wave at her. Shit. They'd already started. She pointed awkwardly to the round conference table. "Let's all have a seat."

As they each took a chair, Melissa asked, "Why are you meeting with all of us at the same time? Shouldn't it be more personal than that?"

"I like to be efficient. Sometimes we will meet individually. For this initial meeting, it makes more sense to be together so I don't have to repeat myself. I need to get to know each of you beyond your audition videos. I need to know where you're from and what you want in a guy. Why your past relationships didn't work out."

"Okay." Jennifer leaned forward. "I'm divorced. My husband cheated on me. I'm successful, and that intimidates men. I need to find one who won't be, because I'm not going to dumb myself down to get a man."

"What kind of guy are you drawn to?"

"I tend to go for quiet types."

"So, no rock stars for you?"

Her eyes shot wide. "Lord, no."

Nat smiled. "Why do you think you intimidate men?"

"I like intelligent men. I like to be able to carry on a conversation beyond where I had lunch. Because I have opinions I can back up, and I can stand on my own, I've come across too many men who want to be leaned on more than I'm willing to do."

"Obviously, you want an educated man, then, someone successful in his own right who won't be threatened by you."

"Of course. My problem is, they all look like that at first. Things tend to take a turn after a while."

Nat knew how that went. She could definitely sympathize with Jennifer. She turned to Melissa. "How about you, Melissa? What are you looking for?"

"Aren't we all looking for the same thing? True love? I've been engaged. Twice."

Nat held up a hand. "Who broke it off?"

Melissa pressed her lips together. "I did."

"Both times?"

"Yes."

"Why?"

She fidgeted with her hands on the table and when she realized she was doing it, she tucked her hands in her lap. "I knew something was off. We were comfortable and maybe even in love, but something was missing. The spark, you know?"

"Was the spark there when you first met?"

Melissa's squinted and looked up at the ceiling. She bit her lip and returned her gaze to Natalie. "Thinking back now, I'm not sure. If you had asked me then, I would've said absolutely. Now, I'm not so sure."

Nat studied her for a minute. Melissa might've been so desperate to settle down and get married that she jumped on any train that came along. Nat began to wonder if she was really ready now. Maybe she needed to play the field a little more. Melissa cleared her throat and Natalie realized she'd left them all hanging.

"Sorry. I was just thinking. Let's move on. What kind of man are you looking for, Melissa?"

"I don't know. I've dated guys from all walks of life. Different careers, personalities...I'm open to just about anything."

Nat smiled. "That's good to know."

Melissa laughed. "I don't know if I like that smile. It looks a little wicked."

Ashley bumped Melissa with the back of her hand. "Wicked can be good."

All three women laughed, and Nat finally started to feel comfortable.

"How about you, Ashley? Tell me about yourself."

"I've dated around for years. I wasn't looking for something permanent, but now I am."

Nat leaned forward with her elbows on the table. "And why are you here?"

"Because I think I've fallen into a rut for dating. I'm so used to having the casual thing that I don't know what to do differently to find the permanent thing."

Of the three women, Ashley seemed the most grounded,

which felt weird since she appeared to be so flighty. Nat tried not to judge, having been on the receiving end too often, but she wasn't sure she could help Ashley. She could teach these women to fish, but they needed to figure out which fish to keep. Nat knew nothing about that. Her self-doubt crept back in.

"Cut!" someone behind her yelled.

Nat turned in her seat. "Is there a problem?"

"We have enough."

"Wait. What?" She stood and turned to completely face the guy. "Who are you?"

She remembered seeing him in Brad's office, but couldn't remember his name.

"Mike. Your director."

"Well, Mike. While it's great you think you have enough footage or whatever, this is my time to meet with my clients. I wasn't told there was some kind of time limit."

"There isn't. Talk away."

The people behind the cameras continued to buzz around and Nat figured they would just have to ignore them. They'd done a good job of ignoring them so far, but it was a little easier when they were all quiet. Although now that the crew was no longer hyper-focused on her and the clients, Nat relaxed and could be a little more herself.

She waved a hand over her shoulder. "Let them do their thing. I'm not done. I want to learn more about all of you. If we're going to get this right, I need to know who you are."

Settling back in her chair, she added, "And I like to get things right."

As she interviewed the women about past boyfriends and best and worst dates they'd ever had, questions continued to pop up in the back of her head. Did they cut Malcolm off during his interview process? What did he ask the women? Would it be unfair for her to get that inside scoop?

She kept a running list of these questions while listening. An excellent multi-tasker, she absorbed it all. Malcolm Sterling might still win this competition, but she was definitely going to keep swinging.

Without cameras running, all of the women loosened up, including Nat. She kept her Gem persona in place, but the conversation became just that: four women sitting around a table dishing on their love lives. Melissa, Ashley, and Jennifer were all open, honest, and vulnerable. Like Jennifer, she wondered if it had been a mistake to meet with all of them at once, but she felt it was important to distinguish herself from Malcolm and interviewing could be a tedious process.

The group thing turned out to be a smart move. The women had become friendly as they shared their war stories. This might be fun after all.

Nat glanced over her shoulder. Biting her lip, she thought about how long she should keep the women. The camera crew had mostly moved out. She suddenly wanted to dig in and start working with the girls. Part of her was afraid the producer would get mad if they didn't get it on camera.

"What's going on?" Jennifer asked. "You look like there's a problem."

Nat's attention returned to the table. Maybe a little experiment might work. "I had this urge to start working with you now that we've gotten to know each other some, but it appears the cameras are all off."

"Work with us how?" Melissa asked.

"Flirting 101."

Melissa's eyes widened.

With a quick look over her shoulder again, she smiled. "Let's start small. It's going to seem cliché, but all those stereotypical moves we see in Hollywood productions actually work. Just don't go over the top."

"Huh?" Melissa asked.

"For example, eye contact is key. However, you don't want to flutter your eyes like you're caught in a sandstorm. Make eye contact, look away, and then look back."

Jennifer leaned forward. "Looking. That's your advice? I make eye contact with people all day. So what?"

Nat bit back her sigh. "Melissa needs to practice eye contact. You have it down pat. In fact, we might want to soften you up some. Your eye contact tends to border on the aggressive side."

Jennifer snorted. "One more problem men have with me."

Nat smiled and turned back to Melissa. "You dodge eye contact. Even talking to me, you meet my eyes and then dart away. You're not shifty, but it comes across as you being unsure of yourself. That second look—that's the one that tells a guy to come over."

Nat spun in her chair and wished they'd met anywhere but in the studio. Slim pickings here. One of the production interns was clearing off a table in back. She leaned closer to the women. With a thumb hitched over her shoulder, she said, "See him?" They nodded. "Watch."

Nat angled her chair so she wasn't completely turned around, but she could see the intern, which meant he could see her.

She watched him move for a couple of minutes and like clockwork, he felt her attention on him and their eyes met. Nat put on her slow smile and dragged her gaze away. Then she shifted her chair a little more in his direction and looked over again.

When their gazes locked, it was like a tractor beam. His feet shuffled forward until he stood in front of her. "Uh, did you need something?"

Nat's smile widened. "No, thanks. I was just talking to my clients about getting a man's attention. You helped me prove my point."

His cheeks grew pink. "Uh, anytime, I guess." He returned to whatever cleanup he had to finish.

"You make it look easy," Melissa said.

"Men *are* easy." At least initially. But Nat refused to say that out loud for fear the women would give up before they had a chance to start. "Next time, we'll go out in the field and practice basic flirting techniques."

"I thought you were going to help us find the men of our dreams," Ashley said.

"I am. Who better to pick the man than you? Who am I to tell you who to love? My goal is to help you cast your net in the right places to catch the right type of guy. Then it's up to you to decide who's a keeper."

Jennifer stood. "That makes sense. We'll see what you've got."

Nat guessed that was as good as it was going to get with Jennifer. At least for now.

CHAPTER 5

Over the next week, Natalie did everything she could to give the women lessons in flirting. They needed to learn how to attract men before they could fall in love with them. She didn't believe in manufacturing a connection like Malcolm did. Speaking of Malcolm, she hadn't seen him at all, so she almost sighed in relief. The girls told her he was off picking out suitable men. Typical of a man to think he would know what's best for a woman.

Melissa, Ashley, and Jennifer should be picking out their own men. Natalie was proud of their progress. She was excited to take them out in the world to test out their new skills. Unfortunately, the producers decided Malcolm's parties with the women had to be filmed first.

No, she wasn't feeling like second string. Not at all. And it didn't make her bitter. She'd expected as much, right? Malcolm was the star. So he got to choose the clients, except Ashley. He met with them first. Now he got to have his little dating party. Whatever.

Even as she had the thought, curiosity had gotten the better of her. She wanted to see who Malcolm picked for the women to date. Melissa had told her the name of the bar where the party was being held. A small cocktail, get-to-know-you gathering in a small room in a swanky bar.

Natalie debated crashing. Jillian cautioned her against it at first, but then when Natalie explained the party was at Slate, she changed her mind. Jillian had been wanting to check the place out and a bit of recon was a good enough reason. So they dressed up and headed out.

The place was packed and as Jillian shimmied toward the bar for a drink, Natalie strode toward the back room. A guy stepped in her path. "Sorry, ma'am. Private party."

Nat tried not to grind her teeth at being called ma'am. Like she was old. "I know. I'm part of the show."

He offered a slight shake of his head. "I was told everyone was here. No one else gets in."

Just then the intern she'd flirted with stepped out.

"Hey, how are you?"

"Uh, fine."

Natalie looped her arm around his. "This guy won't let me in. He doesn't seem to understand that I'm part of the show."

"She is." But intern guy didn't look so sure of himself.

She blew a kiss to the doorman and eased past him before anyone else could stop her. Inside the private room, she waited to check out the situation. She didn't want to burst into the middle of the party and draw attention. She just wanted a peek.

Cameras and crew were set up around a dance floor. In the middle was a high top table where Melissa sat. Natalie stayed in the dark behind the crew so she could go unnoticed. The guys standing around Melissa seemed to have her attention, so at least Malcolm listened to what Melissa wanted.

As her eyes tracked to Melissa, Natalie saw red. There

was Melissa, using every tip and trick Natalie had designed for her to use in a bar. But not *this* bar. She was using the skills Natalie taught her to help Malcolm win. Nat took a half step forward before she caught herself. She couldn't barge in and cause a scene.

She edged back to leave before she made a mistake, but her movement itself was the mistake because suddenly Malcolm's eyes were locked on her. He whispered something to a woman at his side, and he made his way around the edge of the dance floor. He headed straight for her. Natalie side-stepped to try to get out the door before he caught her. Although there had been nothing in her contract that prevented her from watching what Malcolm was doing, they both knew it was a sneaky move.

Her hand landed on the door leading to her escape at the same time firm fingers wrapped around her elbow. Fuck.

She turned to face Malcolm.

"Spying on the competition?" His voice was low and if she had heard it in any other situation, she'd think it was seductive.

"Yes." His eyes widened and she realized her honesty caught him off guard, so she plowed on. "Good thing I did. Now I know who I'm dealing with." She paused and added, "A cheat."

He released his grip on her arm and his eyebrows lowered over his eyes. "What the hell are you talking about? How could anything I've done here be misconstrued as cheating?"

"All you've done is fill a room with eligible bachelors. At least as far as I know. You haven't given the women anything they need." She poked at his chest. "Melissa is over there using every technique I taught her this week. Techniques I knew would specifically work for her because I took the time to get to know her."

Malcolm inhaled, causing his chest to push back against

her finger. She should move. Definitely. It took an extra minute for her hand to get the message before she finally dropped her finger.

"I spent plenty of time with our clients. I can't help if Melissa decided your games were a good idea to use here."

"Games?" Her voice rose a notch before she caught it. "This isn't about playing games. I'm teaching them to use their God-given tools so they can find a man to fall in love with and find their happily-ever-after crap. I'm not telling them who they should want."

"Neither am I." He stepped closer and lowered his mouth to her ear. "I'm doing my job just like you are."

Her heart picked up and thundered in her chest. His breath was warm on her neck and he smelled wonderful.

And she didn't like this reaction to him. At all. With a palm flat against that hard chest, she gave a shove. "You better get back to your little party. Watch what Melissa does. You might learn a thing or two."

"About what?"

"About how women work."

"I already know quite a bit about that. I definitely don't need tips from you."

"I doubt it." Nat pressed her lips together. If she continued to talk, her mouth might get away from her. She reached behind her back and twisted the knob. With her eyes on his, she slipped back through the door.

On the other side, she took a deep breath and still smelled Malcolm. Infuriating man. She muscled her way through the crowd to the bar to find Jillian. As she squeezed past people she scoped out her options. It was automatic. Even though she hadn't come to the bar tonight to find a partner, her eyes took in the crowd.

She forced her gaze back to the bar to find Jillian. The last thing she needed right now was a guy to mess up her anger.

Jillian caught sight of her and pointed to a stool beside her. She had a drink waiting. It was one of the many reasons that made Jillian such a good friend.

"How'd it go?"

"Don't ask." Nat gulped her martini and held up her hand to order another.

MAC STARED AT THE DOOR THAT CLOSED BEHIND GEM'S CURVY ass. He shouldn't even notice things like that, but he couldn't help it. The woman annoyed him and poked at him and yet, there was something about her that made him want to move closer every time she was near. Tonight he wished he could blame it on the siren-red dress that skimmed lovingly over her curves. And of course the fucking heels to match. Those alone could bring a man to heel.

As much as he wanted to go after her to explain all the ways in which she was wrong about him, he was in the middle of a meet-and-greet for his client. He turned back to the party. Damn. One of the cameramen spun back to the guests. Mac had an unsettled feeling. Had they caught him arguing with Gem? Shouldn't surprise him, really. She dressed to draw attention.

He quickly scanned his memory for anything that would make him look bad while he pasted on a smile. Nothing he'd done or said had been inappropriate. He neared Melissa's table and he suddenly caught a glimpse of what Gem had been talking about.

Melissa angled her head and looked at a man from under her lashes as she traced a line down the side of her glass with her index finger. She kept eye contact as she licked her lips before spreading them into a smile. It all looked manufactured.

But the men at the table were eating it up.

Melissa wasn't being herself and there was no way for a real relationship to happen under false pretenses. Mac watched for another moment. At least Melissa was giving them her full attention. He'd known her lack of confidence would be an issue. It appeared Gem had tackled that problem for him.

And that was why she'd thought he'd cheated. How the fuck was he supposed to control how these women acted? Talk about infuriating. It wasn't as if she'd found the perfect man for Melissa, and Mac stepped in to introduce them.

He checked his watch. He needed to get things moving. Melissa needed to narrow the field, knock out the men she wasn't interested in so she could spend time with those who had a chance. He waved her over, painfully aware of the cameras shifting to capture everything.

One day he'd get even with his mother for this.

Melissa scooted closer and said, "This is so much fun. I never thought I'd actually enjoy this. There's something to be said for having a captive audience."

"I need you to tell me which three men you're most interested in. Then you'll have a sit down with each of them individually, get to know each other a bit and decide if a date is in order."

"Three, huh?" She glanced over the crowd of men who were looking at Mac and Melissa and trying hard not to appear to be watching. "So I have to tell the rest they're all losers?"

Mac couldn't hide his grimace. "No. They're not losers. I'll keep them in my database for future get-togethers. And once you make your decision, my assistant and I will tell our remaining guests they can go home."

Melissa released a deep breath. "Whew. I didn't want to

be in charge of a mass rejection. Kyle, Thomas, and Will are the three men I'd like to spend more time with."

Mac held his tongue. He'd expected her to choose Kyle and Will, but he hadn't wanted her to choose Thomas. "Can you tell me why you decided on them?"

"Kyle is funny and Will had a way of talking to me that made me feel like I was the only woman in the room." She clasped her hands in front of her and twisted her fingers.

"And Thomas?"

"I'm not sure why. I'm attracted to him physically. But it feels like there's more to it. He has an easy way about him."

Which was exactly why Mac hadn't wanted her to choose him. Melissa wanted a man who would take charge, not sit back and wait for things to happen. Yet she continued to be drawn to mild-mannered men. He waved his assistant, Amy, over. "Can you take Melissa back to the small room?"

When the women left, Mac moved through the room to gather Melissa's choices. Then he clapped his hands to draw the attention of the rest of the men. He thanked them all for their time and had Amy pass out his business card so they could keep in touch. Based on their interactions tonight, Mac knew he probably wouldn't be calling some of them back. There had been a few who were looking to be on TV and he'd hoped the cameraman was good enough to avoid them.

The three remaining men sat at the table Melissa had vacated.

"Gentlemen." Mac stood before them and wondered where his mother always found the right words for this moment. "Melissa is interested in getting to know each of you further. I'll take one of you back to have some time with her in a few minutes. Do you have any questions?"

They all shook their heads. Mac nodded and turned back to the small room off the to side. The production staff had converted a manager's office into a quaint space for their show. The bar owner agreed to let them do whatever they wanted as long as Mac used the bar for all of his meet-and-greets for the series.

When he walked in, Melissa was pacing. She looked up at him with wide eyes. "What am I supposed to do here? This is nerve wracking."

"Have a seat." He pulled out the chair for her. "When I send someone in, just talk. Stay away from superficial stuff. Talk about what you're looking for, what you enjoy doing. Step it up from the conversation you had before." He sat across from her. "Most important, be yourself."

"Of course. Who else would I be?"

"Gem."

"What?"

"Out there I saw you playing the field. There's nothing wrong with that when it comes to breaking the ice and looking at options. These men are here because they're interested. You don't need games and ploys to pull them in. Let them see you."

She nodded solemnly. He briefly wondered what it would take to get Gem to let her guard down and be the real her. He had little doubt the Gem she showed the world wasn't the real woman. He'd seen glimpses of the real woman, and he had a feeling he'd like her a whole lot more than what he was getting.

"Ready?" he asked Melissa.

"I guess I have to be."

He rose, patted her shoulder, and went back to the men. He sent Thomas in first with the hope that by the time she met with the other two men, Thomas would be gone from her mind.

The crew had cameras set up to be unobtrusive during the one-on-one sessions. Mac sat at a monitor and watched Melissa interact with Thomas. At first, he saw the struggle she had with the idea of being herself. How the hell had Gem managed to flip a switch on this woman after a couple of sessions? He'd have to undo everything in order to make this work.

At least Thomas seemed put off by it as well, so Mac didn't worry about a love match there. The scene was almost painful to watch, but he was pretty sure it would make for good TV.

By the time his night ended and the cameras were off, Mac was exhausted. Melissa had managed to settle on asking Kyle on a date, so she was ready for the next phase of the show. He stood to leave the room and almost dropped at the thought of having to do this two more times. This was so much more intense than what they usually did to match people. The meet-and-greet was typical protocol, but having cameras watch his every move added to the stress.

Instead of walking through the crowd in the front of the trendy bar they'd chosen as a location, Mac slipped out he back door. The quiet of the alley was the best sound he'd heard all day. Laughter at the corner grabbed his attention and when he looked up, he saw Gem again. Her giggle was high pitched and an affectation. Too bad the guy she was with didn't see it. His hand kept sliding off her hip and onto her ass.

Mac watched for a moment to see if this was something Gem wanted. She was a pick-up artist after all. Maybe this was all part of the game to her. Unfortunately, if they didn't move on soon, he'd have to walk past them to get to his car. Another round of ridiculous giggles and he'd had enough. He'd walk around them and hoped to avoid notice.

He edged around the man's back, carefully keeping his gaze to the ground or the street in front of him. He got as far as the curb when she spoke.

"Malcolm? Is that you?"

Shit. More phony stuff. He turned his head. She stepped forward, away from the grasp of her handsy companion. She walked until she was inside his personal space, close enough he could smell her perfume.

"It's so good to see you again."

He answered with a lifted brow. Her eyes pleaded with him to play along. Part of him wanted to watch her squirm, but he could never leave a woman like this. "Yeah, it's been a while," he answered quietly.

The other man shifted behind her.

Mac flicked his gaze up to meet him and then settled back on Gem. "Can I give you a ride? Maybe we can catch up."

"That would be great!" she said with such enthusiasm that Mac almost stepped back.

She spun quickly and spoke to the man. "Thanks for a fun night, but I haven't seen my friend here in a long time."

Mac coughed and Gem's shoulders stiffened before saying, "I'll talk to you soon."

The man lifted a hand. "Whatever." Then he turned away, weaving as he did.

Gem returned her attention to Mac. Gone was the flirtatious woman who needed him to play along. She actually looked pissed. "Thanks. The guy couldn't take a hint."

"And what would you have done if I hadn't happened along?"

"I would've pulled that scene with a total stranger. You'd be amazed at how well it works. When a guy gets to be a hero and believes he has a shot at getting laid for playing the part? Works every time."

Mac shook his head. Nothing but games with her.

"Anyway, thanks for playing along. Have a good night." She stepped away from him.

"Uh-uh. I'm not leaving you here to have to do that again. My car is right across the street. I'll drive you home."

"I don't need a ride. I'm capable of grabbing a cab."

"I'm sure you're capable, but why bother? I'm right here. It won't cost you a thing."

"I doubt that." Unlike some women, she didn't mumble it but said it to his face. Her gaze darted up and down the street as if to gauge how long it would take to get a cab.

"Come on." He placed a hand on her lower back and pressed to get her to move. She didn't fight it.

At his car, he unlocked the door and held it open for her. She slid in with barely a glance at him. He settled behind the wheel and asked for her address. He typed it into his GPS. North side, not too far, but not nearly as upscale as she tended to dress. Another piece of the Gem puzzle. Mac started to wonder if any of her was real.

They drove in silence. Blocks from her home, she cleared her throat. "I appreciate the ride. I came to the bar with my roommate and she drove. She left a while ago."

"She left you at a bar?"

A sneaky smile slipped onto her face. "Well, she met someone and asked if I would mind. She drove so she would have her own escape if it didn't work out." She flipped a careless hand in the air. "It's not like it's hard to get around the city. There's always a cab or the el."

She pointed at a brick building, a simple three flat. "That's me. I'm on the third floor. Not a great view, but it's a nice neighborhood."

He parked in front of her building. The neighborhood was nice. Just not what he'd expected from her.

"Thanks again for the ride." She moved to leave the car.

Mac jumped out and met her on the passenger side as she opened the door. She seemed startled at his presence. Then her back stiffened. With a tilt of her head, she said, "I wasn't trading one man for another tonight."

Her comment was like a punch to the gut. "I wasn't

suggesting I follow you into your bed. I was merely opening the door for you and offering a hand." He eyed the short dress she wore. "I wouldn't want you to get indecent."

"So you don't just play the hero? This is who you are?"

"I'm no hero. Just considerate."

A light shade a pink filled her cheeks.

Huh.

She touched his arm and said quietly, "Thank you." The she moved to the door of her building with her head down.

Mac stood at his car and watched her walk inside. A simple act of kindness put Miss Gem off her game. Something to think about.

~

Natalie had enjoyed her day away from TV and cameras and most of all Malcolm. At least she tried to, but then yesterday afternoon she'd received the message that Brad wanted to see her in his office first thing in the morning.

Her immediate thought was that he'd found out she'd crashed Malcolm's party for Melissa. She spent the rest of her evening rereading her contract to make sure she hadn't done anything wrong. She was in the clear. No breach of contract that she could find. So Malcolm could just suck it.

Before walking through the door of the studio, she applied a fresh coat of lipstick and fluffed her hair. Gem would *not* lose this contract. Natalie's life was circling the drain a bit, so Gem had to hold it together.

In reception, she didn't even get a chance to sit and relax to gather her thoughts. Malcolm leaned against the wall and smiled when he saw her. She tried to forget the last time she'd seen him. She'd wanted to invite him up to her place.

She'd tried to convince herself it was the alcohol she'd

consumed and the fact that he'd been nice to her, but looking at him now, she knew better.

"Good morning," he said, tucking his phone back in his pocket.

Damn. Even his voice was smooth. First thing in the morning. Life wasn't fair.

"Is it? A good morning?" she asked. "Did you think that by tattling on me to Brad you'd get rid of me? Think again. I read my contract."

He angled his head slowly and narrowed his eyes. "Tattled on what exactly?"

"That I crashed your party. What else?" Nat's stomach flipped. What else indeed?

Malcolm pushed away from the wall in a smooth, graceful motion and stepped closer. He made Nat nervous with the movement. But nervous in a good way, like anticipation, which was horrible.

"You believe your little spying session worried me? I have nothing to hide." He took another step, putting him as close as they had been the other night outside the bar.

Nat locked her knees so she wouldn't move. The problem was she wasn't sure if she'd step away or toward him.

He lowered his head, his mouth close to her ear, and spoke quietly. "How about you? What are you hiding?"

A shiver skated down her spine. "Nothing," she whispered. Then she swallowed hard.

"They're ready for you," the receptionist called. "Conference room one on the left."

Nat stepped away from Malcolm. This had to stop. She didn't know what game he was playing, but she didn't want to be a part. At least that's what she kept telling herself.

Malcolm turned and held out a hand for her to go first. As she passed, his hand landed on the small of her back, right at the curve of her ass, like it had the other night. The touch caused a hitch in her stride, and she glanced at him over her shoulder, going for a haughty look.

She wouldn't let him know the warm brush of his fingers made her heart race.

"Problem?" he asked.

"Not at all."

They arrived at the room and Malcolm reached around her to open the door.

"Are you always a gentleman?"

He lowered his head again and she braced for the sensation of his breath on her skin. "Not always." He paused for a blink. "But I do always allow a woman to go first."

Nat clenched her teeth. Her mind raced at the innuendo and all the ways he would be a gentleman and when he wouldn't. She inhaled deeply and walked into the conference room.

Brad and Mike sat at the table looking at the screen on the wall. Nat's heart sank. There she was big as life, crashing Malcolm's party.

"Come in," Brad said. "Have a seat." At least he didn't sound pissed.

She moved to a chair, but again, Malcolm beat her to it and pulled it out for her. "Thank you."

He took the seat beside her. Couldn't he at least have left a chair between them? A little distance so she wouldn't be able to smell his cologne?

"You're probably wondering the purpose for this meeting," Brad started.

Nat pointed to the screen, getting riled up all over again. "I didn't do anything wrong. I didn't even know the camera crew was aware I was there. I didn't disrupt anything."

Under the table, Malcolm's hand landed on her knee and gave a soothing pat. He leaned his other arm on the table. "Is there a problem?"

"Not at all." Brad's face lit up. "Show them," he said to Mike.

Malcolm slid back in his seat, taking his warm hand with him. Nat watched the screen as the film fast-forwarded.

Mike rolled the tape and paused as Malcolm on screen stalked toward her. The camera closed in on his face. He looked determined, but not pissed.

Since Malcolm was the only one with a mic, their conversation was muted but sound wasn't needed to know they were arguing.

Then Mike froze the playback. Malcolm and Nat were locked in a staredown.

"Holy crap," Brad said. "It's even better the second time. Do you see that? You can't pay for that kind of chemistry."

"What?" Nat yelled as her chair slid away from the table.

Without a word, Malcolm reached for the arm of her chair and moved it back into place.

Brad stood and pointed at the screen. "That kind of fire and rivalry. That's what's going to make this show."

"What?" Nat asked again. Yeah, she could see the chemistry on screen. Hell, she lived it every time Malcolm was near. No way would she act on it. Definitely not on tape.

"We need more of this." Brad tapped the TV. "More of the two of you as competitors. The audience will eat it up."

Nat's stomach settled. She'd read the whole thing wrong. "So you want us to fight more?"

"Yes!" Brad was a little too excited at the prospect.

Nat snorted. She shot a look at Malcolm. "That shouldn't be too difficult."

Malcolm scooted forward again. "I get what you're saying here, Brad, and I certainly see the appeal."

Nat felt his gaze land on her. Her skin prickled with awareness, but she wouldn't return the look.

"But my concern is for my clients. Isn't the show supposed to be about them?"

"Yes and no. They're important, of course, but the show is about how the two of you work, how different you are." He hitched a thumb at the screen again. "That's what's going to sell."

"Are you going to script these fights?" Nat asked.

Brad took his seat again. "I don't think that'll be necessary. There's enough spark between you two to start a fire."

"What do you expect?" Malcolm asked.

Nat heard the reservation in his voice. Why would he be nervous? All he had to do was more of the same: piss her off.

"From now on, you'll be together for all of the events."

Oh, crap. Without having time to process Brad's request, she didn't know what she'd thought, but she hadn't imagined more time with Malcolm.

She glanced at Malcolm. His smile was full and devilish. He winked at her. Seriously?

Brad slapped his palms against the table and stood. "If there are no other questions, get to work. Exchange numbers and plan the dates for your clients. Use the room as long as you need." He left with Mike following.

Natalie inhaled through her nose and closed her eyes. Calm didn't hit her, just another whiff of Malcolm.

"You okay?" he asked.

"Fine." Determined to do the job, she pulled out her phone and accessed her planner. "I have plans to meet with Jennifer later today and then head to a bar with her."

One of Malcolm's eyebrows quirked up. "Okay. Send me the details."

"Number?" she asked, opening a new contact on her phone. She entered the digits and scrolled back to her planner. "When is your next party?"

"Jennifer's meet-and-greet is scheduled for Thursday evening. Same time and place."

Natalie stood, wanting to get away from Malcolm and this whole situation. She had to figure out how to let the sparks fly without getting drawn in by him. With one more look at him before she left, she realized just how hard that would be.

CHAPTER 6

Mac decided he didn't need to barge in on Gem's individual session with Jennifer. It would've been too distracting for all of them. This little competition became infinitely more interesting as the attraction between him and Gem grew.

She was obviously trying to avoid it, and while he hadn't immediately considered pursuing it, she intrigued him. She was hiding plenty, regardless of what she'd claimed outside the conference room this morning. He wanted to peel back the layers and see who she was underneath. If that meant he had to agitate her every time they met, so be it.

He straightened his tie and ran a hand over his hair before leaving the car. That was a huge downside to this TV show. Having to constantly worry about how he looked wasn't his style. They were only a couple of weeks in and he was already annoyed.

Inside the bar, he easily spotted Gem. She definitely commanded attention. He didn't, however, immediately see a camera crew. They had a tendency to take up half a room. He looked around and then spotted two guys, one in each corner of the room. Damn, how had she managed to get minimal coverage? Mac had to find out her secret.

He stayed on the perimeter, trying avoid drawing attention to himself. He watched Gem talk to Jennifer. Then she nodded and gave Jennifer little push. Interesting tactic. He sat at a table and ordered a whisky from the waitress. He stared at Gem, waiting for her to take notice of him. She would. She noticed what was going on around her and this would be no different. Plus, she was aware he was coming.

Over her shoulder she eyed him and then returned her attention to the bartender. She raised a hand and waited for her drink. Once it was in her possession, she turned and looked at Mac again. He could almost hear her sigh. She strode his way and sat across from him.

"I expected you earlier today."

"I didn't think you needed the intrusion in your *lesson*. For me, this is the interesting part."

She sipped her drink. "Why? It's just a bar."

"That's what makes it interesting. Most women have spent countless hours in bars hoping to find the love of their lives. Mostly they end up disappointed." He sipped his own drink. "A bar is definitely the wrong place for Jennifer to meet someone."

"That's where you're wrong. A bar is the perfect place for anyone. This is practice. She gets to experiment here with no expectations about what will happen. She's not going to meet the love of her life here tonight." Her eyes moved to where Jennifer sat alone at the bar. "But she'll get the chance to figure out how to act and what to do when she's in a situation where Mr. Right might be."

They sat in silence for a few minutes and watched Jennifer. The woman was clearly uncomfortable. She tapped a man on the shoulder and introduced herself and shook his hand. Gem groaned. When Mac turned his attention back to

Gem, he couldn't help the smile. She might be an expert on picking up men, but she was out of her depths here.

"Shut up. She'll be fine."

Jennifer shifted from one foot to another and after a minute of conversation the man backed away. Jennifer turned and stared at Gem with wide eyes. Gem waved her over to the table. When she arrived, Jennifer shot a look to Mac.

"Would you like me to step away?"

"Why is he here?" Jennifer asked.

"The producers want more time with the two of us on screen. It has nothing to do with you," Gem said.

Mac stood. He didn't want to make a client uncomfortable. Brad would have to accept that.

Jennifer straightened. "You can stay." She turned to Gem. "This isn't working."

Gem stood and grabbed Jennifer's shoulders. "You need to loosen up. You approached that guy like you were on a job interview. You're here to flirt. Don't worry about what happens next. There is no next. It's just about tonight."

Jennifer inhaled deeply and closed her eyes. "I'm not good at this. Obviously. That's why I volunteered to humiliate myself on TV to be able to work with a matchmaker."

"I'm going to help you, Jennifer, but you have to be a little more open-minded. What good will it do for me—or Mr. Sterling—to find a great guy if you can't open yourself to possibilities?"

Mac grudgingly had to admit Gem made some valid points to Jennifer. He still believed a bar was the worst place to take her, but Gem must've had a plan. He said nothing and tried to keep his expression neutral as he listened in.

"Just for tonight, pretend every guy you meet is a MacArthur Genius Grant fellow. He's not only smart, but he's also successful and rich. He doesn't need your money and he's not intimidated by your success. What's more, he'll be intrigued by it."

Jennifer's stance loosened, but she didn't look convinced. "But they're not."

"How do you know?"

Jennifer rolled her eyes.

"For all you know, I convinced the producers to contact every Genius Grant recipient they could find and filled the bar with them."

Gem was so sure of what she was saying, Mac almost believed her.

"Did you?" Jennifer asked.

"I'm not telling." Again she took Jennifer's shoulders and spun her to face the bar. "Look at all the options. Who looks most interesting?" She waited a beat. "Your mission tonight is to talk to no fewer than five guys and get their numbers."

"What?" Jennifer squeaked.

Gem sighed. "Okay. It counts if they ask for your number."

"How do I make that happen?"

"First take a seat at the bar. Choose your five guys. Or more if you're so inclined. Then talk to them. Let nature take its course."

"Are you sure about this?"

"Yes. Now go."

When Jennifer returned to the bar, Gem took her seat. She looked at Mac. "Comments?"

"Nope." He took another drink of whisky.

"Liar."

"What difference does it make?"

"You never hold your tongue. You get off on telling me everything I'm doing wrong."

He set his glass down and leaned closer to her across the table. "First, I don't tell you what you do wrong. I might not agree with your methods, but I've never corrected you. Questioned, but not corrected. And second," He looked over his shoulder and made sure the cameras weren't close enough to catch what he was saying. "That is nowhere near anything that will get me off."

Gem blushed again, but clamped her jaw. For someone who was a self-professed pick-up artist, talk of sex seemed to put her off her game. Interesting.

They sat in silence and watched as Jennifer attempted to follow Gem's directions. The first conversation was almost as horrific to watch as the handshake she'd given the man earlier, but before she moved on, she rallied herself mentally. Mac noted the physical motions as Jennifer took deep breaths, closed her eyes, and then squared her shoulders. When she approached the next man, she was confident but not overbearing.

Gem leaned forward with an elbow on the table as if she was watching a key play in a game. When Jennifer continued to speak to the man for more than two minutes, Gem settled back in her chair.

She raised her glass. "And that's how you teach a woman to flirt. I think you're in trouble, Sterling."

"Not likely … Damn. I have no idea what your last name is, so I can't toss that back at you."

She smiled and sipped from her glass. "A little mystery never hurt anyone."

"Mystery? That's why you only use one name?"

After a quick glance at Jennifer, Gem returned her attention to him. "No. In all honesty, the pseudonym is to keep my online dating and vlog life separate from my real day job life."

And the plot thickened. Mac hadn't considered her viral videos weren't her main source of income. "What do you do?"

She paused and then said, "I'd rather not say."

They slipped back into silence and Mac studied her while she studied Jennifer. To his surprise, Gem pulled out a small notebook and began scribbling as Jennifer made her rounds. It took over an hour, but Jennifer returned to their table with a triumphant smile on her face.

She slapped two business cards and a napkin on the table and turned her phone to face Gem. "Five numbers. And I got them all."

Gem smiled. "I told you it was possible."

"I can't believe you were right."

Gem lifted a shoulder as if to say *all in a day's work.*

"That being said, I don't think I'd actually call any of these guys. Pretending they're Genius Grant recipients and having them be geniuses are two vastly different things."

Gem laughed. It was louder than what most women would do, but it was pure enjoyment. When she calmed, she said, "I never said you'd do anything with those numbers, unless of course you want to. The dude with the broad shoulders and tight jeans is still checking you out."

Jennifer glanced over her shoulder and smiled at the man in question.

"This was about getting you out of your comfort zone and making you at ease with a different M.O. What you used to do no longer worked. Now you have new tools to utilize."

"Thank you. Anything else for tonight?"

"Nope. You're free to go." She stood. "I'm going to let the crew know we're finished."

Mac ordered another round for them. Although Gem was done with Jennifer, he wasn't quite finished with Gem. When she returned, she eyed the drink.

"I didn't order that."

"It's a celebratory drink. You did a good job with Jennifer. And that's saying something because she's been resistant to you from the beginning."

"No, really?" Even her sarcasm was cute. She sat and took a sip.

"Why won't you tell me what you do?"

"Defeats the whole purpose of keeping my two lives separate."

Mac looked around the bar. "Cameras are gone. Just the two of us talking, getting to know each another."

"Since when do you want to get to know me? I thought you had everything figured out."

"So did I. But you surprise me."

"How so?"

Mac stood and moved into the chair beside her. Much more conducive for private conversation.

Natalie wanted to gloat. She did a great job with Jennifer and Mr. High and Mighty Sterling knew it. But her desire to brag waned as he stood and moved to the chair adjacent to her. A new desire washed over her. Malcolm stirred her senses in a way that had her leaning toward him, even though she knew it was a mistake.

But the man sent mixed signals. Half the time, he acted like he was so much better than her. The other half the time, she couldn't tell if he liked her or if she amused him.

"As I was saying, you surprised me tonight. I've been watching you, and I owe you an apology."

Whoa. She hadn't seen that coming. She smiled and waited, all while staring into his deep blue eyes.

"I'm sorry I underestimated you."

"I'm impressed." She inched away from him and took a sip of her drink. "Most guys say they owe an apology and they believe that will suffice. Kudos for actually saying the words."

"Does that mean I don't have to explain anything else?"

"Oh, no. I definitely want you to explain in great detail not only in what ways you underestimated me, but also in what ways you've discovered how utterly awesome I am." She tossed him her flirtiest smile.

He twirled his glass twice before speaking. "I saw a couple of your videos. I thought you were simply a..."

"A what?"

"There's no way for me to put this in a politically correct way."

Nat snorted. "Do I strike you as a politically correct person?"

"A flake."

Nat laughed. No, it was more of a guffaw.

"Not quite the reaction I expected." He continued to watch her with careful eyes.

Nat inhaled deeply. She dabbed at her eyes with her middle fingers. "I expected something much harsher than *flake*."

He angled his head again and Nat felt a warm flush flood her body. He always made her feel like he was studying her. "Such as?"

"Such as what?"

"What exactly were expecting me to call you?"

She lifted a shoulder. "Slut. Floozy. Something along those lines."

He stiffened. "Now I think you owe me an apology."

"Really?"

"Just because I believed your dating methods won't find genuine love, doesn't mean I think it's wrong for you to enjoy your life."

"Always so stiff and proper. Why can't you just say what you mean? That you don't hold it against me that I have sex whenever I want with whomever I want."

He leaned closer again. "There's more to enjoying life than just sex."

She patted his cheek and restrained herself from stroking his bearded jaw. "Oh, I know, but sex is the best part, don't you think?"

"I can't disagree." His voice was deep and quiet.

Was he flirting with her? Nat shook her head a little and leaned away from him. He answered with a smirk. He was toying with her. She downed the rest of her drink and moved to gather her things.

"What's your hurry?"

"As much as you think I like games, Mr. Sterling, I don't like to be played."

His eyebrows lowered. "I'm not doing that. I'm talking to you, trying to get to know you."

Nat's heart thumped in her chest. He looked sincere.

"Don't go."

She huffed out a slight breath. "Fine. But you owe me another drink."

He smiled and waved the waitress over to order another round. When she left, he said, "I've never been here. Do you come here often?"

"I've been here a few times. It's a nice atmosphere. Not too loud. You know, you can actually talk to people."

"I'm not much of a bar person myself."

"Why?"

He lifted a shoulder. "Too much façade for my liking."

Hmm...another interesting statement by Malcolm. "I don't mind it. I think people put on a façade no matter where they are. We all have a public face. In some ways, it's easier at a bar because you know everyone is putting up a front. Out there," she pointed toward the door of the bar, "you never know who's being genuine and who isn't."

"I'm well aware. It's part of the reason I hate pretense."

Something flickered in his eyes as he spoke and the idea of deep thoughts with Malcolm pulled Nat in deeper. "So who played you, Malcolm?"

An eyebrow arched in response. He took a sip of his whisky. She about gave up on him answering when he said, "My ex-wife."

She hadn't expected that. Although she hadn't investigated Malcolm Sterling's personal life, she'd almost assumed he was happily married. At the mention of his ex, though, he looked downright miserable. "So you poke fun at me for not finding true love for myself, and you haven't been able to do it either?"

He shook his head slowly. "I don't poke at you because you haven't found it but because you don't even believe it exists. I don't understand how you expect to help your clients when you don't buy into what they're looking for."

She let that thought roam through her head for a few minutes. She knew how she wanted to answer. She helped people all the time as a librarian, helped them research subjects she didn't know anything about. But if she revealed that, she'd be letting Malcolm in to her personal life, and that wouldn't do.

So she chose her words carefully. "It's not that I don't believe love exists. I personally haven't found the evidence or proof."

He licked his lips before he spoke and she told herself the movement wasn't enticing. He was back to studying her.

"I'm like the albatross. They preen and point and dance around the other albatrosses to find their perfect mate."

Malcolm laughed. Actually laughed. Nat was beginning to think it was something he didn't do.

"Where the hell did you learn that?"

She smiled and lifted her glass. "I like to read and learn

things." She drained her glass. "But when the albatross makes his choice, it's for life."

The alcohol buzz flitted through her system, and she knew she needed to stop before she made an epic fool of herself. "Unfortunately, human beings don't play by those rules."

Malcolm was staring at her again.

"What?" she asked, trying not to be unnerved.

"I'm piecing things together. You won't tell me what your day job is, but you reveal your hobby and that you like to read. You make jokes when conversation gets too personal in order to keep your distance. Who hurt you?"

She crossed her arms. He was like a detective, but so was she. "Much like you, and most of the population, I have an ex."

"What was his name?"

The question startled her because it was so irrelevant. And Malcolm didn't do irrelevant. "Why?"

"Because although I've asked you repeatedly to call me Mac, you always use my whole first name, or worse, Mr. Sterling. I was beginning to think maybe your ex's name is Mac."

"Breathe a sigh of relief. You do not share a name with my ex."

"Then why?"

She stood, tucked her purse under her arm, and leaned close. "Because I like to keep my distance and I haven't yet decided how much of you is pretense."

He pushed out of his chair, forcing her back or she'd get a face full of his chest. Straightening his jacket, he said, "None of it is pretense. What you see is truly who I am."

"That's what everyone says. Sometimes it's so ingrained in who we are that we aren't even aware we're doing it."

"One more question before you go."

She waited, eyes locked on his.

"Do you believe people are ever their true selves?"

Again she smiled. "Most people are real when they're naked. Having sex—even if it's *just* sex, no strings, no relationship—forces you to be vulnerable. In those moments it's hard to maintain the façade. Some can do it, but not most."

Natalie didn't wait for him to respond. She knew she didn't want to hear his response. The conversation was getting too real. She had almost reached the door, thinking she'd escaped, when a hand landed on her lower back.

"Let me walk you out."

"I'm fine."

"Of that, I have little doubt."

Outside in the fresh air, they paused again. For the life of her, Natalie couldn't figure out what the hell was going on between them.

"Can I give you a ride?"

"I'll call a cab, thanks."

"My car is right there."

"Fine. On one condition."

He slid his hands into his pants pockets and rocked back on his heels.

"No more deep conversation. I took this job because I thought it would be fun."

"I thought we were having fun."

An unmistakable spark lit his eyes that Nat could see, even in the dark night.

He was right. She'd had an excellent evening. When was the last time she spent a night with a guy talking about anything real? And he wasn't even trying to get her into bed.

He pointed toward his car and they began to walk.

"Are you not having a good time?"

"I think I was wrong about you too, Malcolm. You do

have a sense of humor. It's the teasing kind and I didn't see that coming."

He held the car door open for her—always the gentleman—and Nat had the unsettled feeling Malcolm had much more going on that she wouldn't see heading her way.

She just couldn't decide if the feeling in the pit of her stomach was anticipation or dread.

CHAPTER 7

ac paced the reception area of the studio, waiting for Gem. Just like earlier in the week, they'd been summoned to Brad's office. They'd spent all the filming hours together, crashing each other's plans with the clients. What Brad wanted now escaped him.

Gem pushed through the door, looking a little harried as usual, but when her eyes met his, they lit up as she smiled. His heart gave an unwelcome lurch. Over the last few days, they'd managed to find a balance of some kind of friendship. He was still uneasy because he wasn't sure with whom he was forming this friendship.

But like he had said to her the other night, they were having fun.

"Good morning, Gem."

"Right back atcha, Malcolm."

"Are you ever going to call me Mac?"

She shrugged with a smile and eyes that were a little glazed.

"Are you ever going to tell me your real name?"

"Don't see any reason I would."

She stood close now, close enough for him to get a hint of her perfume. "I'd like to know who my friends are. We both agreed we don't like pretense."

She chuckled. "I like *my* pretense just fine. Any idea why we're here today?"

"None." He let the rest of the conversation drop. Some day soon he'd get her to confess her real name, her story, so he could know the real her. He had a feeling he would like who she was when she wasn't Gem.

"Mr. Winford is ready for you," the receptionist said. She pointed down the hall. "He's in his office."

Mac followed Gem down the hallway and when they reached the door she paused, as if she was waiting for him to open it, then reached for the knob. His hand beat hers to it and he flashed a grin. "Do you have a problem with a man being polite?"

"Maybe I was the one being polite. I arrived at the door first, so I planned to open it."

As he swung the door open, she sneezed. And sneezed again. Two more times. When her fit stopped, she shook her head and sniffed. Her eyes were watery. She dug in her purse and pulled out a tissue. She dabbed at her eyes and wiped gently at her nose.

"Bless you," Brad called from behind his desk. "Hope you're not getting sick. We have a lot of work to do."

Gem waved a hand. "I don't get sick."

"Mike's not joining us today?" Mac asked.

"No. He's started editing the rough cuts. He doesn't need to be here for this. Have a seat."

Gem plopped into a chair and crossed her legs. "So why are we here?"

Brad waited until Mac sat.

"When we talked earlier in the week, I thought you understood what we were looking for."

Gem straightened her shoulders. "We've done what you asked. We spent every minute filming together."

"I know, but...you didn't disagree, argue, or fight."

Gem chuckled and it turned into a cough.

Mac glanced at her, a little worried that she was, in fact, getting sick, but he spoke to Brad. "I thought you weren't looking for us to manufacture fights. You didn't want to script anything. We were being ourselves."

"I don't want it scripted. I don't think either of you can act well enough to make it look good. While you both have a great onscreen presence, you're not actors. But the last two days of filming haven't given us the spark we were expecting from you." He leaned his forearms on his desk.

"How do you want to remedy this?" Gem asked, still sniffly. Her voice was scratchy.

"Unfortunately, I don't have an answer. That's why I asked you to come in today. I hoped you'd have ideas."

Gem's gaze slid to Mac.

What did she expect from him? He still didn't know what Brad found so fascinating from the other day. Mac and Gem stared at each other for a moment. Assessing. Thinking. Until she started to sneeze again.

Brad suddenly stood. "I'm starting to think you are sick, Gem. You should probably go home."

"Maybe you're right."

"When do you film next?"

"The day after tomorrow, I think." She glanced back at Mac for confirmation. Their schedules were mostly synced.

"Sounds right."

"Get well. Figure out what the two of you can fight about. If all you're going to do is get along, then the great footage from the first meet-and-greet is a waste."

Mac had nothing to say. He hadn't intentionally avoided

conflict with Gem. They'd just gotten to know each other a little better. He shook Brad's hand and Gem waved.

Back out in the hall, Mac walked beside Gem. "Any ideas?"

"None. My brain's foggy. I have no idea what's going on. I was fine when I woke up this morning. I think I'll go home and crawl into bed."

Images of her in bed assaulted him, and he mentally kicked himself. She was sick. He wasn't supposed to think about having her naked.

"I'll give our little problem some thought and give you a call later. Let me know if you come up with something."

"I doubt I will. A sick brain might be delirious."

"Delirious would keep things entertaining."

"Funny." She waved at him and trudged to her car.

Mac drove to the office. He hadn't been spending enough time there because of filming and the latest requirement to spend so much time with Gem. When he got to the door of his office, his mom called for him, so he continued down the hall. He walked into her office, took a seat across from her desk and crossed an ankle over his knee to wait while she finished whatever she was working on.

"We need to talk about this show." Her barely restrained disgust echoed through the room. Why should she be irritated? It was her idea.

"What about it? I'm doing what you and the producer have asked."

"Bradley sent me the rough cuts of the last meet-and-greet. You were awful. Simply dreadful."

He uncrossed his legs and thumped his foot against the cushiony carpet. "What the hell are you talking about? I did everything you do at the meet-and-greets."

She waved her dismissive hand. "Not that. You actually

did a stellar job there. I'm talking about the rest of your time. Your interaction with Gem."

Mac gritted his teeth. He and Gem were fine. Everyone needed to get off their backs and let them do their jobs.

"You come off looking like a dud. Especially beside her. She's so full of life and charm. You, on the other hand, look stiff and borderline bored."

"I do not. I'm not boring. I worked competently with the clients, building their trust." He inched forward in his seat and tapped on her desk. "I look like someone who cares about whether our clients find a true match. I'm not out there to play games."

"Ah, but darling, it is a game. It's supposed to be fun. And I saw the other clips. You and Gem in the hallway arguing about who the clients should be and again at the first meet-and-greet. You're not a dud when you're interacting with her."

Mac didn't have an argument. While he didn't think he was a dud alone, he knew he enjoyed his exchanges with Gem. They were fun. And in all honesty, there were few interactions during the last meet-and-greet. Gem had kept her distance.

"Well, Mother, I can't force the woman to talk to me, much less fight with me, which seems like what both you and Brad want. We talked after her first outing with Jennifer. Simple conversation set us both at ease. I suppose when one of us does something annoying, the other will step in with a comment, but that didn't happen last night. We've only been at this for a couple of weeks. One with the clients. I'm sure we'll hit our stride."

"Malcolm, hitting your stride isn't something you can wait for in the world of streaming TV."

As if she were some expert now?

"If Bradley doesn't see what he's looking for, he might

look in a new direction. And none of us wants that." She sat with her back perfectly straight, hands folded on her desk. But her eyes held some fire. She was warning him.

"What do you expect me to do?"

"Find something to criticize about her."

"I will not demean a woman to make viewers happy."

Again with the dismissive wave. "Not a personal attack. Her style. The way she deals with the clients. Point out her lack of experience in finding love. For others, of course. I would never approve of you attacking her for her personal lifestyle."

His conversation with Gem from the other night echoed in his head. He had little experience as well. And they all knew it.

"Maybe you should review some footage and see where you could've argued. Then you'll know what to look for to spice things up." She stood and a look of genuine concern crossed her face. "We need this, Malcolm. I'm trusting you to get it right."

He stood and nodded. Their business was solid but word of mouth had become harder and harder over the years because of apps and online matchmaking sites. This success would put them on the map in Chicago again. And it would prove to his mother that he was serious about taking over the business.

Mac left his mom's office and went back to his. He studied files of potential clients his mother would be meeting with over the coming days. His job was to start digging into their database to find appropriate matches. Unlike the silly TV show, no one expected to get it perfect on the first try.

He worked for a few hours but was distracted by his conversation with his mother. Lydia, his mother's secretary, had dropped off a disk of the rough cuts his mother had referred to. He wondered what kind of relationship Brad and

Gail had that allowed her access to footage he hadn't been able to see.

Sighing, he realized that until he dealt with the show, he wouldn't be able to focus on his real job. He stared at the disk. He should watch it, but it would give him an unfair advantage, again, and he'd told Gem he would do everything in his power to keep the playing field level.

He sent her a text asking if she wanted to meet up and watch the video.

No. Came her quick reply. *I look and feel like crap.*

I doubt it.

Watch without me and give me the highlights.

Sure?

Yeah. I'm not fit to be in public.

Mac gave it some thought. If she didn't feel well enough to go out, he'd go to her. He scooped up his things and the disk and headed to Gem's apartment.

Mac parked his car near Gem's apartment and realized he should've called ahead. Yeah, she was probably home, but no one liked unexpected visitors, especially when sick. He hoped the spicy Asian chicken soup he brought would be enough to balance her irritation.

At her door, he rang the bell and waited, looking for a call box or buzzer. A minute later, a beautiful woman came to the door. Had he rung the wrong bell?

"Can I help you?" she asked, only opening the door an inch.

"Uh, I'm here to see Gem." He suddenly felt ridiculous that he didn't have a last name to offer. "She told me she lived on the third floor."

The door swung wide. "It's you!" she yelled.

Mac wasn't sure if that was supposed to be good or bad, so he waited.

"The matchmaker guy. Na—Gem told me all about you. She didn't say you were coming over."

"I didn't tell her. I know she's not feeling well, but I need to talk to her about the show."

"Oh, well, come on in. I'm her roommate and best friend, Jillian." She spun on her heel and jogged up the stairs.

Mac followed, careful not to jostle the soup too much. Jillian reached the apartment before he did and from the hall, he heard her calling, "Hey, Gem, your matchmaking buddy is here for a visit."

"What?"

Mac stepped through the door and closed it behind him. Hushed whispers crept in from the other side of the living room. Gem didn't sound happy he had come by. She rounded the corner, and he did a double take.

She wore big, dark-framed glasses. Her hair was piled on her head in a sloppy knot. The usually perfectly styled Gem wore flannel pajama bottoms with cats on them and an old Northwestern University sweatshirt. Cute.

"What are you doing here?"

"I brought you soup." He held up the bag. She didn't seem impressed. "You said you didn't want to go out, so I came to you."

"I was being polite. I don't want to see anyone." She sounded congested, but she didn't look like she was on death's door. "Like I said, I look and feel like crap."

He smiled. "It's a good thing I don't care what you look like. The soup will help you feel better. We need to talk about the show. Brad wasn't kidding about needing something more from us."

She huffed and crossed her arms. "Why couldn't this wait?"

"Because we have two days until we're filming again. If we don't have a plan, we'll keep doing what we did for the last two days and it obviously wasn't good enough. They want spark, remember?"

She blew a breath up and her bangs fluttered. She held up a hand and waved over her body. "Let me go change—"

"Don't. You're fine. Do you have a DVD player or should I get my laptop out to watch the footage?"

"We have a DVD player." She held out her hand.

He looked over to the TV, saw the player, and handed her the bag with the soup. "Go have a seat and relax."

Then he went to the DVD player and slid in the disk. From her perch on the couch, Gem used the remote to turn on the TV and get the footage started.

"How'd you get your hands on the this? Brad didn't offer us anything this morning."

"My mother had a copy."

"How did she get one?"

"I have no idea." He checked out his options for seating.

Gem patted the cushion near her. "I promise not to sneeze on you. The chair isn't as comfortable as the couch." She leaned forward and took the soup from the bag. When she popped the lid off the Styrofoam container, she took a whiff.

"Spicy Asian chicken soup. It'll help."

She nodded. "The spices will clear my sinuses while keeping everything from drying. The veggies offer vitamin C to fight the virus. I should've thought of this before. Thank you."

She settled in the corner of the couch with her knees pulled up and the soup cradled against her chest.

The disk started and the footage was rough, but Mac couldn't disagree that it was boring. The camera zoomed in on Mac watching Gem giving Jennifer instructions at the bar. He listened but didn't comment. Maybe he was supposed to have said something.

"Brad was looking for me to say something to you after that."

"Why didn't you?"

"Because I had nothing to say. Everything you told Jennifer made sense. I told you that over drinks."

They watched in silence as the cameras followed Jennifer's movements in gathering phone numbers from men at the bar. Mac picked up the remote and fast-forwarded to the meet-and-greet.

Mac saw nothing wrong. He was competent and professional. Like always. Then he focused on Gem. She'd been unusually quiet at the meet-and-greet. She was the problem. Now, how could he say that without being a total dick?

He eyed her, sitting curled around her soup.

"This is lame," she announced.

"You don't like the soup?"

"No." She sat forward and put the near-empty container on the coffee table. "The soup was amazing. I feel almost normal again. I'm talking about this show."

"I guess we know why Brad called us in this morning."

"How the hell are we supposed to fix this? They can't blame us for this boring shit. They're the ones who insisted on following us all over."

"At the risk of pissing you off…"

She nailed him with a glare. Yeah, she was feeling better.

"Go on."

"I really don't want to tick you off."

"Ha! Since when?" She waved her hand. "On with it."

The spark was back in her eyes, noticeable even behind her glasses. A smile hovered on her bare lips.

"You weren't engaged. You were lifeless."

She smacked his thigh. "I followed your lead. You said nothing during my session with Jennifer so I figured you expected the same. I was being courteous."

He rubbed his eyes. So it was back to him. "They don't want you to be like me. *I* don't want you to be like me. Be yourself. You're fun."

She blushed and her gaze darted away. "Thanks," she mumbled.

He picked up the remote and paused the disk. "What was that?"

"What?" She suddenly stood and gathered the soup container and bag.

Instead of pushing, he waited until she returned from the kitchen. She handed him a bottle of water. "Sorry I don't have anything stronger."

"Water's fine. Now tell me what that shy mumbling was about."

"Huh?" She cocked an eyebrow, but it wasn't enough to hide the insecurity.

"You're not quite yourself."

"I'm sick."

"It's more than that."

She sighed. "I'm stressed. My day job situation isn't good and being *on* as Gem all the time is overwhelming. More than I thought it would be."

"Then why do it?"

She bit her lip. "Because Gem is the fun one. She's who everybody wants."

He chuckled. "It's creepy when you talk about yourself in the third person."

She shrugged. "It's easy to do because I'm not really Gem. You know that."

The stare she offered told him she knew he saw beneath the cover. She didn't mind. But he wanted to know instead of guess what was under there.

"Not true. I don't think you're that good an actress. You

are Gem. At least partially." He settled against the back of the couch beside her. "But I have to ask again, why?"

~

THIS WAS IT. NAT KNEW HE WAS ASKING FOR HER STORY. SHE didn't know if the cold made her delirious or if she was having a reaction to the soup, but she wanted to tell Malcolm everything. She'd become comfortable with him without trying.

"Gem started as an experiment. I was divorced and needed to get back out in the world." She wasn't sure if she was ready to talk about the divorce or why it happened, so she pushed on without that bit of information. "I was always the quiet girl. A bit of a wallflower, if you will. I'm a homebody, and while I dated some when I was younger, I was out of practice, and in all honesty, I was never good at it."

Malcolm's stare weighed on her. He didn't interrupt, just listened intently.

She twisted the cap on her bottle of water and took a sip. "So I did what I do best. I researched dating and flirting and how to pick up men. I read and watched videos, and when it was time to go out and practice, I did. But I didn't have a way to process the efficacy of what I was doing. So I created a blog where I could discuss my dating successes and failures. I titled it *Dating Gem* because my grandma used to dole out bits of ridiculous advice about men."

"You modeled your blog after your grandmother?"

"No. It was more a homage to her. I wanted to pass on my own dating gems to other women who were in the same place I was. I acted as the experiment. And it blossomed. I went from writing the blog to making videos to making money from the videos to having a few go somewhat viral."

"And you still don't think you're Gem?"

"No. I'm Natalie—" As soon as her name slipped out, she clamped her lips shut. How could she be so stupid? She didn't want anyone to know her real name.

A slow smile etched its way across Malcolm's face. It was almost a *gotcha!* smile, but he managed to soften it. "Thank you," he said.

"For screwing up and letting my name slip?" She couldn't hide the irritation in her voice, nor did she want to.

"Yes. I told you I want to know who you are. It's hard to do that when I don't even know your name." He stared for another beat and then added, "Natalie," like he was testing it out.

"Yes, I'm Natalie, the boring librarian who couldn't keep her husband. Happy?" She shot off the couch and went to the kitchen to make a pot of tea. Her throat was still sore. The rawness had nothing to do with her outburst. Definitely not. She sniffed as she lit the burner under the kettle.

Where was Jillian when she needed her? Jillian had routinely rescued Natalie when she opened her mouth in ways she shouldn't have. As soon as Malcolm stood in their living room, Jilly made excuses and disappeared into her room. Nat had thought she'd come out and investigate, but she hadn't. Now Nat had to face Malcolm after admitting who she really was.

Of course, the man couldn't give her time to regain her composure. Before the water was anywhere near boiling, he stood in the kitchen doorway. "I'd love a cup of tea."

She didn't turn to face him. "I don't remember offering one."

"But you would have." He shuffled behind her. "Why did you run out?"

She lifted a shoulder.

"Turn around, Natalie."

What, like he couldn't get enough of saying her name

now that he knew it? She took a deep breath through her mouth and turned. With her arms crossed, she faced him.

"Why?"

"Don't you know any other questions?" she asked.

"I do, but this one is my favorite."

"Why what?"

"Why did you run out?"

"Because I'm embarrassed."

"Of?"

"Everything." She ticked the reasons off on her fingers. "The fact that I pretend to be someone that I'm not. That I let my name slip. And I told you my profession, so my anonymity will disappear. That you're seeing me like this." Her voice rose as she spoke, and she waved her hand over her disheveled appearance. Her lip quivered. She recrossed her arms and stared at her feet. "That I admitted I can't keep a man if I'm Natalie."

She was breathing heavy, and she wasn't sure if it was her anger making its way through her system or the cold laboring her lungs. A wave of mixed emotion washed over her. A sense of relief over letting go of all the crap mixed with trepidation of the repercussions of doing so.

Malcolm's fancy dress shoes came into her field of vision at her feet.

"Natalie." He waited.

He didn't touch her, but Nat felt like he wanted to. She straightened her shoulders, clenched her jaw, and met his eyes.

"You have nothing to be embarrassed about. We all have a history that has shaped who we are, one that we've hopefully learned from."

She tried not to roll her eyes at his comments, but failed.

Again, he waited for her gaze to return to his. Damn his patience. She looked into his eyes again.

"I might not have known your name, but I've seen you, Natalie, hiding beneath Gem. Natalie is the woman I've been trying to get to know, because she's the fascinating one. As far as your concerns about anonymity, you have no worries. I would never betray a confidence."

The heat in his eyes told her he was being honest. It also caused a swirl of lust to tumble low in her belly. They weren't touching, but they were close enough that they could. If she pushed up on tiptoe, they could kiss. Her eyes wandered to his mouth, framed by that sexy trim beard. He licked his lips.

She was entranced.

He inched a fraction closer, his arm moving behind her back. Her eyes fluttered closed. Then the whistling registered and died. He'd reached around her to turn off the stove.

"I'll take my tea black." Then he spun and left the room.

What the hell? Nat blinked repeatedly. She did not imagine that. He was going to kiss her. She rolled her shoulders and grabbed a couple of mugs from the cabinet. She dropped a tea bag into each and filled them with scalding water.

With the steaming mugs in hand, Natalie walked back into the living room. Malcolm paced back and forth in front of the window, pausing to peer out onto the street. She handed him the mug. "What was that?"

"What?" he asked as he accepted the cup of tea.

"In the kitchen. You were going to kiss me, but didn't."

"I was not." It was almost a scoff, and if he had been more successful at pulling it off, Nat might've been hurt.

"I might not be able to keep a man interested forever, but I know when one is about to make a move. You were definitely on the move."

He didn't respond.

She took a step closer. "Why did you stop?"

"Because this isn't a good idea."

"Wrong again, Mr. Sterling. Why is it wrong to act on attraction?"

"Because we work together."

She rolled her eyes again.

"But more importantly, right now, you're feeling vulnerable and that's the wrong time to act. You're not comfortable being you, so you become Gem and anything goes."

Being turned down never felt good, but somehow, Malcolm made it worse. He tried to be all logical and shit. She just wanted to have fun. So she told him so. "It could be a great time, we'll only be working together for the next few weeks. Who knows? It might even add to our on-screen spark." She wagged her eyebrows at him, but he wasn't buying.

He drank his tea and maneuvered around her to go back to the couch. "If we don't figure out what to do about the show, neither of us will be working much longer."

She sighed. Again, his logic won out. The moment of intensity was gone. "Let's watch the video again and see what we could've done differently. Then we'll be armed going into this week."

"Are you suggesting we plan our arguments?"

"Not exactly. But if we know where each of us is headed with the women, we'll have ideas about how to ignite the spark that Brad loves so much."

They spent the next hour reviewing footage and talking about how to improve. By the time Malcolm left, they had a handle on the situation. Brad had no idea what was coming his way.

CHAPTER 8

Nat ran a hand down the short skirt she wore while she waited for Ashley and Malcolm. After their chat the other night, Nat and Mac had decided to meet Ashley together. If anything could create a spark between them, Ashley could. The techs all walked around adjusting lighting and microphones. When the door opened again, Nat knew it was Mac without turning around. She felt his gaze on her, and she was glad she chose these heels to wear.

Mac strode up beside her and handed her a cup. "Feeling better?"

She took the cup, lifted the lid, and sniffed. Tea. "I am, thank you."

"You definitely look better." Without shifting, he ran his eyes all over her.

"Careful. You might give a girl a complex." She took a sip of the hot tea. She'd spent the last couple of days in bed, well medicated, so she was almost back to normal. The tea soothed her dry throat.

Moments later, Ashley came in. Her smile was broad and friendly. "So how do we do this?"

Mac raised a hand. "We'll explain everything once we're in front of the cameras. The producer gets irritated if they miss anything good."

He led Ashley over to the conference table. Mike directed people and then started rolling.

Mac cleared his throat. "Ashley, Gem and I decided we might try something different. Instead of meeting with you separately, we thought we'd talk to together."

"Cool," Ashley said. "Where do we start?"

"I have a mixer set up for you. I've invited twenty men who I believe might be a good match for you."

"Okay."

"My concern lies in how you conduct yourself at the mixer."

"How do you mean?"

Nat watched as Ashley's defenses came up. She leaned back in her chair and crossed her arms. Nat, on the other hand, leaned forward to make sure she heard every silly syllable dripping from Mac's lips.

"You project a certain amount of casualness based on your dating experience. I think you need to soften some of that to project the right level of responsiveness to the men at the party."

Nat snorted. She could've kept it in check, but both Brad and Mac had told her not to hold back. Mac shot her a look from the corner of his eye, one eyebrow twitched.

"So she shouldn't be herself?" Natalie asked.

Ashley's face tightened.

"That's not what I'm saying."

"Really? I just heard you tell her not to be herself. You said she needs to project the right image."

"That's not what I said. She's dated a lot of men. She said she doesn't take dating seriously. If that's the attitude she has at the mixer, that's how the men will treat her."

"What way?" Ashley asked.

"As someone who's looking for a good time, not a relationship." He clasped his hands on the table in front of him.

The crew around them shifted, but Nat didn't know what they were doing. What she did know was that she was getting angry on Ashley's behalf. "That's BS. She needs to be herself. Having a string of casual relationships has played a role in developing who Ashley is. She can't just forget, pretend they didn't happen. And if your guests can't see that, maybe you're working with the wrong guys."

"I know what I'm doing. The men I've invited are of the highest caliber."

"Highest caliber of what? Man whores? You just said if Ashley appeared to be looking for a good time, they'd treat her like a slut."

"What?" Ashley shot up out of her chair.

"I said no such thing." His voice was low, but his cheeks were flushed.

Nat began to think maybe she'd gone too far. "Ashley, what you need is a man who won't be bothered by your past. Preferably one who won't even ask about it."

"Am I supposed to be embarrassed about my past? About the guys I've seen and slept with?"

"No. Of course not. I'm simply voicing my opinion about how to handle the mixer with Mr. Sterling."

Mac's shoulders stiffened at her use of his name. He turned to face Nat, fury in his eyes. "You need to stop putting words in my mouth. At no point did I even insinuate Ashley should be embarrassed by her social life. I wouldn't look down on *any* woman for enjoying her life."

Nat's breath hitched because suddenly, it didn't feel like he was talking about Ashley anymore.

With his eyes locked on Nat's, he continued, "But I do know a thing or two about people and the judgments they make. First impressions matter. It's where the first decision is made. If she appears flighty and cute, no man is going to consider her a serious prospect."

Now Nat really didn't know if that was supposed to be a dig at her or not.

Mac startled her further by leaning close and getting in Nat's face. "And furthermore, as a professional matchmaker, I spend a lot of time making sure I've chosen men who are worthy of my client."

Ashley's hand came down hard on the table. "You're both jerks. I'm not sure either of you knows what their doing. I'm done." She unclipped her mic, spun, and stomped out the door.

"Cut!" Mike yelled. "What the hell was that? What are we supposed to do?"

Mac and Nat looked at each other and both started laughing. They had gotten completely carried away. Nat rose. "Don't worry, Mike, I'll go talk to her."

Mac stood and rebuttoned his jacket. The man looked damn fine in a suit. The smile he sent her made her question all the thoughts that had run through her head during their argument. His mouth was soft and his eyes friendly. Maybe she imagined the attack.

With a small wave and a promise to be right back, Nat rushed from the room. It didn't take long to find Ashley. She stood in front of the vending machine contemplating poor choices. Nat knew what Ashley was thinking because Nat had found herself in the same position many times.

"Can I talk to you?"

Ashley didn't speak, but she didn't walk away either.

Nat took a deep breath. Honesty was the way to go. "What happened in there had nothing to do with you and the way you live your life. That was about me and Mr. Sterling."

Ashley turned. With a snap of her fingers, she smiled. "I knew it. I knew you guys had a thing."

"No, it's not—"

"Even so, he was still being a dick. Kind of misogynistic, don't you think? I mean, I suppose he has some good qualities, but…"

"Ashley," Nat said quickly before anyone could hear Ashley's theory and spread rumors. "That's not what I meant. What I was getting at is that this is TV. The producers wanted some more conflict between Malcolm and me. That's all."

"You were just playing it up for the cameras?"

"Yes. Things might've gotten a little more heated than we planned, but we're hoping the executives will be happy. For the record, I've seen nothing in Malcolm to make me believe he's misogynistic. He does know what he's doing. And while I might not agree with his methods, he wouldn't do anything to hurt you."

Nat paused and waited for a reaction, but when Ashley finally spoke again, it wasn't what Nat had expected.

"You guys *don't* have a thing going?" A look of confusion filled her face. "I'm not usually that far off base." Then she waved a hand. "I suppose I was tuning in to the passion. You're both passionate about your work. That must've been it."

"Must've been," Nat replied. "So you won't quit, right? I kind of promised I'd get you to come back."

"Of course I'm not quitting. I'm having a great time. You two aren't the only ones with a flair for the dramatic."

Tension seeped from Nat's muscles. "That's good."

They went back into the studio. The rest of the prep time with Ashley was calm. No more accusations were handed out and although Nat and Mac continued to disagree on what

Ashley should do to find her happily ever after, they managed to keep their tempers in check.

They responded to each other with friendly banter, which left Nat more confused than she'd been in her kitchen the other night when she'd thought Mac was going to kiss her. They were attracted to each other, he as much as admitted that. He just didn't want to act on the attraction.

Then why the hell did it feel like he was goading her into something?

WHEN THEY FINALLY CALLED IT A DAY WITH ASHLEY, MAC WAS in need of a drink. Natalie had walked out with Ashley, leaving him alone. They'd agreed that after the bickering this afternoon, he would handle Ashley's mixer alone and she would arrange something with the women later.

Whatever format Brad had originally envisioned for this show had been thrown out the window. Mac wanted to succeed, which was why he'd put in the effort to reignite the spark he and Natalie shared. He hadn't counted on the professional engagement to spark flames personally. He'd never gotten involved with someone from work because it was messy. No matter what people said about handling it, it always got messy. He couldn't afford for this to go sideways. Not only was his mother counting on him to succeed, he wanted to prove that he could hold his own in helping others find happiness.

He knew his relationship with his wife had been a disappointment to Gail. Getting involved with Natalie wouldn't help the situation.

Natalie. The name fit her so much better than Gem. He felt like they'd finally made some headway the other night, getting to know each other without cameras watching them.

The fact that he had, in fact, almost kissed her was beyond the point.

But then today, when he was explaining how important first impressions were, she looked like he'd attacked her, and he had no way to back out or make her feel better.

As he poured himself a whisky and loosened his tie, he considered calling her. Before he had the chance to make up his mind, the phone rang in his hand. Brad calling at this time couldn't possibly be good.

"Hello."

"Malcolm, you did it. Mike showed me the footage from today and it was amazing. I just wanted to call and say keep up the good work."

"Wait. What?"

"The footage today of you and Gem going at it. Whoa. It could almost be a show unto itself."

"I'm glad it's working. Did you already call Gem and tell her?" Mac wasn't sure she would share Brad's enthusiasm.

"I just got off the phone with her. She told me you two are doing the next segment solo with the women. I'm not thrilled with the idea, but after she explained why you each needed time with the clients, I understand. But I'm telling you, as I did her, you need to get back in front of the cameras together soon."

Mac told Brad he understood and hung up. He drank his whisky and poured another. Then he dialed Natalie's number. When it rang three times, he braced himself for leaving a message.

"Hello, Malcolm. What can I do for you?"

He smiled. "You can start by calling me Mac."

"Where would be the fun in that?"

"Are you busy?" He sank onto his couch.

"Nah. I'm getting ready to watch TV with Jillian. Are you calling because of Brad?"

"Yes and no. I was about to call you when he interrupted. I guess we gave him what he's looking for."

"Definitely. He was thrilled. I felt like I had my own little cheerleader. What were you going to call me about besides that?"

"We're okay, right?"

"Why wouldn't we be?"

He heard shuffling on her end and imagined her curling up on her couch, pulling her knees up to her chest.

"Things got a little heated today during filming."

"That's what we're going for, remember?"

"I felt like you were misinterpreting what I said."

"All fodder for the camera, babe."

Her light explanation should've put him at ease, but it didn't. Then he realized why. He was speaking to Gem, not Natalie. He rubbed his forehead. "I thought we were past this."

"What?"

He sighed. "You being Gem with me." When she didn't respond, he went on. "When we were arguing today, you looked...I don't know...hurt. Like I had insulted you."

"In a way, you were," she said softly. "We both know Ashley and I are not all that different. It's part of why I picked her. So an attack on her personal life hit me."

"I wasn't attacking. I was trying to get her to understand that if she wants to find something different, she needs to treat the situation differently." He sipped his whisky.

"And had you said that, it would've been fine."

This wasn't going any better than it had when the cameras were on them. Mac pinched the bridge of his nose. "I'm sorry. I should've been more careful with my words. I don't think a woman who has sexual experience should be treated any differently than a virgin."

Natalie laughed in his ear, but it wasn't the snarky, hard-edged snicker of Gem's. "That's good to know since you'd be hard-pressed to find too many adult virgins. I want to make sure Ashley gets a fair shake with you."

"I treat all my clients with respect." He paused. "I do respect her, Natalie, as I do you."

"Thank you," she said quietly. "Good night, Mac."

She disconnected, leaving him feeling like there was so much bubbling beneath the surface for them. But it wasn't lost on him that she'd finally called him Mac.

NATALIE HAD NEVER BEEN AS NERVOUS AS SHE WAS RIGHT NOW. She and Mac had worked with the women separately for the remainder of the week, for which Natalie was grateful. She needed to put some distance between her and Mac. Things were getting muddled and it messed with her head. Ever since she let her guard down, she felt like she was more Natalie than Gem around him, which was a dangerous prospect.

Today, she had to do a solo shot with the cameras to set up the individual dates she'd arranged for Jennifer, Ashley, and Melissa. Her plans were different than what Brad had expected, but then again, he'd hired her because she wasn't a run-of-the-mill matchmaker. As she sat in a tall chair, makeup and hair people came and fussed over her and it took a bit of doing not to swat at them. The lights were bright and she could only see the edge of the set, but it didn't look or feel like Mac was there.

A few new faces were hovering just on the edges, so she couldn't get a good look at them. She chose to pretend they didn't exist. Instead, she focused on what to say to the cameras as she described the plans for each woman. Later, they would edit in footage of the places.

After the success the women had had at a bar she'd taken them to, Nat finally had some confidence in her ability to pull this off. She'd taken everyone to a bar and set them loose. The cameras were tucked in around the bar and the women knew they were still being filmed, but they accomplished more than Nat thought.

Mike waved at her to let her know they were about to start. Nat rolled her lips in and took a deep breath. This was the first time she'd had to go solo in front of the camera. It shouldn't be a big deal; she did videos by herself all the time.

In the back of her head, a nagging voice reminded her that Mac would see this video. As much as she didn't want to admit it, she wanted to impress him.

She shook the thoughts loose and became Gem. Looking directly into the camera, she said, "I'm so excited about what I have planned for each client. I've already said, numerous times that I don't think I should decide who my clients should date. I've spent hours working with each woman to prepare her and give her the tools to attract the kind of man she's looking for."

Being Gem in this atmosphere was easy. She winked. "To keep things interesting, I've planned to give Melissa, Jennifer, and Ashley unique experiences. Melissa will be going rock climbing." Nat paused to allow filler for the video clips. "Jennifer will take an art class." Another pause. "And Ashley will be going to a book store."

Somewhere behind the camera, someone snickered loudly enough for her to hear. For a second, she thought Mac had arrived after all, but her gut told her it wasn't him. Her body was on full alert whenever he was around. She had no inkling of his presence right now.

Ignoring the small outburst from the intruder, Natalie continued with a brief explanation of why she'd chosen each of these activities for the women. They managed to get everything in one take, so she hoped Mike was good at his job as he chopped all these segments and assembled them into a TV show.

Nat hopped off her chair and looked for Jillian. Jilly had been wanting to check out the whole TV show filming, but her schedule didn't usually allow for her to pop in. Nat intentionally set this time up on Saturday so Jillian could come. Unfortunately, she only got to witness Natalie do what she'd been doing in their living room for years.

"That was awesome!" Jillian said as she came into the lights. She lowered her voice and added, "Except for the asshole who laughed at you. Who the hell was that?"

At least she was assured that it wasn't Mac. Jillian would've recognized him. Nat shrugged. "Don't know. I can't see much when I'm in the lights." She looped her arm around Jillian's and led her away from the camera. "Point him out."

Jillian lifted her chin and looked around. "I don't see him."

"No big deal. I'm sure plenty of others will laugh at me. Gem can handle it."

"Can you give me a tour?"

"I would, but I don't know much about anything." Then she had a thought. She glanced around to find the production intern who'd gotten her into Mac's mixer. She found him cleaning up the table from food services. "Hi. Remember me?"

"Uh, of course. Do you need something?"

"First, I don't think we've ever been formally introduced. I'm Gem." She extended her hand.

He shook it. "Spencer."

"Nice to officially meet you, Spencer. This is my friend Jillian. I was wondering if you could give us a tour of the place. She's never seen a TV studio before." She giggled. "Neither have I, but that probably sounds silly coming from someone who's on camera all the time now."

"I'd be happy to." He turned away from the table and led them through the entire studio, offering more than the dime tour. He launched into all kinds of technical details and the information junkie in Natalie ate it up.

When they finally left the studio, night had fallen, but Natalie was still ramped up. She felt good about her taping, she'd learned all kinds of interesting information about television production, and she managed to not see or talk to Mac in days. She was back in her element. "Let's go to a club. I feel like having a good time tonight."

"Lead the way," Jillian said.

MAC GOT READY FOR HIS TAPING. THINGS WITH THE CLIENTS had been smooth for the last few days, mostly because he and Natalie had not been in the same room since the debacle with Ashley. As he looked over his notes to prep, Paul came into his office.

"Got a few minutes?"

Mac glanced at the clock. He had to leave for the studio soon. "A few."

"You might need to rethink your approach with the show."

Mac set down his note cards. "How so?"

"I went to Gem's filming. She's got some unusual things planned." He took the seat across from Mac.

"We knew that going in. That was Brad's whole purpose in bringing her on board. So what?"

While he shouldn't be bothered by anything Gem—Natalie—had planned, something in Paul's demeanor was unsettling.

"Even if what she does flops, the activities will play out

well on film. She'll grab the audience's attention because visually, it'll be a hit."

Mac considered asking what she had planned, but he didn't want to care. He bit his tongue and waited. Paul would've stood to leave if he'd said everything on his mind. Then he asked his friend, "Why were you there anyway?"

"Gail asked me to stop by. She's worried about you."

Mac rocked back in his chair. "More like she's worried I'll screw up her reputation. Maybe remind her that this was all her idea. I'm playing this the way I would with any client. That means no switching things up to compete with ... Gem." Good thing he'd caught himself. He'd almost used Natalie's real name, and although he'd trust Paul not to say anything, he didn't want to betray her confidence.

"Gail is worried about you. *I'm* worried about this competition."

It was unlike Paul to worry. "Why? I'm doing everything my mother would do if she were in my place. Would you have these concerns if she were the one in front of the camera?"

"Yes." Paul stood and tucked his hands in his pockets. "It's not you or how you do your job. I'm sure you're competent. Gail wouldn't let you do this otherwise. It's the other players here. We still don't know anything about Gem or what she's capable of."

Now Mac was totally confused. "Gem isn't doing anything."

"You don't know that. The studio isn't keeping a tight lid on things. I walked into Gem's taping and no one even looked at me."

"It's a TV show. Are they supposed to have security check points? I think you're overreacting."

"I hope I am. But I know Gem brought someone to watch her film. What if she's there to spy?"

"First, we're not trading government secrets. Second, most of what Gem and I do happens together, so no one's hiding anything. Third, she probably brought her roommate to the taping. She'd mentioned earlier that Jillian wanted to see the set."

Paul turned abruptly in his pacing route. "You know her roommate?"

Mac nodded. "After Brad called us in to talk about our lack of excitement on camera, we met and came up with a plan. That's why the last meeting went so well. Brad was thrilled with the footage."

Mac, however, was still concerned about how his remarks had affected Natalie. She's said they were all right, but since they hadn't seen each other in days, he wasn't sure.

"You spent time with Gem?"

Mac nodded, checked the time, and stood.

"Without the cameras?"

"Yes," he answered as he gathered his notes. "I have to get to the taping. Are you joining me?"

"I think I might. I want to hear what else you have going on behind the scenes with Gem."

"There's nothing going on." Mac worked to keep the irritation out of his voice because Paul would sniff that out as an indication he was on to something. Mac led the way out of his office.

"Where did you meet for your little pow-wow?"

"Her apartment. That's where I met her roommate."

"If you give me her address, I'll be able to find out her real name."

Mac pressed the button for the elevator. "Don't need you to do that. I already know. You don't need to do any digging on her. We're in this together to make a good show."

"Wrong. You're both on *Love Match*, but you're in direct competition with each other. Don't forget that. She has no reason to make you look good. In fact, she bonuses if you look like an idiot."

"Gem wouldn't do that." *Gem* would, but Natalie wouldn't. Crap. Now he was thinking about her as two separate people.

They stepped onto the elevator. Paul leaned against the rail and studied him. "Are you into her?"

"What?"

"Are you into her? Do you want to screw her?"

"What's next? Are you going to ask me if I *like her* like her? I thought we were adults."

Paul checked his phone. "Nice deflection. Don't think I didn't notice your lack of an answer."

When they reached the lobby, Mac turned to him. "We have chemistry. She's a fascinating woman. However, it could ruin my career to get involved with her. I'm not an idiot."

"Hmmm," Paul said.

"What now?"

"Just thinking how we could use this to our advantage."

"Stop. You're starting to sound like my mother. I'm not a client and neither is Gem. We're going to do this job, draw positive attention to Everyday Love, and bring in tons of clients. That's it."

"If you say so."

He did say so. He was an adult, and so was Natalie. They both had a lot at stake in this venture. An exciting night together wasn't worth the risk.

At least that's what he kept telling himself.

hen Natalie came home hours later, she was fuming. Every single woman had stories of dates gone wrong. It was part of the game. However, this guy tonight…she couldn't believe him. Natalie walked into her apartment and threw her purse at the couch. It hit the back and bounced to the floor.

"Are you okay?" Jillian asked. "Steam has been rolling off you since we left the bar. So the guy was a dick. It happens."

"No, Jilly. It was more than that. It was his assumptions about women and everything. Agh." She threw her arms in the air, then stomped over to her laptop.

Jillian raced across the room and slapped a hand on the computer. "Oh, no you don't. You can't do a video when you're like this."

"Like what?"

"Half Gem, half Natalie."

"I'm fine. This is exactly what Gem would talk about." She inhaled deeply and smiled at Jillian. "See? I'm fine." As the words tumbled from her lips, she became Gem and her smile turned flirtatious.

Jillian backed away shaking her head. "I give up. Good night. And remember—no real names. I don't want to defend you in a lawsuit."

"I know the rules."

As soon as Jillian closed her bedroom door, Natalie booted up the computer and opened her video program. She took a minute to gather her thoughts so she wouldn't come across like a screaming lunatic. Then she hit record.

"Hi, everyone. I have a bit of rant for today's Dating Gem. It's pretty simple, really. Come close so you don't miss it." She leaned forward, knowing she offered the camera better cleavage. "Here it is...No one owes you anything." She paused, smiled, and sat back.

She waved her hand. "I know, you're all sitting there thinking, 'Hey, Gem, tell me something I don't know. Or at least explain what that has to do with dating.'"

Natalie took another deep breath. "I've been feeling out of sorts, so I went out looking for a good time. I danced with my roommate and we met a couple of guys at a bar. This one guy—let's call him Dick—he bought a few rounds of drinks. Then he suggested we go somewhere a little quieter to get to know each other."

She leaned toward the camera again. "We all know that's code for making out. And I'm okay with that. He was cute. We had some chemistry. And you all know how I feel about a kiss." She clenched her jaw and then forced her face to relax. "But then this guy..." She shook her head. "We didn't even get to a kiss. He starts pressing against the back of my head telling me to go down on him. When I tell him no, he says I owe him at least a hand job."

She laughed a thin, little laugh. "And yeah, a hand job isn't much. I might even enjoy it." She winked at the camera. "But to tell me I owe you? I think not.

"I give myself freely to whomever I want. Yeah, I've gone

down on guys before without any reciprocation because we were having fun. I've given a hand job in a dark corner of a crowded bar because it was exciting. But those were things I *wanted* to do. Not because someone expected me to."

Natalie inhaled slowly. She nodded at the screen as if someone had spoken. "I know, guys. You're complaining that women expect you to pay for a date, buy them dinner or drinks. And some do. I'm not saying it's right. But I didn't expect Dick to pay for my drinks tonight. I have my own money. Hell, I didn't ask for a drink at all. He did that because he *chose* to. But to expect sexual favors in return for some drinks?"

She crossed her arms on the table in front of the computer. "This isn't some feminist screed, so trolls, step on back. This is basic human decency. Guys, you want to get somewhere with women, don't treat them like hookers."

Running her tongue over her lips, she studied her face in the screen. "I'm all for fun and games and having a good time. But always remember—it's about the fun, not what someone owes you.

"And poor little Dick. He missed out on a whole lotta fun tonight."

Natalie clicked to stop recording and sat back. She felt better. She usually did after making a video. There was something cathartic about spilling your guts to thousands of strangers.

She hit play and watched herself to see if the video needed any editing, but she just got irritated all over again listening to herself talk about Dick. Adding the lead-in with titles and her music, she titled it "I Owe You Nothing," and then saved it.

Jillian was right. This wasn't her normal type of video. She offered advice based on her research and experimentation. What worked and didn't work for picking up a guy.

How to go after what you want. She talked sex and flirting and fun.

But something about the whole episode with Dick was wrong. She knew she should consider herself lucky to get to thirty years old without experiencing something like this or worse. And if that had happened when she was younger, she would've felt ashamed, not indignant. She'd learned a lot about herself and men, and dating in general over the last couple of years. Thankfully, Dick was not the norm. He was the kind of guy that ruined the dating pool for everyone.

So she'd sit on the video for a while. When she was clear-headed, she'd decide whether it should be uploaded. In the meantime, she got ready for bed. Her irritation with Dick reminded her of her irritation with Mac. She hadn't heard from him in days, and she was glad. She'd needed a break from him.

They shared a ton of chemistry; she felt it every time they verbally sparred. But his reaction to Ashley struck a nerve with her. He'd explained himself easily enough, and his words on camera didn't jibe with her perception of him, but they still irked her. She didn't know what to think of Malcolm Sterling.

Mac was different for her, but she couldn't quite put her finger on why. He'd treated her with respect in every interaction they'd had, and it had never felt phony. That was part of why his comments about Ashley hit her. She sighed and took off her make up.

The day was over. She had dates set up for Jennifer, Ashley, and Melissa, but she didn't know if Mac planned to tag along. She barely planned to be part of the night. Her clients needed to fly on their own if they wanted to be successful. The more she guided them, the less likely they were to find the right guys.

Regardless of Mac and his experience, she firmly believed

each woman needed to discover who was right for her. And maybe they could teach her something in the process. Every time she stepped in front of the camera, she still felt like a fraud. She knew nothing about finding forever love. But maybe with the right tools, her clients would be successful.

~

Days passed and Mac hadn't heard from Natalie at all. Brad had agreed it would be awkward for the clients to have Mac and Gem with them on dates. Since they didn't tag along on the dates Mac had set up, it was only fair that they not attend the events Gem had scheduled. That meant there had been no reason for him to call Natalie, which irritated him. He shouldn't need a reason, but he found himself searching for one because he missed spending time with her.

Then his reason came in the form of rough cuts of the clients' dates. He'd called Natalie and asked if she'd like to come to his place to watch the tape. She'd agreed, and now he paced in his living room trying to figure out what else he needed. He had snacks and drinks. He looked at the room and imagined how Natalie would view it.

Masculine, without a doubt. He had no frilly pillows or soft blankets hanging on furniture the way she had. The leather couch was comfortable and his flat screen had a much better picture than hers. He scrubbed a hand over his beard. Why was he trying to impress her? Hadn't he told Paul starting something with her would be too risky?

Forget it. He never worried about what the place looked like when Paul came over, so he wouldn't be concerned now. Natalie was a coworker, a friend.

One he was attracted to.

Shit. He needed to turn off that part of his brain. The bell rang and he buzzed her up. He opened the door and waited in the hallway for the elevator to arrive.

When she stepped off the elevator, she was in full Gem form from high heels to perfectly applied eye makeup. He didn't know why, but it bothered him. He'd expected her to be dressed like she had been while sick.

As she neared, she looked at him with a smile. The smile was pure Natalie. "Nice digs. I think I'm in the wrong line of work. Had I known matchmaking was so lucrative, I would've gotten into the business a long time ago."

"My mother has built quite the nice empire." He held the door for her.

She stepped into his condo and let out a low whistle. "It's even nicer than I imagined. You probably had a good laugh coming to my place."

"I didn't laugh at your apartment. If it makes you feel any better, my mother owns this building."

"Thanks for trying, but that doesn't help. This place is amazing and nothing like where I live."

"But your apartment suits you."

She turned and looked at him with a raised brow. He didn't know how she did it, but she routinely made him sound stupid. The words in his head didn't come out the way he wanted them to. "I mean that your apartment is comfortable, lived in."

"So something *used* and rundown suits me."

He froze. Every time he opened his mouth to fix what he'd said, he only made it worse.

Finally, she let him off the hook. She smiled. "Lighten up, Malcolm. I know what you meant. And you're right. My place does suit me. It's cozy."

Cozy. Why hadn't he thought of that? Maybe because she was looking anything but cozy right now.

She turned away again and swept through the room. "But

what I could do with a space like this. I could have a whole wall of books."

Ah, the librarian in her shows. "My mother actually has a library at home. It's always been one of my favorite rooms in the house."

She looked at him. "You grew up in a house big enough to have its own library? Like in *Beauty and the Beast*?"

"Not quite that big. I don't come from royalty." They stood awkwardly for a moment. "Can I get you something to eat or drink?"

"Sure. Whatever you have is fine."

"I have wine or whisky. Water."

"I'll have some wine."

"White or red?"

"Jeez. Aren't you full service? Since Jillian and I usually drink whatever's on sale, I'm not picky."

Mac was grateful to have a task that would get him away from her for a minute to gather his thoughts. He didn't like feeling out of step with her. They'd found rhythm for work and it had stemmed from the personal foundation they'd forged. He had no idea how they'd gotten here.

"Can I help with anything?"

So much for his reprieve. He pointed to the selection of snacks he had laid out on the counter. "Decide what you'd like."

"A man after my own heart. Salty and sweet. The best kind of snacking food." She opened the box of popcorn and put a bag in the microwave.

He grabbed the bottle of white from the fridge and opened a drawer to get the corkscrew. Natalie stepped around him. She tore at the package of chocolate chip cookies and opened a cabinet to get a plate. She moved through his kitchen as if she'd been there before.

They worked around each other, nearly colliding only

once as they readied their feast. When he had glasses poured and she had cookies plated and popcorn in a bowl, they filled their arms and carried everything into the living room.

"I'm glad you agreed to come over tonight."

"Yeah?" she asked.

"We haven't talked in days, and I think watching the rough cuts together is a good idea."

"Is that the only reason?" She set the food on the coffee table.

"No." He handed her a glass of wine. He stared into her guarded blue eyes. "I wanted to make sure we're really okay. I know you were bothered by what I said to Ashley. And you were right, I could've said things and handled the situation better, but I don't know. You make me tongue-tied and then you poke at me, which makes it worse."

She took a sip of wine, but it wasn't enough to hide her grin.

"Now you're going to laugh at me?"

"I'm not laughing." She sighed and set her glass down as she sat on the couch. "I'm glad I'm not the only one affected by this." She pointed between them.

"What have I done to you?"

She laughed. "You look at me. No—you study me. Every move, every word. I haven't been able to tell if you do it because you like me or because you're looking for my weakness."

He hadn't thought he'd been that obvious. He couldn't keep his eyes off her whenever she was in the room. "I think we've already discussed the fact that I like you."

"I like you too. Friends, right?" She winked. "Now let's watch the dates."

He settled beside her and turned on the TV. As the video started, Mac put the idea of her being Gem out of his mind. They were friends. That's what they had to be.

Since they were viewing the rough cuts, there was a lot of extra footage of the women getting ready for their dates. Natalie kept a running monologue about their wardrobe choices.

Each woman had dinner at a different restaurant, each quiet and romantic, allowing ample time to get to know their dates.

"Kind of repetitive, huh?"

"I'm sure for the final show they won't go back to back with these dates." He hadn't even thought about how that would play out on screen. No wonder Paul had been worried.

Melissa's date was first and inside the first ten minutes of the date, she'd mentioned her desire to get married and talked about her past relationships. He'd specifically told the women not to bring up the past unless their dates asked a question.

Natalie didn't comment, but shook her head.

Both he and Natalie saw the man, Greg, begin to distance himself. Watching the remainder of the date was almost painful. Natalie drained her glass before they cameraman got to the point of solo interviews. Melissa said she enjoyed the date, but didn't feel any chemistry. Greg said he wouldn't be calling Melissa again.

Without a word, Natalie got up and went to the kitchen. She returned with the bottle of wine. "I think we're gonna need more to get through the rest of this."

Unfortunately, she was right.

By the time they got to the third date, the bottle was empty and they'd resorted to fast forwarding through the worst parts. Natalie had moved closer to him on the couch, making it difficult to keep his focus on the TV. Her soft scent wafted over to him every time she shifted.

When they reached the end of the three dates, Natalie

smiled. "You know, this whole time, I've been treating it as a given that you would win this competition."

"Really?"

"Yeah. I mean, let's face it, I know nothing about setting people up. But after watching this train wreck, I think I might have a chance."

"That sure of yourself?"

"No, but I think it's a possibility. I can't be that bad, right?"

"You're funny. Not every date is a homerun. I'll go at it again. I'll find men more suited to the women. As soon as I figure out where I went wrong."

Natalie shook her head. "I'm probably going to regret saying this, but let them help."

"What?"

"These women need to play a part in finding their partners. Sure, they've had no luck on their own thus far, but who's to say you know what they like and what they need better than they do?"

Damn if she didn't have a point. What if he let the women go through the database with him, watch the interview tapes the men submitted. It might work, especially with the time crunch the TV show created. He'd have to run it by his mother to see what she thought.

"Are you up for staying to watch how your event went?"

Nat checked the time, but what difference did it make? It wasn't like she had a job to get up for in the morning. However, the wine made her feel friendlier towards Mac, and she wasn't sure if it was a good thing. He'd apologized a couple of times now for his words to Ashley, but she remained self-conscious about what he'd said.

"Something wrong?" he asked quietly.

When his voice got deep like that, it hit her low in the belly with a desire she shouldn't have.

Calling on her full ability to be Gem, she smiled. "I'm nervous about what's going to happen when we turn this on."

Her double entendre wasn't lost on him. Clearing his throat, he settled back on the couch, extending his long legs in front of him and one arm along the back, close, but not touching her. "Can't be any worse than what we've seen."

"One can hope."

He reached and tugged her hair. "Only one way to find out."

His touch sent signals through her body where they didn't belong. Her breath hitched, unsure of the rules for this game. She wasn't used to the playing field being quite so even. She didn't like it.

He tossed the remote in her lap. "Press play."

Point Malcolm. Any other man would've made a move. She sighed and pushed the button.

For each woman, Nat had worked with a reputable organization that put together events for singles. It allowed Chicagoans to meet other singles without it being filled with the pressures of a date. In exchange for allowing Jennifer, Ashley, and Melissa access to the events, Natalie gave the organization free advertising on her site and she promised a call out to them in her next few videos.

Ashley was first, which made Natalie feel a little better. She was most confident in Ashley's abilities to strike up a conversation with a man and get a date. Her event took place at a bar that hosted literary events, which was a natural fit for Ashley since she was a writer. Books n' Brew was a regular event at the bar, but that night, the place had been packed with singles.

By the time Ashley had chatted with a handful of men,

Nat couldn't hold back her smile. When Ashley made a date to get to know one guy better, Nat jumped up and danced.

Mac's attention was glued to her expertly executed hip swivel. "Don't get too excited there, Gem. You still have two more clients to get through. And considering you have a special bond with Ashley, I'd worry if this hadn't been a success." He stood. "But I like the dance. You should consider doing that for the camera."

"You're a funny guy, Mr. Sterling. At least I'm having fun." She plopped back on the couch.

He left the room, so she hit pause on the disk. She wouldn't want him to miss any of her success. When he came back, he was carrying another bottle of wine. "What's that supposed to mean?"

"You're always so stiff and formal. Do you have fun doing anything?"

"I'm enjoying myself," he said with a smile. He refilled their glasses.

The grin was friendly, but the look in his eyes was anything but. The way he looked at her made her warm all over.

She took a deep breath and a healthy sip of delicious wine. It wasn't like her to be that off track. Rarely did she look into a man's eyes and be unsure of what he wanted. She hated questioning herself.

Jennifer spoke directly into the camera before her event. *"I don't know what Gem was thinking with this. I'm an accountant. I have zero art skills."*

Nat shook her head. She'd explained the philosophy clearly when she'd met with Jennifer. The woman needed to get way the hell out of her comfort zone. Nat hoped an art class might loosen her up.

The screen cut to the class where the project for the week was working with clay.

"Were you hoping for the love scene from *Ghost*?" Mac asked.

"With her? Hell, no. I wanted her to dig in and get dirty." Nat glanced at him. "She's a lot like you."

"How so?"

The incredulous look on his face forced a smile onto hers. "Oh yeah. You both have these ultimate shields up. You hide behind perfect manners and polite conversation. Damn. Even when you're insulting me, you sound nice about it." She couldn't believe she was saying this. Another sip of wine fortified her. "There's never anything real and raw. Uncensored."

Although the video continued in the background, the air between them filled and expanded with tension. Mac stared long enough and deep enough that she knew he was ready to break.

But a shriek on the TV broke the moment instead. Slowly, they both turned to the screen where Jennifer had clay splattering everywhere, including all over the cute guy sitting next to her.

And she did nothing.

"Ugh. You'd think I didn't teach her anything. That was the perfect moment. Cute chit-chat, get his number..." Nat waved at the screen. "What is wrong with her?"

"You're trying to get her to be something she's not. Much like you warned me against doing with Ashley."

That stung. Partly because he had a point. "I don't want her to be something she's not. I want her to be fearless and try new things."

Mac inched forward on the cushion. "Not everyone can be like you."

The snort slipped out before she could stop it. How little he knew. Their gazes locked again and the same thick sexual tension peaked. She swallowed hard and leaned closer.

"What are you doing?" he asked, his voice barely a whisper.

"Being fearless." Closing her eyes, she moved in for a kiss, but he grabbed her shoulders as he backed away.

Her eyes snapped wide open.

"We can't do this," he said.

"Why the hell not? We have hot chemistry going on here."

"We have to be able to work together." He released her shoulders.

"So we should get rid of this distraction."

"I'm not the kind of man who has sex to purge my system. I like you, but this won't work."

"Hey, babe. Your loss." She scooted to the other side of the couch. She knew he felt the attraction. He didn't deny it. But damn. A girl can only take so much rejection. Of course, he was aware of her as Natalie, and as usual, she wasn't enough.

They watched Melissa's date play out on screen, but Nat had a hard time focusing. She'd made all the right moves again to spark something between her and Mac. Yet he wouldn't play ball. It was irritating to say the least, especially since he didn't say he wasn't interested.

Melissa's date was at an indoor rock wall climbing event. Nat gave Melissa credit for at least trying. The woman gave climbing a real try and Nat guessed she was probably mighty sore now. When they reached the end of the disk, Nat stood. "They might not have found true love on their dates, but no arguing, they had a good time."

Once again, Mac was still sprawled in his corner of the couch, all long legs and arms. "Gloating doesn't look good on you."

"You're wrong. Everything looks good on me." She gathered up their dirty glasses and took them to the kitchen. When she turned, Mac was behind her with the remainder of the snacks.

"Are you okay to drive?"

Other than still being turned on by your presence? "I'm good. Thanks."

He stroked his beard, which Nat had been dying to do.

"About before—"

She raised a hand. "Over and forgotten. See you whenever we get summoned to the office. I'm sure Brad will want to see us soon."

"I'm sure."

Then Nat waltzed out of his condo. Yeah, waltzed. She wouldn't let him see his rejection bothered her. She was better than that. A man could no longer determine how she felt about herself. Her failed marriage had taught her that much.

Malcolm Sterling didn't want her. So what?

Except as she got into her car, she still felt like she missed out on something really good.

MAC HAD EXPERIENCED TWO OF THE MOST RESTLESS NIGHTS OF sleep he could remember ever having. He knew he was right in turning Natalie down, but he knew she didn't fully understand why. He'd hoped to be able to talk to her before meeting with Brad again, but she'd dodged his calls. Turning her down also made him miserable.

He got to the studio before Natalie, waiting outside until five minutes before they were expected, and she still hadn't arrived. Surely she wouldn't blow off the meeting. After letting the receptionist know he was there, he went back to the door to look for Natalie. She whipped into a parking spot with a minute to spare. When she walked up to the door, he held it open for her. "Can we talk?"

"We're supposed to meet with Brad."

"I know, but since you've avoided talking to me since you left my house—"

"I haven't been avoiding you. I have a life, Malcolm."

"Mr. Winford is ready," the receptionist said.

"See? No time for chatting." Natalie waved and ducked past him.

She was back to being Gem full-time and it was killing him. He didn't like full-time Gem, but worse was the toll he knew it took on her. *She* didn't like it either.

With a deep breath, he followed her into Brad's office. Mac didn't know what to think. They'd been meeting in the conference room because it allowed for more space for cameras and crew to film. Natalie had the office door open and had already gone through when he'd caught up.

Mac glanced around the office. No crew. Just Brad, Mike, and a lone cameraman.

"Gem. Mac. Thanks for coming in." Brad pointed to the two chairs in front of his desk.

"What did we screw up now?" Natalie asked.

"Nothing," Mike said. "You've seen the footage we've got, right?"

They nodded.

"It looks good. By the time we finish editing, it'll be great."

"So why are we here?" Natalie asked.

Brad leaned his arms on the desk. "We need to move things faster. All of the work you did with the women this week will be boiled down to a couple of episodes. We need to get steamier stuff on screen. That's what's going to draw in viewers."

Mac had been afraid of this since the beginning. "You can't rush this. Falling in love takes time."

"Definitely," Natalie agreed.

Mac froze for a second. He'd thought she would disagree just to oppose him. Her agreement was odd.

Brad said, "Look. We don't necessarily need to see a wedding. Not that I would say no. But I'm trying to be realistic. We need to see enough romance between the women and whoever they pick. We need some steam on the screen."

"We can definitely get that going. I've said all along they should kiss their dates. The first kiss is so important."

Mac didn't have the patience for Gem to push his buttons. "Rushing to kiss a man isn't going to lead to lasting love, just a lot of sampling. They want more than that."

Natalie slapped the arm of her chair and stood. With a finger pointed at him, she railed, "That's enough. What is with you and the slut-shaming? I'm not talking about a gang-bang for the cameras. It's kissing. A kiss is the fundamental basis for finding chemistry. A kiss can tell you everything you need to know about a guy."

When she stopped for a breath, Mac stood. With his eyes on Natalie, he said, "Can you give us the room for a minute? My colleague and I have something to discuss."

He felt them shifting around the room. When the door clicked, Mac looked around to make sure everyone was gone, including the cameraman. When he turned back to Natalie, she had her arms crossed.

"That's rich. You're afraid to lose it in front of the cameras."

"I don't lose it."

Her arms waved wildly. "That's part of your problem. You're too buttoned up to enjoy life and go after what you want."

Mac stepped forward and she backed away, bumping into the desk. But now she was fully within reach. He burrowed his fingers deep into her hair and brought her mouth to his. He started slow, brushing her lips with his and she sucked in a breath.

She was exactly where he wanted her—no longer talking

like Gem but acting like Natalie. When her eyes fluttered closed, he angled his head and took the kiss deeper, opening her lips and sliding his tongue into her mouth.

Then she sighed and her hands found their way under his jacket and circled his back. Time stood still and the world faded to background around them. Why the hell hadn't he done this sooner?

Natalie was right. A simple kiss did tell him everything.

In that moment, he decided Natalie would be his.

CHAPTER 10

A sharp knock on the door had Nat jumping away from Mac. In the process, she knocked over a cup of pens. She stared at Mac. "What the hell?"

She barely got the words out and Brad was opening the door. "Are you okay in there? Everyone decent? We're coming in."

Nat grabbed the pens she'd spilled and shoved them back in the cup. Mac just stood, staring at her with an unusually intense expression, her lipstick smeared on his lips. Which meant her lips were smeared to the high heavens. She put a trembling finger to her lips as the door swung wide. Brad and Mike came back in, looked at Mac and her and back to Mac.

Grabbing her purse from her chair, she kept her head down and said, "I'm sorry. I have to go."

She practically ran out of the office, tripping in her heels, and almost colliding with someone coming down the hall. Once in her car, she flipped down the visor and studied her face. If she hadn't actually been involved in the kiss, one look at her face, and she would've thought a whole hell of a lot more had happened. Her hair was wild around her face, her lipstick had vanished, and her lips were swollen.

What the hell was that? That was no regular shut up kiss. She'd had guys kiss her before in an effort to shut her up. Hell, she'd done it to guys who were boring. But that? She had no idea what that was. Her hands were still unsteady when she started the ignition.

In the rearview mirror, she saw Mac come through the door, so she put the car in reverse and screeched from her spot. She couldn't talk to him. Not now. Not until she had her shit together. All the way home, she replayed the kiss in her head.

Maybe it had been so intense because they'd been fighting it for so long. That was probably it. Nat took a deep breath. Finding a reason for the unsettling emotions hitting her made her feel better. Then her phone rang. Mac's name lit the screen and an avalanche of rocks tumbled through her stomach, so she ignored the call.

At her apartment, Natalie kicked off her heels as soon as she cleared the door. Stupid shoes. She'd been walking in heels since she was a teen. Gem's wardrobe required heels all the time. She never stumbled, let alone tripped.

She threw the shoes at the closet door.

"What did the poor shoes do to you?"

Jillian's voice scared a scream from Nat. "What are you doing home?"

Jillian lifted a shoulder. "Playing hooky."

"What?"

"I needed a mental health day."

"But you never take a day off. What's wrong?"

"Nothing. Why are you throwing shoes? Was the meeting at the studio that bad?" Jillian squinted and studied Natalie's face.

"So much worse. He kissed me!" Nat walked to the couch and flounced on it.

"Who kissed you?"

Nat rested her head on the back of the couch and closed her eyes. But that was a mistake because she envisioned the kiss. Again. "Who do you think? Mac. He sat in his freaking living room the other night and flat out rejected me, but today, in Brad's office of all places, he plants a kiss on me. Who does that?"

"This is good." Jillian joined her on the couch, curling her legs under her. "Tell me it was good. He looks like he could make it really good."

Three goods didn't nearly begin to cover it. Nat rolled her head to face Jillian. "So good." Closing her eyes again, she groaned.

"What are you moaning about? I thought you wanted this." She smacked Nat's thigh.

"I wanted it on my terms."

The doorbell rang.

"I'm not here," Nat said as she grabbed a pillow and put it over her face.

"Well, I have to answer. What if my boss is checking to make sure I'm sick?"

"He wouldn't. He's a big important lawyer."

Jillian stood. Nat jumped up and grabbed her arm. "No."

"You don't even know it's him."

Nat held tighter. The doorbell rang again.

"He doesn't sound like he's going anywhere." Jillian pulled from her grasp. "Plus, you have to face him sooner or later. It's better here. You have home court advantage."

Jillian had a point. Nat still had to work with him for weeks. So while Jillian went to let Mac in, Nat raced through the apartment to fix her hair and her clothes. She even put on the offending heels again. As Gem, she could face anything.

When she came back into the living room with her full armor in place, Mac was standing there, not looking any better than she felt.

Jillian cleared her throat. "I'm running out. Be back in a couple of hours. Might take in a movie."

Before Nat could protest, Jillian waved and closed the door behind her.

She and Mac stood on opposite sides of the room staring at each other. Finally she asked, "Why are you here?"

"Why did you leave?"

"You kissed me." She stepped forward.

He nodded. "But why did you leave?"

Nat faltered. She couldn't tell him why she ran out. "Why did you kiss me? The other night you turned me down."

"Gem made that offer, and we both know it."

"What are you talking about?" she asked, but in her gut she knew.

"You decided to be fearless with me, but you only did it as Gem. If it had been Natalie, the night would've ended differently." His voice was strong and sure, his words definite.

Her heart thumped from her chest up into her throat. She swallowed hard and said, "You were the one who said I'm not two people."

"But you've convinced yourself you are. You can say and do things as Gem and keep everyone at a distance." He took a step toward her. "Today in Brad's office, you walked in as Gem, but when you yelled at me, you were Natalie." He stepped closer and kept getting nearer.

Nat wanted to back away, but her legs locked. She was trapped in his gaze.

"I kissed Natalie in the office. It's Natalie I can't resist." He stood within inches of her touch. "Natalie is who I want."

Nat stopped breathing. She was sure of it. But she wasn't losing consciousness. She'd be aware if it was happening, right? He stood close enough now that she had to tilt her face up to continue to look into his eyes.

He pulled out a handkerchief. Rubbing at her lips with it, he said, "This is camouflage to hide Natalie. It's a convenient shield."

He swiped again and she wanted the touch to be his lips.

"Tell me what you're thinking. Please tell me you were as affected by that kiss as I was."

Instead of answering with words she didn't have and probably wouldn't offer even if she did, Nat angled up and kissed him. Twining her arms around his neck, she pulled him closer. She'd show him how affected she was. His strong arms wrapped around her back as their tongues tangled.

They kissed until Nat couldn't take it any longer. She needed more. Sliding her hands from his neck, down his chest, she moved until she could stroke him through his perfectly tailored pants. He was already hard under her palm and the pressure from her hand was enough to spur Mac on.

His hands were suddenly all over her, brushing over her hard nipples, gripping her ass.

She pulled away, gasping. "Bedroom." Afraid he might put a halt to their activities, she grabbed his hand and dragged him through the apartment to her bedroom. She stepped out of her heels and kicked the door shut as soon as they were clear.

Mac said nothing, but immediately tossed his jacket on the chair and kicked off his own shoes. As he pulled off his tie and shirt, he continued to stare at her while she shimmied out of her dress. When she reached for her bra, he said, "Let me."

His arms came around her body, the warmth of him sending tingles through her, or maybe it was his gentle caress on her skin as he flicked the clasp on her bra. He peeled the satin away and kissed from her collarbones across her chest and to the stiff peak of her breast.

Then he continued to trail open-mouth kisses down her torso. She gripped his shoulders for balance as his breath whispered across her damp panties. His thumbs hooked the sides and slid them down. His hands got the fabric clear of her knees, but his mouth nuzzled her pussy, licking and stroking without warning.

Her whole body trembled with want. Her knees started to buckle and he pulled away. Once on his feet again, he nudged her toward the bed. Stepping from her panties, she turned away and lay on the mattress. Crooking a finger, she smiled.

MAC STARED IN AWE AT THE BEAUTIFUL WOMAN LYING IN front of him. At the moment, he wasn't sure if she was playing and acting as Gem. He'd like to think she wasn't, but whether Gem or Natalie, he couldn't stop. Her beckoning had him licking his lips and tasting her. He wanted more. Standing beside the bed, he dropped his pants and underwear and kicked them free of his body.

When he crawled over Natalie's body, she sighed and he knew Natalie, and not Gem, was lying under him. Her strong, sure fingers wrapped around his hard dick and stroked. A deep groan rumbled in his chest. He didn't know what it was about this woman, but she made him lose control too easily.

"I like that sound," she purred.

He shifted out of her grasp and stared into her eyes. "Are we sure about doing this?"

"I'm damn sure. Are you?"

He kissed her again and her legs wrapped around his

hips. He wanted nothing more than to slide home, but he needed a condom, so he pulled away. "Condom?" he asked.

She clucked her tongue. "I never thought of you as the kind of guy to show up unprepared."

"I didn't plan on this."

"Really?"

"I thought I'd show up and we'd talk. Which, by the way, we're still going to do. Later." Bending, he kissed her neck. She bucked and squirmed.

She gave his shoulder a shove. "Condom in the nightstand. Now."

He went into the drawer and grabbed a condom. She took it and slid it on for him, offering extra strokes as she did. He thrust into her hand before reluctantly pulling away. He wanted this to be good for her as well. Pushing her gently back he allowed himself time to explore her body and adequately work her into a frenzy.

She quivered and trembled under his touch, and when he finally sank into her, he knew he was where he belonged. The startling realization had him frozen in place.

This feeling, this unmistakable feeling was what his mother had always talked about. Finding your home, your final destination. He'd dismissed it because he'd never experienced it. And now, it was with a woman he barely knew.

Natalie's breathing had returned to normal and she shifted under him, pulling him from his thoughts. He moved inside her and she held him close. He was in no rush to finish, especially now that he knew he was caught up in something different—not simply having sex with a woman he liked.

Fear hit him at the same time. Fear that she would laugh if he told her. Worse, that she wouldn't feel the same. Lowering his lips to hers again, he allowed his body to reveal what his mind wasn't prepared to say aloud.

Sweaty and out of breath, Mac lay beside Natalie, stroking her skin. He buried his face in her hair at the crook of her neck and sniffed. "I love the smell of your hair."

"Did you know the human nose can remember fifty thousands different scents?"

"No, I've never heard that before." He waited, and when she didn't say anything else, he propped up on an elbow and asked, "Any other nose trivia?"

She cocked an eyebrow in challenge. "An ant has a better sense of smell than a dog."

"What's going on?"

"What do you mean?"

"Why are you spouting off random facts?" As the words left his mouth, he saw her shields coming back up.

"I wasn't spouting anything. I mentioned something after you sniffed my hair. You asked for another fact."

"Natalie."

She blinked and turned her face away.

Gently, he turned her back. "Why are you running from this?"

"Because I'm not sure what this is anymore," she whispered. She swallowed and he watched her throat work.

"What did you think it was?"

"I thought we were friends having a good time, working through some sexual tension." Her chest rose and fell rapidly.

Mac moved so he covered her again, keeping most of his weight off her, but trapping her just the same. "And what is it now?"

She shook her head slowly.

"This is real, different, but we don't have to label it yet. Let's just be."

She nodded and smiled, relief softening her body. He kissed her again, loving that her whole body responded to his every touch.

"What do you have planned for the rest of your day?" he asked against her lips.

"I don't have plans. Figure out the next dates for the show. Look for a new job. The same stuff I do every day."

"If you don't have anything pressing, I'd like to spend some time with you."

"Don't you have to work?"

"We can plan the show together. That's where most of my energy is spent these days. I'm still proving myself to my mother."

"Proving yourself?"

He rolled off her and lay down, pulling Natalie to his chest. If they were going to talk, he needed to remove the distraction of her naked body. "How much do you know about Everyday Love?"

"Just what I read on the web site."

"My mom and dad founded the company after they'd been married for a couple of years. My dad was a psychologist, but my mom, she just gets people. It's like a sixth sense with her. She's an excellent matchmaker. But in recent years, with the advent of dating web sites and apps, the business has taken a hit. I hadn't realized how bad it had gotten because I was living in New York."

Natalie brushed her fingers through his chest hair and rested her chin on him to be able to look up. "You lived in New York?"

"For three years. My ex-wife wanted to be in New York, so we moved there. Anyway, when I came home after my divorce, I wanted to help with the business more. I'd grown up at Everyday Love. My mom had been doing everything by herself since my dad's death. I told her I wanted to take over, let her retire and enjoy her life. Although she hasn't outright said it, I don't think she believes I can do it."

"What did you do in New York?"

"I had my own practice."

"Practice?"

"Psychologist."

"Like your dad." Her eyes softened as she said it.

He nodded and played with her hair as it trailed down her back.

"Why not continue that here?"

"It was never what I wanted." He took a breath, unsure of how to explain this. "I became a psychologist to follow in my dad's footsteps. He used his education to do what my mom does instinctively. I only started my own practice in New York because it was what Ariel wanted. I wanted her to be happy."

"Since you're divorced, I'm guessing it didn't make her happy."

"She wanted me to be someone with power and influence. What I wanted was a wife and family. I wanted the love I saw my parents share. Ariel wasn't it. It took me a long time to figure it out. She wasn't who I thought she was." For the first time in a long while, he considered what had really happened. "I don't think she ever outright meant to lie. What she wanted for life was nothing like what I wanted. Looking back, I think maybe I was so desperate to find that perfect love I saw what I wanted to see."

NATALIE PUSHED UP AND SAT NEXT TO MAC. WHAT HAD SHE gotten herself into? This was so much worse than she feared. Mac was looking for his perfect penguin.

"What are you thinking?"

Knowing that this might ruin what might have been a damn near perfect morning in bed, she told him the truth. "I'm like your ex-wife."

"No, you're not."

"You're looking for your perfect penguin."

"What?"

She licked her lips. As crazy as she sometimes sounded when she rattled off useless knowledge when she was nervous, those facts often came in handy. "Some penguins mate for life. They search for the right penguin, and then the male will search all over the entire beach to find a perfect pebble to present to his prospective mate. He'll spend as long as necessary to find the smoothest, prettiest rock. If she accepts it, she'll put it in her nest and then they're together."

"What does that have to do with me?"

"You believe in your one true love."

"Of course. Well, not necessarily one, but true love, definitely."

"I don't."

"You don't believe in love?"

"Not true love, meant to be together forever, no."

He stared at her in that intense way he had, making her want to tuck under the blanket because he might see right into her soul.

"And yet you're filming a show where we're supposed to help women find true love."

"I'm an out-of-work librarian. It's a paying gig."

"That's not entirely true."

"Yes, it is. Do you think they ever would have come knocking on my door as Natalie? No. They wanted Gem."

"Why Gem?"

"I told you that story already."

"Only the beginning. Not why you created her."

"I needed to be someone else for a while. As Natalie, I had no idea how to date. I married young, fresh out of school to my college sweetheart. We were fine for a while, but then he became distant, and we were leading separate lives. He wanted a divorce because I was boring."

Mac chuckled.

She lightly smacked his arm. "That's not funny."

"Sure it is when you think about what an idiot your ex is. You're anything but boring."

"Thank you for saying that, even if it's not entirely true. I'm okay with being boring. It's who I am. But Gem allowed me to experiment and try new things."

"So you don't want anything permanent, just one experiment after another?"

Surprisingly, she heard no judgment in his voice. "I don't know what I'm looking for anymore. I can't focus on my personal life when my career is up in the air like this."

"Okay. I understand."

His words sank in and left a bitter feeling behind. She didn't know why his words bothered her, but she was annoyed they did. "What does that mean?"

"That means I'm willing to be your next experiment."

"Huh?"

He surged forward so their faces were close. "You're not getting rid of me that easily. I'm not running off because you're unsure of things in your life. I'm here and I'll wait."

Her heart jumped in her throat. "Wait for what?"

"For you to be ready."

"Ready for what?"

"To accept my perfect pebble." He kissed her cheek and smirked. "Is it okay if I use your shower before we head out?"

Nat stared at the empty space where Mac had been sitting. What was going on?

"Natalie?"

"Huh?"

"Can I use your shower? Maybe then we can go grab some lunch and make a plan for the show."

She blinked at him and tried to focus. "Yeah, sure." She climbed from the bed. "Wait? Lunch?"

He set the clothes down that he had been gathering. Stepping close to her again, he grabbed her shoulders. "Yes, lunch. You know, sustenance to replenish the fuel you sucked from my body." He bent a little to be eye-to-eye. "Are you okay?"

"Fine. Lunch sounds good." She grabbed a T-shirt and led him from her room.

He stopped. "Is your roommate back?"

"I'm sure Jillian would've announced herself if she came home."

He continued to stare from the doorway of her room.

"Hey, Jilly, you home?" she called. Of course, no one answered. Jillian would've come in banging and making a ruckus to make herself known. They rarely brought men back to the apartment. It wasn't a rule or anything, but both she and Jillian felt more comfortable sleeping with a guy and being able to leave without him having her address.

Confident that they were still alone, Mac headed for the bathroom, pressing a kiss to her cheek as he passed. "Feel free to join me."

Nat considered his offer. Things had gotten kind of heavy and she never wanted heavy in the bedroom. She'd become adept at keeping things light. With a smile, she decided to join Mac in the shower. A good blowjob should get his mind off penguins and forever love. At least with her.

As light as she tried to feel, it didn't work because part of her was drawn to everything Mac offered.

❧

MAC HELD NATALIE'S HAND AS THEY STRODE DOWN MICHIGAN Avenue. It was a warm late spring day and a breeze kicked up, blowing her hair. With every lift from the wind, her scent tickled his nose, reminding him of their morning in bed. She was skittish when it came to talking about or considering a serious relationship. He'd give her time to adjust because he wasn't in a hurry for anything. His thumb stroked her hand as he led her to the restaurant.

"Do you want to sit out on the patio?"

"I'd love to."

The host sat them outside. After taking her seat, Natalie scooped her hair up into a loose knot. Mac's gaze was drawn to her neck and his mouth watered.

Natalie seemed oblivious to his attention as she picked up her menu. "I've never been here before. What's good?"

"I've never been disappointed with anything I've ordered."

They looked over their choices and after they placed their orders—Cobb salad for her and salmon for him—they discussed the show.

"What do you have planned now that Brad wants more steam?" Natalie asked.

"I have no clue. I'm going to talk to my mother. We've always approached matchmaking as a journey to find the right person, not ramming someone into a person's life."

She angled her head as she listened. "Isn't that kind of cheating to ask your mom?"

"It's not about winning. This whole show isn't about winning or losing."

"Ha. Every man I've ever known is always about winning."

He took a sip of water. "Of course I enjoy winning. Who doesn't? But for me, winning is about taking over Everyday Love."

Natalie put her arms on the table and leaned forward. "You never did get around to explaining that. Why do you have to prove yourself to your mom? She's a smart woman. You look like you mostly know what you're doing."

"Thanks for the lukewarm vote of confidence," he interrupted with a smile.

"You know what I mean. She's the expert. Even though you've been around her your whole life, learning. There's no substitute for experience."

"I know. She doubts my ability to do this because I married Ariel against her advice."

"What?" She sat back in her seat and crossed her arms. "Your mother doesn't think you can run her matchmaking business because you married a chick she didn't like?"

Mac appreciated her defensiveness on his behalf, but he tried not to read too much into it. "It was more than Gail not liking Ariel. They actually got along quite well. But my mother warned me early on that Ariel wasn't the kind of woman I should be with. Looking back, the signs were all there. I refused to see what my mother saw."

"I didn't peg you as a mama's boy."

"You're a riot today. Not listening to my mother in matters of the heart is the equivalent of being sick and not taking your mother's advice when she's a doctor."

"I suppose you have a point. So you think winning the competition on this show will prove to her that you should take over the business."

"That's the agreement we have." Although he had no reason to believe his mother would back out, she didn't seem ready to loosen the reins.

The waiter returned with their food, and as Natalie poked at her salad, she asked, "What kind of woman does your mom think you belong with?"

Her eyes never left the bowl in front of her, and Mac wondered if she truly wanted the answer. He waited until she looked up to meet his eyes.

When she did, fork poised to enter her mouth, she said, "Well?"

He set down his own fork. "According to my mother, I need someone, and I quote, to remove the stick from my ass and teach me to live."

Natalie's eyes shot wide and she dropped her fork with a burst of laughter. He'd expected such a reaction, which was why he chose that little nugget from his mother's arsenal. He and Natalie had already showed many of their scars to each other, and he was well aware it made her uncomfortable.

Natalie laughed so hard and loud that heads were turning in their direction, but Mac didn't care. He loved the genuine happiness pouring from her. This was the woman he was falling for, smart and funny and real.

When she finally calmed down and dabbed at her eyes, she offered an apology. "What your mom said was kind of mean, but the way you said it…it was funny."

"You don't need to apologize. Seeing you let loose with a laugh like that was worth it."

"Does you mom talk to her clients that way?"

"Never. You've met her. Gail Sterling is always refined and classy." He leaned closer and lowered his voice. "But don't let her fool you. Get a couple of martinis in her and she talks like a sailor. No one is safe from her opinions."

After a few bites of her salad, accompanied with a moan of appreciation, Natalie said, "I think you should host a cocktail party. Invite everyone, including your mom. *That* would make for great TV."

"I don't think so." His mother would kill him if film ever appeared showing any form of impropriety. Which, now that he thought about it, seemed ridiculous because it made her look like she had the stick up her ass.

Mac didn't want to waste this valuable time talking about

his mother, so he switched tactics. "How's the job search going?"

"Not great. I've applied for a bunch of positions, but I haven't had any nibbles yet. I might have to expand my search."

Something about the look in her eye didn't sit right with him. "Expand how far?"

She shrugged. "I've already been looking into some of the suburban areas, but if something doesn't happen soon, I might look out of state."

"You'd pick up and move?"

"I don't want to. I love living in Chicago. But I don't want to be unemployed either." She returned to eating, making it clear she didn't want to talk about her job situation any more than he wanted to talk about his.

The thought of her moving away bothered him in ways he couldn't put into words yet. He'd often laughed at his mother when she talked about people being soul mates or falling in love at first sight. He'd admit that immediate lust was possible and he'd even allow a quick connection, but he'd never thought he'd experience it. While he'd known Natalie for a couple of weeks now, nothing was quite *at first sight*, and this connection he felt with her was new. He definitely wasn't ready to lose it.

"Would you consider working at Everyday Love?"

She choked out a laugh again, but quickly sobered when he didn't join her. "What?"

"Would you consider a job working with me?"

"You mean for you?"

He lifted a shoulder.

"I'm not a matchmaker. I have no idea what you do."

"But you're good with people. You know how to get dates. You're good enough they brought you on for *Love Match*."

"I don't believe in what you're selling."

"How's that?"

"I told you. I don't buy into forever love. You convince people you can help them find their perfect penguin."

He smiled. "I'm going to talk to my mother about changing our slogan. Find your perfect penguin at Everyday Love."

Natalie snorted.

"Just think about it before you take off out of state."

She studied him for a minute while she ate her salad.

"So how do you plan to make your dates steamier?" Natalie asked.

"I have no clue. I prefer a hands-off approach during the actual dates. I can't very well tell the women to go make out with men because the studio wants sexier scenes."

"Why not?"

"That's not how we work."

Natalie answered with a quirk of her eyebrow, but said nothing.

CHAPTER 11

After lunch, Mac went back to the office. He needed to talk to his mother about what the studio wanted. All he wanted at this point was to spend the rest of the afternoon—and night—with Natalie. He whistled as he headed toward his office, but Paul stopped him before he got to the door.

"Why the hell are you so chipper?"

"Is there a problem with me being in a good mood?" Mac asked.

Paul stopped abruptly and stared at him. "Who the hell did you fuck?"

Mac clamped his jaw shut and pushed his office door open, motioning for Paul to go in. When he closed the door behind them, Mac said, "You're not going to be happy."

"Hell. Do I need to sit down for this?"

Mac didn't answer, but moved toward the couch himself. "I slept with Natalie."

"Who?"

Mac shook his head. "Gem."

"Fuck me. What are you thinking?"

"Do not tell my mother."

"This is going to be a mess."

"No it's not. Our relationship is separate from the show."

"Are you sure she's not using you to try to win?"

"What?" The thought had never crossed his mind. "No. How would she even do that?"

Paul sat next to him and crossed an ankle over his knee. "I know you. If you like a woman, she can sweet talk you into just about anything."

"Like what? Sabotaging myself and my chances to win? Not going to happen. I need this win. Natalie knows this. And while she's not going to give up, she doesn't need the win the way I do."

Paul didn't look convinced. Mac knew his friend had more to say, but was holding back.

"There's something between us. We weren't looking for it, but we're not ignoring it either."

Paul eased back on the couch. "You're falling for her? You barely know her."

Mac almost opened his mouth to say he'd already fallen, but didn't want to hear Paul's laugh. "I know enough."

"You didn't even know her real name until what? A week ago? You have no idea what's real and what's for show with her."

Mac felt a growl pushing up in his chest, but he pushed it down. He knew Paul was watching out for him. "I know her. I know who she is when she's not being Gem. It's Natalie I'm interested in, and I put up with her acting like Gem."

Paul continued to stare at him.

"I know what I'm doing. Be happy for me."

"I'd be thrilled for you finally finding someone else after Ariel if I thought it had a chance of working. But this is crazy. She's the enemy."

It was Mac's turn to laugh. While he knew Natalie was

capable of fighting, she was far from an enemy. "We only have a few weeks of filming. As long as we keep it to ourselves until that's done, we won't have any problems."

Paul scrubbed a hand over his face. "What about Gail?"

"What about her?"

"She'll flip the fuck out if she finds out you're sleeping with Gem."

"Natalie."

"Whatever."

"So don't tell her. Contrary to what you think about my mother, she's not a psychic. Natalie and I already spend a lot of time together because of the show. The cameras only follow us when we're in the studio or with clients. No one will know."

Paul stood. "Hope you know what you're doing."

"Not a clue, but that's half the fun, right?"

Mac left the office right behind Paul. He still needed to talk to his mother. And he needed to put on his best game face because regardless of what he'd said to Paul, if Paul figured out he'd gotten laid, his mother would surely know something was up. Outside her office, he thought about his ex-wife, which sobered him quickly.

He knocked twice and then turned the knob. His mom was on the phone and she waved him in. Taking the seat in front of her desk, he waited for her to finish her conversation.

When she disconnected, she folded her hands on the desk and asked, "What's the problem now?"

"Brad called us into the studio this morning to tell us that although everything we're doing is good, and they have great footage, we need to move things along faster."

"How so?"

"He wants sex. Or at least something close."

Gail pressed her lips together and inhaled through

flared nostrils. "He promised me this show was going to be different. He didn't want wild parties. True love. The real thing. That's what he said." She picked up her phone, but before dialing, she said, "Is Paul still here? He needs to look at our contract. If Bradley pushes for this, we'll pull out. I will not allow them to make Everyday Love look like a sex party."

Mac raised a hand. "They're not looking for porn, Mom. Relax. The clients didn't even kiss their dates. Brad needs something to sell to audiences. People kiss, they grope, they have sex, often long before they have the real thing. Brad knows this."

"We're different."

"I know. Which is why I'm here. I want to brainstorm ideas for how to move things faster, find the chemistry Brad needs to see on screen."

Gail set her phone down. A spark lit in her eyes as a smile spread across her face. "I like the way you think."

For what might've been the first time since coming back to Chicago, Mac finally felt like he was at home working with his mother.

~

WHEN NATALIE GOT HOME FROM HER LONG LUNCH WITH MAC, Jillian was back in the apartment. It felt weird to have her there in the afternoon. Nat had gotten so used to being alone most of her day. She'd barely kicked off her sneakers before Jillian pounced.

"Well, what happened? I thought about calling when I got home and you weren't here, but then I thought you might be busy." She ended with a wiggle of her eyebrows.

The swell of emotions Nat had been pushing down since Mac walked into her apartment flooded her. "Oh my God. It was so much, Jilly. There's a fire between us, and wow is it hot."

Jillian grabbed her hand and dragged her toward the couch. "Spill. I want details."

"He said all the things, Jillian. Things I didn't think I ever needed or wanted to hear. And then it all just felt right."

Jilly's eyes widened, but she didn't say anything. Nat flopped back on the couch. "I thought him kissing me in the office was bad, threw me off my game. Sleeping with him? Colossal mistake."

"What do you mean? You just said it felt right."

"Too right. That's the problem. It wasn't just raging hormones and wanting to get off. I don't know how else to explain it. It was deep and scary and I'm not in a place to want anything like that."

"What was his reaction?"

"That's what made it worse. Most guys would've been scared off. Not Malcolm Sterling. No, that man is all like, 'Cool. I'll wait for you to be ready.' Who the hell does that? He's not normal."

Jillian's hand came up. "Wait. You need to explain this."

Nat took a deep breath and then explained her bedroom conversation with Mac. How understanding he'd been about where she was in her life and how she couldn't be his perfect penguin. Jillian, of course, laughed at her.

"It's not funny."

"Sure it is. You're falling for a sexy, intelligent, employed guy. Even you have a hard time saying no to something so good. I don't see what the problem is." She stopped for a second and then added, "Except for the whole competition, TV show thing."

"It's all a problem. Yeah, we have great chemistry. But we're not supposed to be anything more. And the whole TV show thing is a big deal. I'm having a hard enough time being taken seriously as it is."

Jillian scooted closer and patted her leg. "This show is a paycheck, not your life. If you have a chance for a real relationship with Mac, why not take it? You deserve to be as happy as the women you're working for."

She wasn't sure how to explain her feelings to Jillian. Natalie knew if roles had been reversed and Jillian came to her with such a problem, Nat's advice would be the same. The difference was Natalie had already tried for her happily ever after and it didn't work out. She didn't know if she was ready to try it again.

"You don't have to think about perfect penguin forever stuff right now. Enjoy your time with him. Have a relationship. You remember those, right?"

"Still not funny."

"Did you guys talk about how your relationship might affect the show?"

"No. We talked about a lot of things, but that wasn't one."

"Talking. Is that what we're calling it these days?"

Natalie sat straighter on the couch. "You're a riot today. Maybe you should take the day off more often." She sighed. "I mean, we talked. Had genuine conversation about things I never mention to guys. He listened like I mattered and then he talked to me, answered my questions without hesitation."

"Sounds like an adult relationship. Isn't that the way it's supposed to go? What we all search for?"

"I wasn't searching. I was happy with what I had going."

"You keep telling yourself that, but no one's believing it. Not you. Not me. But as your lawyer, I would advise you to keep it away from the cameras and the studio executives. They'll exploit everything they can."

"Thanks." Just what she needed—something else to add another layer of worry to the pile she carried.

She'd enjoyed everything about her afternoon with Mac. The sex was great. The conversation matched it in intensity. Jillian had a point, though. They had a job to do and they couldn't let a relationship interfere with it. She needed to figure out what she wanted and what she could offer Mac.

Sure, he'd said he'd wait until she was ready, but what if she never was?

~

FOR THE NEXT TWO DAYS, NATALIE STRUGGLED TO AVOID MAC. They had a great afternoon together and they clicked in ways she hadn't seen coming, but the fast connection they'd shared scared the pants off her. If it were just her pants and she was getting laid, she'd be fine, but her conversations with Mac led her to understand so much more about him. Being a match-maker wasn't just a job or a family legacy for him. He totally bought into it.

And when he looked at her, she wanted to let him sell it to her too. Which was why she was standing in Brad's office alone, prepared to beg him to let her work one-on-one with the clients. She thought she'd have to make her case, but he agreed as soon as she said she'd be able to provide sexier situations without Mac's presence.

"I like the way you think," Brad said.

"You said you needed the women to move faster. Mr. Sterling is a little old school. He wants the women to be courted. I come from the swipe left and right generation. I'll get things moving along."

"Has something happened between you and Mac?"

"What? No. Why do you ask?"

"The two of you seemed to be getting along well, but this proposition of yours reeks of competition. It's what I've been hoping for from the beginning." He leaned forward and tapped on his desk. "I want more of that spark I see when you argue with Mac. I wish I could bottle that stuff."

"The show is about the clients, not me and Mac. I'll make sure you have good footage moving forward." As she left the studio, she dialed the clients and made arrangements to meet them all for drinks later. It might be against Mac's way to tell them what the studio was looking for, but she was willing to do whatever she needed.

A sleek black town car was parked beside her car, and when she got near, the rear window rolled down and Gail Sterling called to her. "Hello, Gem. May I have a word?"

Natalie looked over her shoulder and saw no cameras were following her. "Hi, Gail. How are you?"

"Have a seat in the car. I'd like to have a talk."

Although the words were said with a smile, Natalie didn't feel as though she was being given a choice. "Does Mac know you're here?"

"Of course not. Please get in."

Natalie walked around the car and slid in beside Gail. "What's with the secrecy?"

"I feel horrible about the way things are going, dear."

"What do you mean?"

Gail waved her hand and shook her head. "They chose you because you were inherently at a disadvantage. I want to offer you a chance to level the field a bit."

Natalie heard the words, but she couldn't process them. Never in her life had she felt as stupid as she did right now.

Gail released a slow breath. "You don't have a chance to win. While I want Everyday Love to look good, I don't want you to pay the price. I'm here to offer you some advice. Malcolm told me the producers want the clients to move faster, get more serious, et cetera."

Natalie nodded.

"I know my son, and he'll do whatever it takes to win. He

wants to prove to me he can take over Everyday Love, and I'm concerned he'll do anything to make that happen."

Natalie opened her mouth to argue because she knew Mac wouldn't. He had ethics. She'd seen them in play time and again. Before she had the chance to say anything, Gail continued.

"If you tell the women to go out and have sex with their dates, you'll accomplish that goal, but you'll look like a tramp. Malcolm will win by default."

"I wasn't—"

"You can't tell them to do it, but if they choose to on their own, the audience will make their assumptions about the clients and not about you. All you need to do it set the stage. Get each client on a date in the most romantic setting possible with the possibility for clothes to come off."

"I don't know."

"The producers and audience alike will eat it up."

"Are you sure?"

Gail gave one quick nod and a half a smirk.

"Why are you doing this?" Natalie wondered if Mac had told her about them, but quickly had decided against that thought. "Why would you sabotage your own son?"

"I'm not sabotaging him. He's been doing this his whole life. He has a skill set you haven't even thought about developing. It's like expecting a toddler to run a marathon. You aren't prepared for this. Malcolm will be fine. In addition, as a man, he can get away with doing things you could never do. Like flirt with the clients to get them to do what he wants."

"He doesn't do that."

"Malcolm shows what he wants you to see. That's his job as a matchmaker. He makes every woman feel unique and special. It's part of the job."

Natalie no longer knew whether Gail was speaking about

the competition or Natalie's relationship with Mac. Could Gail know they had slept together? Was it like a sixth sense mothers had?

More worrisome than whether Gail knew was whether she was right in her assessment of Mac and his feelings. Natalie got behind the wheel of her car with a sinking feeling Mac might be playing her. He might be toying with her emotions to keep her off-kilter so he could win. Hadn't he told her repeatedly how important this competition was to him?

Later that evening, Natalie met with Ashley, Jennifer, and Melissa. She'd decided to put Mac completely out of her mind and focus on using Gail's advice. The woman had been in business almost as long as Natalie had been alive. So instead of telling her clients to get sexy on their next dates, she asked them what their idea of a sexy romantic date would be. She planned to use that research along with Gail's information to take to Brad to pitch her next idea. She'd choose the men for the clients if Brad could stage the dates.

Ashley swirled the straw in her drink. "I never thought about what would make a date romantic. I mean, if I'm looking for romance, anything can become romantic, you know?"

Natalie nodded. She definitely understood. Picking up a man was easy. It didn't have to be romantic. But that wouldn't look good for TV.

"Think about it this way. You're looking to settle down, right? You want a guy who is your forever. This is the date story you'll pull out and tell at family parties for years to come. It needs to be romantic. Not we got hot and heavy in a restaurant bathroom."

Jennifer's jaw dropped. Ashley slapped a hand over her mouth to contain the drink she'd just sipped. Melissa's eyes widened and she asked, "Do people really do that?"

Natalie raised her glass. "To each her own."

Melissa said, "I can answer. Quiet music, a fireplace, a bottle of wine, and good conversation."

Ashley made a gagging noise.

Melissa glared at her. "I know it sounds cheesy, but when the conversation's good—when it's real and vulnerable—it's hot. There's something about a guy who's not afraid to let his guard down and let you see scars."

Natalie thought she made a good case, especially as she thought of the scars Mac had revealed to her. It had been real —real enough that she'd been hiding from him.

Jennifer chimed in. "That's a good start. But I'm not one for staring into each other's eyes longingly. Maybe a movie. Alone at home."

Ashley nudged Jennifer's shoulder. "Netflix and chill. I'm with you."

Jennifer shook her head.

Natalie looked at Ashley. "You must have some ideas."

"I want something different. Exotic. Like a whirlwind vacation or weekend getaway. Something where there are no distractions. Real life and the real world can't intrude."

"Oh, that's good." They finished their drinks and went their separate ways. Natalie built a mental proposal to take to Brad the next day.

Natalie rose the following morning and stared at her phone. She had another text from Mac asking if she wanted to meet for lunch. She knew he found out she asked Brad to work alone. Jillian had told her Mac had stopped by yesterday. Nat knew she couldn't avoid him forever.

The problem was she had no idea what to say. At this point, she wasn't even sure why she was dodging him. Originally, she needed to gather her thoughts and fortify her defenses because Mac struck a chord in her she didn't want strummed—the note that made her think of happily ever afters.

But after meeting with Gail, she began to have a completely different set of doubts. The first time Natalie met with Gail, the woman had seemed lovely and friendly. This time, however, the friendliness had an undercurrent of cutthroat competitiveness that she'd accused Mac of having.

The upside of those doubts was that they put a damper on all the sunshiney thoughts of happy endings with Mac. Now she had to figure out how to get through the next few weeks of working with him.

First, she'd meet with Brad and talk to him about the romantic dates for their clients. Then she'd deal with Mac.

So she dressed up in her usual costume wear for Gem, shoving thoughts of sweat pants and her couch aside and went back to the studio.

When she arrived, Brad was ready for her, and he had a cameraman ready to shoot. She'd been hoping they could have another private meeting, but her luck wouldn't hold out.

"Hi, Gem. I hope you have some great ideas for us today."

"I hope so too."

Brad chuckled in that fake way men in suits behind desks did.

Nat licked her lips and crossed her legs. "You want sexy, but the women need romantic. I think we should plan a romantic date for each of them. I spoke with Ashley, Jennifer, and Melissa last night to get some ideas. Jennifer and Melissa will be easy enough to coordinate, but Ashley might be a little more difficult, but not impossible."

"Sounds intriguing." Brad leaned forward.

"The women need alone time with a date. Something

that's staged, but doesn't feel staged. A night at home watching a movie on the couch. A shared bottle of wine in front of a roaring fireplace. A handholding walk on the beach." She pushed it a little with the last one, but she had to say something.

Brad's reaction was nothing she'd expected. He burst out laughing. "Did Mike put you up to this?"

She stared at him waiting for an explanation while he laughed.

"What's next? A rose ceremony?"

In that moment, she knew she flubbed. This wasn't anything he was looking for. So she did what she did best— she played along. She laughed. "Gotcha!"

"You had me going there for a minute."

"Sorry. I thought I'd have something more by now, but spending time with the clients didn't help in the way I thought it would. I didn't want to blow off our meeting."

"I appreciate that, but next time, just call. One thing we all agreed on when we developed the concept for the show was that we needed to stand out and be different than the other matchmaking shows out there. What you proposed is almost verbatim what we told Gail and Mac we didn't want."

Nat held her smile and nodded. That old lady played her. She couldn't believe it. "I'm sorry I wasted your time. I'm definitely going to figure something out."

"Check with Mac and see what he has planned. The two of you make magic together. I was a little surprised you wanted to go solo."

She nodded again and stood. Walking stiffly out of the office, she focused on her plan of attack. No, she didn't need to attack. Gail wasn't her problem. Mac was. And this damn show. At the moment she couldn't have been more grateful for being Gem, because Natalie would've fallen apart in that office. Embarrassment would've had tears pooling in her eyes.

Not Gem. Gem got pissed. She no longer knew who to believe. Gail and Mac had been in on the development of this show, so they both knew Brad's stance on the expectations. Of course, they had all failed to fill her in on it.

And Nat thought Gail was sabotaging her own son. It figured. She should've known better. She had no reason to believe Gail wanted to be fair and kind. It made no sense.

CHAPTER 12

Mac had chased his tail for two days. Or chased Natalie. She barely answered his texts. When he went to the studio, Brad informed him Natalie requested to work alone with the clients for the next round. That night, Mac showed up at her apartment to confront her, but Jillian said she was meeting clients. He left feeling even more frustrated. They'd had a great time together. Better than great. They had connected in a way that didn't come along often.

He knew she'd felt it too. She might not be ready to admit it, but she'd felt it. So now she was running scared. She wasn't the first woman he'd known to run from her feelings. Even though it was frustrating, he knew how to handle it. His mother had taught him well.

Often a client came to them saying they were looking for love, but when presented with the real thing, they freaked out. A good portion of their time at Everyday Love was spent holding hands and talking clients off metaphorical ledges.

So he planned to ambush her at the studio. Brad had mentioned Gem was coming back in to talk about the next round of dates—that she planned to coordinate without him.

Mac would just show up at the studio and confront her. Then she'd either have to admit she'd been avoiding him or she'd have to cave and actually spend time with him. He counted on the latter.

He arrived at the studio earlier than her meeting was supposed to be finished, but Natalie was already hurrying to her car. He knew that look. He whipped into the spot beside her and hopped out. "Natalie."

She spun and looked at him. Yeah, she was mad.

"I've been trying to talk to you for days. Why have you been ignoring me?" He came around his car to talk to her.

She crossed her arms. "You're really the last person I want to speak to right now."

"Why?" He couldn't have possibly done anything to tick her off since he hadn't even spoken to her.

She rolled her bottom lip into her mouth and bit down before taking a deep breath. "Look, I'm not in a position to have a rational conversation."

"So have an irrational one. Tell me what the hell is going on." He reached for her, but she pulled back.

"You want to know what's going on? I'll tell you. Your mother showed up here yesterday offering me advice in the name of leveling the field. Told me how I should approach making things happen for our clients. Planted plenty of seeds of doubt where you're concerned as well."

"About me?" Everything she said made no sense, but he wanted her to continue, so he crossed his own arms to match her stance and waved her on.

"I used her advice and just got laughed out of Brad's office. She gave me every cheesy romantic idea that the women would like that has already been played out on reality TV, which Brad happens to hate. Of course, Gail already knew." She winked at him. "So when you see your mom, thank her for making me look like a fool."

She turned to get into her car.

"Stop right there."

She paused, but didn't turn back to face him. He stepped closer. Close enough to feel the heat of her body through the thin dress she wore. He lowered his voice as he spoke. "Do you really think I would do something like that to you after what we shared?"

"I don't know. I'm not sure what to believe anymore."

He tugged her arm to make her face him. Her bright blue eyes glistened. "After everything I've said about how honesty is important to me. Probably the most important thing."

"When your mother made little innuendos during our conversation, I completely discounted them. But now, after listening to Brad and how everything had been discussed and *everyone* knew what he wanted—and didn't—for the show, it makes it a little harder to swallow that you weren't in on it."

He slid his palm along her jaw, the simple contact centering him in a way he'd been missing for the last two days. As pissed as he was at his mother right now, the woman had taught him to recognize something special when he had it. He bent his knees so he could look directly into Natalie's eyes. She would not mistake anything he had to say right now. "I had nothing to do with the crap my mother pulled, nor would I. I'm here to prove myself. Even if I thought I needed to do something underhanded to win, I couldn't do that to you. Not now."

He closed the slight distance between them and kissed her. Her lips parted and her breath fluttered. Their tongues barely touched and she pulled away. His hands anchored her hips to him. "Stop hiding from me."

"I don't know what to do with you. This is crazy." Her eyes darted to the side. "Especially here."

She had a point about their location, but he hated letting

her leave without her understanding he wouldn't do anything to hurt her.

He stepped back to a respectable distance. "Do you believe me? I wouldn't do that to you."

She nodded. "This is all very complicated."

"Not so much. We need to talk. Can I come by later? I'll pick up dinner."

"I'm free now," she offered.

"As much as I'd love to take you up on that, I need to go deal with my mother."

For the first time since he'd pulled into the parking lot, Natalie smiled. "A battle of the Sterlings. I think I might like ringside seats. Sorry to disappoint you, Mac, but I think Gail is gonna win. She's got years of practice on you."

"That just means she'll underestimate me, like she did you." He reached across the space and stroked her hand. "I'll be by tonight."

"See you later."

He waited until she was in her car and driving off before he did the same. He went straight to the office, calling Paul on the way.

"Hello?" Paul answered.

"Did you know what my mother was up to?"

"Hello to you to, Mac. What are you talking about?"

"Did you know my mother met with Natalie and fed her crap advice to make her look bad?"

"No."

Of course his friend said nothing else. The single word should have been enough. "You're not going to ask what she did?"

"Nope. Then you might want me to get involved and that would be stupid."

"Thanks anyway."

"I'm sure you can handle it on your own."

"I definitely will."

"Is your girl okay?"

"My girl?"

"That's how you think of her. Even though I think it's a bad idea, I know when you've made up your mind. And you've already decided on her."

Yeah, he had, but Gail couldn't know. "You didn't tell my mother, did you?"

"I work for Everyday Love and your mother by extension, but you're my best friend. There are a few things that beat out business loyalty."

"Thanks."

"I hope you know what you're doing."

"So do I." He pulled into the parking lot and went straight to his mother's office. This time, he didn't even bother knocking. He didn't care if she was with a client. He needed to get this straightened out now.

"Malcolm, I know I taught you better manners than to barge into a room."

"You also taught me to be honest and forthright."

"And?"

"And you met with N—Gem yesterday and gave her bad advice so she would look ridiculous in front of Brad. It was underhanded and dishonest." He stood in the middle of her office with his arms crossed to stop himself from ranting like a lunatic. His mother preferred calm logic.

"I did what you are obviously too weak to do, Malcolm. I've seen the footage. She's better at this than we thought. We can't have some Internet pick-up artist beat us, a well-respected matchmaking company. I didn't do anything horrible."

"Yes, you did. You wanted her to look foolish. Unfortunately for you, it won't appear on film. She took your ideas to Brad who laughed at her."

Gail splayed her hands on the desk. "She *is* better than I thought. I was convinced she'd take any information and possible advantage and run with it. I hadn't planned on her running to Bradley."

"Stop. Now. We need this competition to be fair. She's already at a disadvantage because she came into this late and she doesn't have the experience we do. Leave her alone. I can win by myself."

"I have some doubts. Don't let some silly affection for this woman as the underdog get the better of you. We have a plan. Stick to it and win the competition."

"You'll back off?"

"It's your show."

"That's what I thought, but every time I turn around, you're there interfering." He lowered his arms. He considered telling her about his night with Natalie. If anyone could root for a relationship over a TV show, Gail Sterling could. But he decided against it. He wasn't even sure where he and Natalie stood after his mother's stunt.

Gail settled back into her chair. "For what it's worth. I like her. Quite a bit. I think everyone underestimated her and her ability. Don't do it again, Malcolm."

"I won't. I know exactly what I'm up against."

He left the office and returned to his. He had plans for the clients he needed to put into motion. Then he'd go back to Natalie. Hopefully by tonight, she'd be cooled off and ready to talk to him.

~

Natalie spent the rest of her afternoon brainstorming ideas for how to find the magical chemistry for her clients. It was time to just be blunt. If she told them they should allow a guy to kiss them, they might listen. No one expected them to have sex, and even if they chose to, the cameras wouldn't follow. Based on what she'd seen of similar reality shows, they would piece together enough to make the viewers believe sex was happening no matter what.

When her bell rang, it yanked her out of her research. Emails and phone calls had netted her a few unique ideas. Checking the time, she realized it was probably Mac at the door. She'd thought he'd call first. She glanced at her comfy working from home wear. Did she need to transform into Gem for this?

The bell rang again making the decision for her. She didn't have time. She went downstairs and found Mac standing with two full bags. Opening the door, she said, "That's a lot of food."

"I thought Jillian might be home."

Nat shook her head. "She's never home before seven thirty."

"Long hours."

"The glamorous life of a lawyer." She held her arm out for him to come in. They walked into her apartment in silence and Natalie didn't like the level of awkward in the room.

Mac set the bags on the coffee table and sat on the couch, patting the cushion beside him. When she joined him, he took her hand. "I talked to my mother today. She won't be interfering anymore."

"Why did she do that to me?"

"She feels threatened. You're better than anyone expected you to be."

A surge of pride roared through her. She *was* good.

"In all honesty, you worry me. You say you don't care about winning, but you have the potential to kill it in this competition. I'm no longer sure I can beat you."

She smiled. "Suck it up, cupcake. We all fear failure. It pushes us to do better. What happens if you don't win?"

He lifted a shoulder. "I'd like to think my mother would still keep me on at Everyday Love, but who knows?"

"It would be stupid for her to fire you over this show."

He stroked her fingers. "Are we all right?"

"What do you mean?"

"This afternoon, you accused me of being in on my mother's plan. I know what we have is new, but I need to know you trust me enough to believe I wouldn't do that to you."

"I know. I was angry and sometimes my mouth gets away from me when I'm mad."

He leaned forward and toyed with a lock of hair that had slipped out of her ponytail. His fingers lingered near her neck. "I want to keep seeing you. Like this."

"What about the show?" she asked quietly.

"We go to work like any other couple. No matter what happens at work, we don't let it ruin this. Okay?"

She turned her face and kissed his palm. "That sounds a whole lot easier than it's gonna be."

"We only have a few weeks of filming. Then it won't matter."

"So we keep this a secret and date on the sly?"

He nodded, his eyes, filled with lust, locked on hers. He ran his tongue across the seam of his lips. Natalie pushed forward and kissed him.

Two days of not being around him, not talking to him, proved to be too much, especially now that he was here. She rose up and straddled his lap, fitting comfortably against him. She couldn't fight this, so she gave herself over to it. She might not be able to give Mac everything he was looking for, but she was willing to try.

Against her lips, he murmured, "I thought we were going to eat dinner."

"We'll reheat it. I missed you."

"Next time you have a problem, don't ignore me." His

hands were busy under her T-shirt and he stopped. "Why did you?"

She continued to kiss his neck as she unbuttoned his shirt. "Why did I what?"

"Ignore me? You were dodging me before anything happened with my mother."

She'd hoped he wouldn't revisit that, so she tried to distract him by grinding her hips against his.

"Natalie," he said, his voice gruff.

She sat up and stroked his beard. "What?"

"Why did you pull away? You stopped answering my texts and calls before you met with my mother."

She sighed and climbed off his lap. "I needed space to think. About this. Us. It was pretty intense the other afternoon."

He nodded, but said nothing, just waited for her to continue.

She pressed her palms together and then slid them between her knees to prevent herself from fidgeting under his scrutiny. "You said all these great things and even when I told you I wasn't ready, you were fine with it."

"I am."

"It's not fair to you. You want a life I don't know I'm ready for. I don't know if I'll ever want that. I've been there and it didn't work."

"And what you're doing now, how you live your life, does it make you happy?"

She stared at her hands because that question went deep. If anyone had asked her a month ago, she would've said yes. Since losing her job and working with Mac, she began to reevaluate a lot of things. Playing the field might not bring her the happiness she once believed it did. "I'm not sure. You cloud my judgment."

"That's telling in and of itself, don't you think?" He took

her hands from her lap and held them. "You're a bright woman. You know that just because things didn't work with your ex-husband doesn't mean it can't work with anyone."

"Logically, I understand. But it took me a long time to get comfortable being me again. I don't want to lose that because I fall for a handsome, slick-talking man."

"I may be handsome, but I'm not slick-talking. I speak from my heart, like my mother taught me to. Our first marriages taught us things about ourselves. We use that knowledge and move on. I'm not going anywhere."

There were those words again. As if he had the patience of Job. "Did you tell your mother about us?"

"No."

"Why not?"

"Because I don't want things to be more complicated than they already are. I'll tell her as soon as we're done filming."

"What about the last show? Even when we're done filming, we're supposed to go back for the live episode and online voting to determine the winner."

"What about it?"

"According to your plan, everyone will know about us then."

"So let Brad use it as a selling point. Archrivals become lovers. He'll probably love the headline."

"I don't want a complicated life. I want simple."

"Life rarely is."

She knew he was right. "Can we just let this be simple for now?"

He tilted his head and studied her again. He looked like he wanted to argue, but he surprised her by nodding.

She smiled. "Now that we have that settled, dinner first or do you want to take me to bed?"

"It depends. Are you going to throw me out after you have your way with me?"

She laughed. "No."

"I can spend the night?"

She hadn't considered that was what he meant, but she thought about it. Mac had her breaking all of the hit it and quit it rules that she'd been living by, but she liked it. "You can stay if you want."

"Then let's eat first. You'll need your energy because I have all night."

Her blood heated at his words and she wanted to climb back onto his lap, but she followed his lead and helped spread food out on the table. Her time with Mac felt normal and exciting all at once, which threw her off her game. This was unlike any relationship she could remember ever having. It looked to be one hell of a ride.

NATALIE JOLTED UP IN BED AT SEVEN O'CLOCK. MAC LAY NEXT to her, snoring quietly. She looked at him for a few minutes. Her body was relaxed and her head was clear. So clear, in fact, that she knew exactly what she wanted to have the women do for their next dates. But she needed to talk with them without the cameras first. Grabbing her phone, she sent a group text to see if they could all do a video conference call.

Mac's arm snaked around her hip and he yanked her back down against him. "I guess I didn't do a good enough job tiring you out if you have the energy to be on your phone first thing in the morning."

"You did plenty good. I had a flash of brilliance about our clients and I need to talk with them away from cameras."

"You're not allowed to meet with them without Brad knowing."

She smiled and nestled closer to his bare skin. "I'm not

meeting. Trying to go with a video chat." She reached down and stroked his already hardening cock. "Mmm. Maybe I'm the one who didn't perform well enough last night. You're ready to go again."

"You always do this to me." He thrust his dick into her hand as he kissed her. His hands caressed her back and then he stroked her.

Tossing the covers off them, Natalie pushed Mac to lay on his back. When she reached across him to the nightstand for a condom, he sucked her nipple into his mouth. She sheathed him quickly and then straddled him, sinking onto his dick. He filled her and stretched her.

His hands skated up her ribs to her breasts. He kneaded them and pinched her nipples. She began a slow rock against him, keeping their bodies connected intimately. Mac sat up and took a nipple in his mouth. With an arm wrapped around her waist, he lifted her off him and then plunged upward as he brought her back down. He reached for her jaw and pulled her face to his and kissed her long, hard, and deep.

Their lovemaking was languid and Natalie's orgasm built slowly. She enjoyed every sensation Mac's body brought to hers. He set fire to each individual nerve in her body. When she was frantic and falling apart, he continued to cradle her in his arms until she came down.

Then he flipped her onto her back and thrust into her in long hard strokes, drawing out the aftershocks of her orgasm. His arms came under her shoulders and anchored her to him as he picked up the pace, pounding into her. The sounds of slapping flesh and harsh breathing echoed in the room.

Mac's fingers tightened on her shoulders and he buried his face in her neck as his whole body stilled.

For long moments after, they continued to touch each

other, as if they couldn't get enough. Natalie didn't think she'd felt this way about a guy since she was a teenager and being with a guy was new and she just wanted to learn everything. It wasn't just the sex. She loved the way Mac looked at her and held her and talked to her.

He was giving her a relationship like she'd never known. It was still scaring the pants off her, but she was enjoying it too much to care.

They didn't move until her phone kept buzzing with texts.

"You should probably answer that," he said as he stroked a finger down the center of her back.

"You should probably get to work. You need to come up with a plan to beat me and make your mommy proud."

"Ugh. Can we agree we'll never discuss my mother while lying naked in bed?"

Natalie laughed. She was having fun. This was the kind of thing Gem would want to pass on to her viewers. Part of her wanted to jump up and record now, but a bigger part of her wanted to keep this private. She wasn't sure what to do about this.

She and Mac took turns in the shower and when he was dressed again in yesterday's suit—still looking mighty fine in it—she broached the subject. "You know, if we're going to keep this a secret, Gem should probably continue to post videos."

Mac stopped, his tie halfway knotted. "What?"

"It'll be suspicious for Brad and my viewers if I suddenly stop posting completely."

Mac's eyes narrowed and he said, "Are you asking me if I'm okay with you continuing to pick up men?"

Natalie laughed. "No. I'm asking if it would be okay if I posted about us without talking about us? Just talking relationships in general. It's what I do and as it is, I haven't posted in a couple of weeks."

"You want to tell everyone about us without telling anyone it's me. I doubt that'll work."

"Sure it will. Gem always shares what's going on in her life. I've been toying with the idea of doing a series of videos based on my experience with the show. Obviously, I have to run it past Brad, but I think my viewers will eat it up, and it will be good promotion for the show."

Mac bent down and kissed her. "Don't give me a stupid code name."

Natalie smiled and wrapped her arms around his neck. "We're really doing this."

"Yeah. Although I'd be fine if Gem dropped off the planet. I don't think there's room in this relationship for her. Natalie is more than enough for me."

"See? Slick talker."

"Truth speaker."

"Whatever. Now get out of here. I have a top-secret meeting with clients that you can't hear. I'll let you know when we have our dates set in case you want to join us."

"Fine. Enjoy your meeting. I look forward to seeing your plans." He kissed her again and then walked out of her bedroom.

Natalie heard him saying goodbye to Jillian as he left. Moments later, Jillian appeared in the bedroom doorway dressed for work. "Having sleepovers now?"

Natalie smiled. "I'm taking your advice. We're seeing where this goes."

"I'm glad. See you after work?"

"Maybe. I have to book things for the show and I'm hoping it'll happen fast."

"See you later." Jillian left.

Natalie booted up her computer and dialed all three clients. When they were all on, she said, "We need to chat. I'm setting up the next round, but we need to move things faster, or no one will have anything to show for all of this work."

Ashley said, "What do you mean?"

"In order for the show to succeed, you all need to get a boyfriend. We're not expecting wedding bells, but you need to have one guy. Or in this case two if Mr. Sterling happens to find you a guy as well. On the dates I'm setting up this week, I need you to be open. Use all the flirtation techniques I showed you, and don't be afraid to let things happen."

"I'm not having sex for the cameras," Jennifer said.

"I wouldn't expect you to. But you have to give the chemistry a chance to hit. All I'm asking is if you find yourself in a position to feel the chemistry, get there. You have to let these guys make a move and at least kiss you. That kiss can determine so much for you."

All three women stared at her from her screen.

"Come on. You have to know what I'm saying here. If the kiss doesn't do it for you, there's no need for further exploration."

"Okay," Jennifer said. "You have a point. I've been hesitant to do anything because of the cameras, but you're right. Even if I like a guy, if he can't kiss me, I'm not getting naked with him."

The other two nodded in agreement.

"Awesome. I'll text you as soon as I have your dates set. Trust me. You're gonna have fun."

Natalie clicked off and went to work booking events that would hopefully get her clients near the men they would fall for. She tried to stop her own brain from wandering to the guy she was falling for, but she was unsuccessful. All she could think about was when they would see each other again.

CHAPTER 13

*M*ac was surprised to hear from Natalie so soon. She texted to give him the details for the "dates" she had planned for the clients and invited him to come along to spy. After another discussion with Brad, whatever Natalie had said, sold him on the idea of having Mac and Natalie follow along and spy on the dates.

He hadn't yet told his mother about this latest development because she'd already expressed enough doubt in his abilities that he didn't want to give her more ammunition. If he'd been in on the conversation with Brad, he would've argued against being on the dates. It went against everything they worked towards at Everyday Love. Hell, it went against what Natalie had discussed with the clients. She'd been obvious with her desire to teach them and set them free.

He parked beside a small storefront, which didn't look at all like a restaurant, but then he saw the hand-painted sign on the door. GUILLERMO'S. Mac had eaten at a number of restaurants throughout the city, but he'd never heard of Guillermo's. He stepped from his car as Natalie turned the corner with a huge smile on her face.

She rushed up to him and stopped abruptly. She winked and said, "Just know that if cameramen weren't swarming the area right now, I'd wrapped myself around you and kiss you until you couldn't breathe. Then I'd revive you so I could do it all over again."

"Interesting concept. What put you in such a good mood?"

"I'm pumped about the dates I have scheduled. It was like all of a sudden I *knew* what to do. The only thing that would make this more perfect would be if I could've invited the perfect men to attend."

"Still just a roll of the dice, huh?"

"Not really. I did some homework. Neither one of us can control the outcome."

"We'll see." He tipped his chin toward the restaurant. "Shall we?"

She nodded.

"What exactly is this place?"

"It's a pop-up. The chef is crazy skilled but young. So he does these gourmet meals twice a week to gain a following. Everything I've been able to learn about him says he's fabulous. You can't go wrong eating anything he prepares."

"And which client is partaking in this meal?"

"Ashley."

"Hmm…I would've thought Jennifer."

"This is too tame for her."

"She's the tamest client we have." He reached for the door and held it open for her.

"I know. That's why she needs something different."

Natalie was beginning to sound like Gail, not that Mac would say that to either woman. He had no desire to be stuck between them and the storm they would create.

"Why did you agree to sit in on the dates? I'm not comfortable with this."

She huffed a breath. "That's what I get for texting instead of calling. The nuances don't come through. We're not really here. We're spying, like I said. The place is wired with cameras and mics and we're going to be sitting in the office with a cameraman of our own."

Mac opened his mouth, but he had no idea where to even start, so he followed her through the near-empty space. One long table sat in the middle of the room with enough seating for ten guests. Intimate setting.

"Why does Brad want us to spy?"

Natalie lifted one bare shoulder. Even like this—dressed as Gem—he'd started seeing glimpses of Natalie in the small things, like the shrug.

"It's about us. He likes watching us battle over the clients. The only thing he's raved about since we started was watching us fight. So, we're going to give him more."

An unsettled feeling curled in his gut. "I don't want to fight with you."

"Sure you do. You can't stand Gem. Hold onto that feeling and we'll be fine." She swung a door open that led into a small office. How the hell was he supposed to concentrate on anything but being alone with her and getting her naked when they had to practically sit on top of each other? All while a camera was focused on only them.

He unbuttoned his jacket and sat in one of the two chairs that faced small TV screens. He nodded to the cameraman fiddling with equipment on the other side of the cramped room. "Does Ashley get an earpiece so you can coach her through what to say?"

Natalie stuck her tongue out at him. "No. She doesn't even know we're here." She settled in the chair next to him and her scent wafted over. "I think Brad realized the opportunity he missed by allowing us to watch the raw footage in the comfort of our own homes."

"He didn't suggest—"

"Oh, yes he did. I felt pretty confident speaking for both of us when I told him we refused to give up that bit of privacy."

She looked straight into his eyes when she said it, and Mac felt it to his core. They couldn't reveal their relationship while at work, so the only time they could be completely themselves was at home.

"Absolutely," he responded.

The noise from the kitchen eked into the office when their conversation died.

Natalie slowly slid from her seat. Turning to the cameraman, she said, "Um…Stan, I'll be back in a minute. I want to introduce myself to Chef Antonio. Then you can set us up."

"Nothing to set up." He pointed to the camera and then the large mic he had poised overhead.

"Were you recording us?"

"Nothing that'll count. I was getting some B-roll footage and checking the lighting."

Once Natalie was out of the room, Mac looked at Stan. "If you were recording that conversation, I'd appreciate it if you deleted it."

Stan gave him a blank stare.

"Brad isn't going to want footage of us talking about his motives."

"I didn't have the mic on yet. But the footage of you two interacting is awesome. They'll kill me if I get rid of it. You guys look great on camera together."

They were great together anywhere, and Mac knew that, which was why the extra filming bothered him. He wasn't ready to share his relationship with Natalie with anyone, and definitely not with TV viewers.

～

By introducing herself to Chef Antonio, Natalie had hoped to give herself a mental break. She needed to get away from Mac to gather her thoughts. She hadn't counted on the chef being a huge flirt. She thanked him for being gracious and allowing them to film this event. Then she went back to the office.

Outside the door, she took a steadying breath. She hadn't thought being with Mac and not being able to actually be with him would be so hard. She'd almost lost her mind when she saw him step on the curb because she'd wanted to kiss him. Luckily, she caught herself and remembered the cameras were everywhere.

But in that moment, she'd wanted to share her excitement with him. She had a good feeling about this new direction she was taking. Not new, but more focused. It didn't matter to her that Mac was her competition; she wanted to tell him about her plans. And that thought struck her as important.

While she'd already decided to take a chance on starting a relationship with Mac, this revelation—wanting to share her excitement with him because he was important to her—felt as nerve racking as the first time they had sex. Because that was a level of intimacy she hadn't had in a really long time.

Putting on a flashy smile for the camera, she pushed the door to the office open. "Guests should be arriving any minute. Are we ready?"

The two men nodded and she sat beside Mac. She focused on the screens in front of her. The crew rigged cameras to cover the entire dining area. The wait staff was small and they buzzed around setting everything up.

"So what plans do you have for our clients?" she asked Mac.

"I have dates arranged for each woman based on their preferences and everything I've learned."

She knew he was hinting at the conversations they'd had where they worked together. "No more mixers?"

He shook his head. "They weren't very successful."

"That's debatable. I think they were a lot of fun."

"They might've been fun, but we weren't getting the results we'd hoped for, so we're trying something new. Much like you are."

On screen, dinner guests were arriving. Natalie had only spoken to the chef and head waiter about the evening, so they were the only ones aware of the cameras and her plan. Trevor, the head waiter, had explained the usual eating arrangement was alternating male and female guests. While it wasn't a dating event, all of the guests were single.

And because she knew how to research, Natalie had a feeling there were at least a couple men who might work for Ashley.

As the guests sat at the table, Natalie pushed everything else out of her head and stared at the TV screen. She watched as Ashley introduced herself to the people sitting around her. As usual, Ashley was friendly and talkative, but engaging. Within minutes, she had the attention of two men at the table. Natalie turned and winked at Mac.

"Looks like my method works."

"Just because Ashley can chat up some men doesn't mean she'll find love. She has a track record of *not* finding the right man."

"But she should trust you to tell her who the right man is?" Nat laughed. "That's a decision she ultimately needs to make."

"I agree. My job is to narrow the choices."

The dinner party was under way and Natalie couldn't have asked for a better performance from Ashley. The woman oozed sex appeal. Being a bit of a foodie helped. She moaned and oooed and aahhed over ever morsel she ate.

This, of course, not only played out well on screen, but it also entranced the men she sat with.

What she hadn't expected was for Ashley to ask the chef to come out to talk with them. Everyone at the table seemed on board with the idea.

Chef Antonio came from the kitchen wiping his hands and then his forehead on a towel that he then tucked into the apron at his waist. He smiled at each guest and when he got to Ashley, Natalie saw it. The spark.

Natalie's eyes shot up to Stan. "Do you have a camera in the kitchen?"

Stan's eyes widened and he shook his head. Natalie realized he didn't want to be on camera or have his voice picked up by the mic. She pressed her lips together in irritation. "Stan, we need a camera in the kitchen."

Stan's eyes almost bugged out of his skull.

"Oh, geez. They'll cut this out. Trust me. We need a camera there. Go hook it up." She snapped her fingers. "Now. They can't know it's there."

Stan fumbled behind the equipment.

"What are you up to?"

"Something I didn't see coming. Didn't you see the look Ashley gave Antonio? She likes him." Natalie settled back in her chair and folded her hands in her lap. "Watch what happens."

On the screen in front of them, Ashley began asking Antonio about his recipe and joking about whether it was a secret. The chef came to her side and answered every question she asked.

"Oh, yeah," Natalie said.

"The man is being polite and entertaining his guests. No need to drool over him."

Natalie swiveled in her seat. Was that a tinge of jealousy

she heard? "No drool here, Mr. Sterling, just the sweet sound of success."

Mac held up a hand. "Even if the attraction is mutual, that doesn't mean it'll work out. Do you even know anything about this man?"

"I did my homework."

Mac's nostrils flared as he inhaled. He opened his mouth, but shut it quickly when Stan came back into room.

Stan pointed at the screens in front of them, one of which split as Stan made adjustments behind them. The kitchen came to life and Nat loved watching Antonio work.

"Mmm…That man should have his own show. Something about watching a man who's competent in the kitchen is a huge turn-on."

She felt Mac stiffen beside her. This was too easy.

On the screen, the guests were finishing up dessert and Ashley excused herself. Natalie poked at Mac's leg. "Here we go!" She was giddy by the idea that Ashley was interested in someone.

"She might be going to the restroom."

They didn't have cameras in the hallway, so they couldn't see Ashley's progress, but in her gut, Natalie knew. Then she got a text to verify.

A text from Ashley. *Excellent event. Chef is a total hottie. Going to introduce myself and hope he's interested.*

Natalie laughed out loud and flashed the phone at Mac, who shook his head. She patted his thigh. "It's okay. You'll have a good day soon, I'm sure."

"It's not nice to be patronizing."

She gave him another wicked smile and turned her attention to the screen again. Ashley had just peeked into the kitchen.

"Sound. Where's the sound?" Natalie asked.

Stan fiddled with some equipment, but shrugged.

Damn it. Nat wanted to hear what Ashley was saying.

Mac leaned forward and rested his elbows on his knees. "Don't suppose you're a lip reader?" he asked.

Stan did something to toggle the screens and instead of a split screen, they now had the kitchen in full screen. Natalie leaned forward, much like Mac had, as if by being closer, she'd be able to hear something.

MAC TRIED TO FOCUS ON THE SILENT FILM IN FRONT OF HIM, but Natalie's constant prodding and poking kept him from being able to concentrate. Although she had her usual Gem getup on, she exuded pure Natalie. Her excitement over seeing Ashley show interest in the chef wasn't about winning this competition. Natalie was enjoying herself.

She would be an excellent addition to Everyday Love.

Without warning, her hand landed on his thigh, but her eyes continued to face the TV. "I told you. This isn't about her getting lucky. She likes Antonio."

Ashley leaned against the counter in the kitchen and watched Antonio's every move. They were in deep conversation and Mac wished he could hear it. But Natalie was right —the spark was there.

Antonio said something to make Ashley laugh and their playful banter played out well on the screen, even without sound.

"Are you sure they don't know we're recording them?"

"Antonio knows. He gave us permission and signed the waiver. Maybe he assumes Ashley knows. In a way she does. We've been following everything she does. This shouldn't come as a surprise."

Mac sat in silence, still trying to ignore Natalie's hand on his leg, which hadn't moved. He shifted his legs to reposition, and she got the hint.

Moments later, Ashley pulled out her phone. She and Antonio were exchanging numbers. While Ashley tapped on her screen, Antonio reached out and tucked a lock of hair behind her ear.

"He's touching."

"Still not a kiss."

"That's okay. Sometimes a simple touch can be hotter than tongue in mouth." She pointed at the screen. "See the way she leaned in to his touch? It's an invitation to do more."

"Doesn't look like that'll happen tonight," Mac said, pointing to where Ashley and Antonio were obviously saying goodbye.

A grin broke on Natalie's face. "I'm good at reading people. Give Antonio a minute."

Sure enough, Antonio held up a hand to halt Ashley. Then he said something to his employees at the sink and tossed his towel on the counter. He held his arms open for Ashley to lead the way.

Natalie jumped up. "Quick. Grab a camera and follow them."

She didn't wait for Stan to listen before walking out of the office herself. Mac caught her by the arm in the hall.

"Wait. Let the crew do what they do. She doesn't need you bursting outside to watch."

Stan came through the door talking on a walkie-talkie. He nodded at Natalie and disappeared down the hall.

Natalie tapped her foot. "I want to see."

Mac was impatient as well, but for a whole different reason. He glanced over his shoulder to make sure none of the cameramen were coming. Then he backed Natalie up against the wall and lowered his mouth to hers. The taste was much too brief.

She pressed a palm against his chest. "What are you doing? There are cameras all over."

"Not in the hall, remember? Where's your sense of adventure? I've been waiting all night to do this."

"And we still have all night."

He pressed the length of his body against hers. "Did you drive here?"

"Nope. I was hoping to bum a ride from you."

"My place?"

"Sure." With a single finger, she pushed against him again. "Now back off before someone sees. This show isn't supposed to be about us."

"I don't like it when you get all logical on me."

"I'm always logical when I'm working."

He ran a hand down the side of her body. "It's pretty sexy watching you. You're having a great time doing this."

Her face softened as she stared into his eyes. "You're right. I am." She stepped forward, forcing him to back off. "It's a real high kicking your butt."

He laughed, louder than he'd intended, but she had that effect on him. "One date during one round doesn't mean you're winning. I'm not even sure if this could be considered a date. You had her here to meet one of the dinner guests."

"Don't be a poor loser. Even if tonight doesn't count as a date, trust me, they're already making plans to see each other again."

He knew she was right, but he wouldn't give her the satisfaction of agreeing with her. He'd seen what she did on the screen. Ashley was more than interested in Antonio, and it looked to be mutual. "It was still pure luck they made that connection."

"Ha!" she yelled. "You admit it. They shared a connection. Which is more than you had happen on any of your dates. So we're back to me kicking your butt." She danced her way down the hall toward the front of the restaurant. She slowed as she got to the front and peered around the corner. Satisfied the coast was clear, she waved to him.

He followed her until they were back at the dinner table. Stan came back in with a huge smile on his face.

"You were right. That was a great move. The only thing that would've been better is sound, but you got your kiss."

"Yes!" Natalie did a fist pump and turned to Mac. "Kicking. Your. Butt."

She'd pay for that later. He cleared his throat and turned his attention to Stan. "Did you need anything else from us?"

"Nah. We're good. We're going to clear out now."

"See you tomorrow, Stan," Natalie called as she swept past him. There was no denying the cocky sway of her hips.

The thing was, Mac didn't even care. He loved seeing this confident side to her. She paused outside the door and looked up and down the street. Sidling up to her, he asked quietly, "Do I need to drive around the corner to pick you up or is it safe for you to get in my car here?"

"You're quite funny, Mr. Sterling. I don't think there's anything suspicious about a couple of colleagues sharing a ride."

"We'll be sharing a whole lot more than a car."

"I hope so," she answered with a sweet smile.

He unlocked the car and held the door open for her. He wasn't sure what changed in Natalie since yesterday, but he liked it. She no longer doubted their connection or tried push him away. In light of that, losing to her for this show didn't seem like a big deal.

CHAPTER 14

*N*atalie woke in Mac's arms the next two mornings. They were falling into a routine, which involved sharing meals, free time, and a bed. Going to work was becoming harder for her only because she hated pretending they were still adversarial. The banter came easily enough, but she didn't quite have it in her to throw the barbs she had a couple of short weeks ago.

She was falling hard for Malcolm Sterling, and it was both exciting and unsettling.

Over breakfast in his condo, Mac smiled at her. "You're not still cranky about Melissa's date, are you?"

"Why would I be cranky?"

"Because you thought you had everything locked down. You hadn't counted on me actually finding a good match for her."

"I didn't discount it either, I was hopeful." She swallowed another bite of omelet. Who knew the man could cook? "Besides, just because she had a good date doesn't mean she won't enjoy herself on my little excursion."

"Of course. You've been lucky so far. It might hold."

"Better watch how you talk to me or you won't be getting lucky at all," she said, waving her fork at him.

"I'm practicing for the cameras."

She sighed. "I don't like it."

"What?"

"Pretending. It's hard to pretend you still annoy me."

"After last night's date, I have a hard time believing that. You were nearly brutal."

"I was not. Besides, I was channeling my frustration at having to play up for the camera."

"I've watched your videos. Playing it up for the camera is something you do well. Speaking of which, I thought you said you were going to post new videos as Gem." He finished his food and stood with his plate.

"You've watched my videos?"

"Of course. Why wouldn't I?"

"Because you hate Gem." She stood with her own plate and followed him into his kitchen.

"I don't hate Gem. She's part of you. I don't particularly like some of what you say as her, but it's an unvarnished truth. It's a side you don't often share with me." He took her plate and rinsed it.

"You see me as Gem all the time at work."

He spoke as he filled the dishwasher, and Natalie leaned back to watch. How could a simple household chore look so damn sexy?

"I think when I watch your videos, it's easier for me to be objective because it's not about me and us. I can see parts of you shine through."

That was part of why she hadn't made the new videos she'd talked about. She'd thought she could discuss her new relationship, but revealing all of that on camera felt too intimate. She wasn't ready to share Mac. And she wasn't sure she could be Gem and not slip into herself too much.

He turned from the dishwasher. "Problem?"

"No. I've been thinking that I don't know where I go from here with Gem. I have to keep everything going through the airing of the show, but after?"

As soon as she said the words, she wanted to reel them back in. She didn't want to seem like a needy woman, worrying about where they're going, but now it was out there.

"You won't hear me complain if you dump your online persona." He wiped his hands on a towel and stepped close to her. "She served a purpose—to journal your dating adventures while you healed your broken heart."

Nat swallowed hard. He was so good at getting to the heart of the matter. Maybe she didn't need Gem any more, but she didn't know if she was ready to make that call now.

She stepped close and kissed Mac. "I have to get going to make sure everything's ready for tonight."

"Wine tasting, you said?"

"Yeah. It's simple and a little elegant at a new wine bar."

"How do you find all of these places?"

"What do you mean?"

"The Gourmet Connections pop up for Ashley, now some new wine bar."

"Some things I hear about because they contact me because of Gem. I have some pull online. I don't quite understand it, but when I talk about places, it helps. People want me to call them out on my videos. Other times, like this wine bar, I just noticed the grand opening a few weeks ago. I like to keep up on what's happening in the city."

He wrapped his arms around her waist. "I'm telling you, my mother needs to hire you. Your knowledge of the social scene would help Everyday Love stay relevant."

"I think you're pretty relevant." She stroked his jaw,

loving the way his whiskers tickled her palm. She stepped away. "See you tonight?"

"Of course."

Natalie dressed and left Mac's apartment. Even though she wore yesterday's clothes, she never felt like it was a walk of shame coming from his place. Not that she ever really felt ashamed after a night of pleasure.

Knowing this was more than one night mattered. Mac mattered and she still wasn't sure what to do about that.

He obviously had been more serious about them than she had since the beginning. As much as she knew she was falling for him, though, she wasn't ready for a full-on lifetime commitment.

MAC TRIED NOT TO RUB IT IN; HE REALLY DID. BUT MELISSA'S wine tasting adventure was a bust. He didn't think Melissa experienced quite what Natalie had hoped.

Nat grunted next to him. They had a similar setup to the one they'd had for Ashley's meal and Melissa's date. They sat in a cramped office watching small TV screens.

The wine bar was fabulous and he made sure to introduce himself to the owner because it would be an excellent place to suggest for dates. They might even consider holding a mixer there. Tonight they had a tasting for singles, and although she had plenty of chances to interact with men, Melissa kept checking her phone.

"This is ridiculous. Who the heck is she hoping will call?"

"Maybe David. You know they had a great date the other night. According to Melissa, they've spoken multiple times since he dropped her off."

Natalie slapped her thigh. "They didn't even kiss good-night. How good was the date if she didn't even get a kiss?"

Mac shook his head. Sometimes he wasn't sure if she was still playing it up for the camera or if she believed herself.

"I agree a kiss is important, but rushing into it won't accomplish much. How special is a kiss if she's locking lips with every guy she meets?"

Natalie's eyebrow rose as if to say touché. "I'm not suggesting she kiss everyone, just any guy she is seriously interested in. Then at least she'll know if he's worth pursuing."

"I respectfully disagree."

Natalie snorted.

"If she takes the time to get to know someone, and she's falling for him, the kiss will be that much better. There will be an emotional charge behind it, not simple biological lust."

Natalie laughed. "Lust isn't always simple."

On screen, Melissa was engaged in conversation with the man next to her, but she was telling him about her date earlier in the week. Natalie shook her head and then rested her forehead on her hand. "I give up."

Mac reached over and placed a hand on her thigh. His instinct was to stroke her leg, but when she jerked her head to face him, he remembered they, too, were on camera, so he her gave her leg an exaggerated pat. "There, there, you can't win them all."

He reluctantly pulled his hand away.

"One date does not a winner make."

The fact that she routinely spat out such one-liners made him understand why she had a huge following online. She was fabulous to look at and a ton of fun to listen to—even when he was on the receiving end of her zingers.

"One good date will lead to others. My family has managed to build an entire business based on that concept."

The look in Natalie's eyes softened for a second before she flashed him a Gem smirk. "A guy would be lucky to get a second date with me if he didn't even offer me a kiss that could knock my socks off."

Mac opened his mouth to talk about the kiss he'd give her soon, but luckily, her phone buzzed with a text before he could embarrass himself.

"Oh crap," Natalie said.

"What?"

She looked at him. "Melissa's leaving. She says she's not having a good time, no prospects." She released a huge exhale. "Shouldn't they have to finish a date? She didn't even give this a chance."

"If it's not working, it's not working. If I set her up on a horrible date, you wouldn't expect her to stay." He chuckled at the thought. "In fact, you'd probably offer to be her emergency call to get out of there."

"I would. No one should have to suffer through a bad date, but this wasn't even a date. She didn't even try to have a conversation."

"She's preoccupied."

They turned back to the screen and saw Melissa say her goodbyes to the man next to her. She picked up her purse and left.

The cameraman turned off the equipment and Natalie settled in her chair. "What do you have planned for the rest of the week?"

"Well, since Brad wants first dates wrapped up by this weekend, I have Ashley scheduled for a date tomorrow night."

"Shoot. I have Jennifer booked for an event."

"Can't you reschedule?"

"No. I have her going to game night. It won't happen again until next week and I don't think Brad will go for that." She pulled out her phone. "We should just each do our own thing with the clients. I'll email Brad and let him know we'll need two crews tomorrow. Maybe we can stop in the studio and watch the films together and do voiceovers or individual camera talk."

"Camera talk?"

"You know, when they have us talk straight into the camera?"

He smiled as she tapped away on her phone. He couldn't wait until the filming was done. They only had to finish out this week of events and first dates, then with any luck, each woman will have chosen a guy to pursue a relationship with. Then they would only meet with the clients to talk. He and Natalie would be free to openly date.

He'd been dying to tell his mother. She would be thrilled. Natalie was everything Gail had been wanting in a woman for Mac. His mind raced ahead to how quickly he could make their relationship progress. Natalie no longer appeared to be afraid of his desire for a long-term commitment, which he took as a good sign.

"Mac?" Natalie waved a hand in front of his face. "Where were you?"

He blinked. "Sorry. Just thinking. Lots of plans."

"Brad said it's fine for us to do separate shoots tomorrow. We're done here." She pointed to where the equipment was being packed and stacked. The crew was just waiting on the chairs he and Natalie were sitting in.

"Sorry," he mumbled.

They both stood and said goodbye to the crew. When they got outside, Natalie tugged his arm.

"Everything okay?"

He looked down at her, at the concern splayed across her face, and took her hand in his. "I'm fine. I got caught up in thinking about how happy I am we're almost done filming."

"Happy to be rid of me?"

He yanked her until her body collided with his. "Not

funny. I'm happy to be done with sneaking around. I want the world to know we're together."

"What are you talking about? We still have a couple of weeks of filming. Then there's the finale we have to do live."

He led her toward his car. "After this week, we're done filming together. No more playing in front of the camera. We can be a couple. By the time the finale rolls around, no one will care that we've fallen in love."

He pressed the button to unlock the car, but Natalie jerked back, her hand slipping from his.

"What?" she croaked.

He turned. She stood stock still, her eyes wide. "Huh?"

"What did you say?"

He thought back about the words that had come from his mouth without thought. He stepped closer to Natalie and lifted a hand to her jaw. Stroking her cheek, he said, "No one will care that we've fallen in love."

Her eyebrows twitched and she took a stuttering breath. He stepped closer still. Lowering his face to hers, he added, "In case you haven't figured it out, I love you. I'll shout it to the world. I don't care who knows."

He straightened and looked up and down the street. As he was about to announce his love, she gripped the lapels of his coat and yanked him back to her.

Her kiss was soft and exploratory, as if she was experiencing his mouth for the first time. When she pulled away, he'd hope she'd tell him she loved him as well.

Looking deep in his eyes, she said, "We agreed to keep this between us for now."

He sighed. He didn't understand her desire to keep them a secret. Maybe on film, sure, but this was frustrating.

She smoothed his jacket. "I know it's not your style, but there are consequences for me—professionally—that I don't know I'm ready to deal with."

He pulled back and stared.

"I haven't decided what I'm doing with the vlog and Gem yet. Right now, that's my source of income. It'll be hard for me to convince people to listen to me give advice if I'm not out dating."

He took another step back. "Are you saying you plan to continue dating?" His words came out sharp, but he hadn't expected that.

"No. But if I'm in a committed relationship, the whole idea of *Dating Gem* goes out the window. I just...I don't know. I didn't expect this to happen and it's all a little sudden and you're still looking for your penguin and you think I'm it."

"And you don't." He knew this about Natalie, knew she was reluctant to commit to anything, but he hadn't considered she would avoid being honest with him. She'd given zero hints that she was backing away.

She crossed her arms around her middle as if she needed to hold herself together. "That's just it, I didn't want to think it. I didn't want to be anyone's penguin, but you make me believe it's possible."

His brain raced. Had he heard her right? She stared at the ground, which increased his doubt that he understood her.

"Natalie?"

Her eyes rose to meet his. They were filled with worry and fear.

"I'm having a stupid moment here," he said. "Are you saying you think you're my penguin?"

He should've felt ridiculous saying such a thing to a woman, but it felt right with Natalie.

She nodded. "I didn't think I'd ever fall in love again. You make me believe in all kinds of things."

He moved closer again to take her in his arms, but she moved farther. She held up a hand. "This is freaking me out."

She chuckled. "You know, in case you haven't noticed. That's why I want to keep it between us. I don't think I can handle the scrutiny of the world watching us."

"Okay." He didn't care what she asked for. In that moment, he'd give her anything because she as good as admitted she loved him. He had no doubt she'd be saying the actual words soon enough.

"Really?" Relief stole across her features.

"Of course. Anything."

"Thank you."

"Did you think I'd demand we tell everyone?"

She took a slow, deep breath. "I wasn't sure. Some men want their own way, no matter what."

He smiled and held out his hand for her to take. "I think I've already proven I'm not most men."

"That you have, Mr. Sterling. Take me home."

Mac loved the sound of that and he hoped one day soon they would have a home together.

NATALIE SAT IN THE BACK OF THE BAR WITH JENNIFER, WHO was more nervous than when Natalie had forced her into the art class.

"What is this again?" she asked.

"It's game night." In her head, however, Nat thought of it as nerd night. The bar was filled with guys playing tabletop games. Since she wasn't sure how Jennifer would react to teasing, she opted not to tell her. "Games are set up at tables. You play for thirty minutes or so and then switch."

"Oh, God. So it's like speed dating."

"No!" Natalie held Jennifer's shoulders. "No. This is relaxed. You get to meet people. It's not a set up, but like the other events we've done, everyone here is single."

"What if I don't know how to play a game?"

Although Natalie doubted Jennifer wouldn't be able to find something she knew, she said, "Then you ask a cute guy to explain the rules." She turned Jennifer toward the bar. "Go get yourself a drink, so you have something in your hands. Walk the room to check out your options and when you see something interesting, hop in."

"You sure about this?"

"Yes. It'll be fun. Don't think about it as a dating thing. You're just here to meet new people. If something clicks, great, but if not, you have a fun new thing to do."

"Okay. That helps." Jennifer straightened her shoulders and set off into the bar.

Natalie took a seat and sipped a soda. Jennifer ordered a glass of wine and then looked over the tables, but didn't move. Crap. Natalie thought she'd have to go give the woman another nudge.

But much to Nat's surprise, Jennifer walked to a table and took a seat. She smiled and began chatting with the people playing, and Natalie sighed.

"You were really good with her," a deep voice beside her said.

Natalie turned and saw her cameraman standing beside her. "Thanks, uh…"

"Damian," he supplied and held out his hand.

Natalie shook hands. "Shouldn't you be behind the camera?"

He nodded. "Yeah. I wanted to introduce myself." His gaze wandered the room. "Fun event."

"Yeah, seems like it."

"Why don't you go jump in? Without Mr. Sterling here tonight, I only need to focus on Jennifer. You might as well have some fun."

Natalie laughed. "No, thanks. I'm good here."

"How about a drink later, when we're ready to wrap up?"

She shook her head slightly. "I hope to be done before you. That is, if Jennifer can find a man she likes."

He shrugged and moved back behind the camera. Natalie turned her attention to Jennifer. She missed having Mac here. She'd thought after their emotional conversation yesterday she'd enjoy the break, but implementing dating strategies and discussing them was more fun when she had someone to talk to about it. Even if they had to do it on camera.

Sitting here by herself, twirling her straw and being bored was awful. She took out her phone and texted Mac.

How's your night going?

Fine. Yours?

Jennifer is at least interacting with people. Natalie leaned over and took a picture of the room for Mac to see.

What are they doing?

Playing games. It's fun. You should try it. There's Dungeons and Dragons and trivia.

As if I'd ever play a trivia game with you. I don't enjoy losing.

Natalie laughed and slapped a hand over her mouth.

Ashley is not interested in this date. I shouldn't have even tried. She's got Antonio.

Natalie stopped short of a fist pump, but couldn't hold back the smile. *I'll let you get back to it then.*

Coming over tonight?

I suppose if you ask nicely, I might be persuaded.

Pretty please?

I'll be there as soon as we're done.

Have fun. But not too much.

Natalie glanced up at Jennifer who was laughing as she slapped cards on the table. Nat couldn't tell if Jennifer had her eye on anyone, but she was at least engaged in the night. Nat considered it a win.

They stayed for two hours. Natalie was so bored she wanted to cry. But even after moving around to a few games, Jennifer still appeared to be having a good time. Then she stood with a man and they walked to the bar together.

Finally. That was Natalie's cue to leave. If Jennifer chose to extend her night, Natalie didn't need to watch. She slipped from her stool and stifled a yawn. All she wanted was to crawl into bed next to Mac and sleep.

Well, maybe a little more than sleep.

Damian sidled up to her. "Leaving?"

"Yeah." She pointed to Jennifer, who had moved to a small table with the man, drinks in hand. "My job here is done for the night."

"Would you like to get that drink now? On me."

"No, thank you, Damian. I'm pretty beat." She slung her purse over her shoulder.

"How about dinner tomorrow? I'd like to get to know you better. You seem like fun, so I bet we have a lot in common."

His offer held no appeal. It wasn't all that long ago Nat would've taken in his dark hair and the stubble on his jaw and considered whether he'd be fun for the night. Now all she thought about was being in Mac's arms.

"No, thank you, though. It's best to keep dating away from work." The lie almost got stuck in her throat, but she didn't want to tell him she was seeing someone. The last thing she needed was word to get out that Gem, the pick-up artist, was in a relationship.

He stepped closer. "Isn't your whole job based on dating? Mixing it up could be worth your while. Plus, we'd look great on camera together."

Nat swallowed the groan. She hated when a guy couldn't take a hint or worse, a polite let down. "I appreciate your interest. I'm not looking to hook up."

She slid to the side of him and wound through the tables to the front door, smiling at Jennifer as she went past.

The episode with Damian made her realize she needed to decide what to do with Gem. It also reminded her of the video she shot but never released. The "I don't owe you anything" video from her night with "Dick." She briefly wondered if Damian would've been like that. Everyone who knew Gem assumed she was still in the game, looking to pickup or hook up.

In her gut, Natalie knew it was time to let her go. But waiting until the show finished made the most sense. Her vlog provided her platform. And bottom line, like she told Mac, she needed the income. So she'd log on and release her story about Dick.

CHAPTER 15

Mac sat on his couch, sipping a whisky like his father had taught him while he waited for Natalie to arrive. The thought of asking her to move in had been circling his brain. Logically, he knew it was too early, and she would definitely balk at making any decision until after the show was over.

But he really wanted her here every night. When his bell rang, and he rose to buzz her in, he decided he would at least give her a key to let herself in. He waited at the door to greet her. When she stepped off the elevator, she looked exhausted.

She trudged over and sank into his waiting arms. "I've been needing this for hours."

Mac rubbed her back and then turned and guided her into his condo. "Long day?"

She nodded. "I don't even know what was so long about it. I'm just so tired."

"Does that mean you don't want to talk about how the night went with Jennifer?"

Natalie leaned away and looked up at him. "You want to tell me how it went with Ashley?"

He laughed. "I already did. It went nowhere. She showed up out of obligation. I have the impression she's serious about Antonio."

The smile Natalie offered was so sweet and genuine, he wanted to capture it. It was the kind of smile she never gave the cameras, so he felt like it was just for him.

"It's a good feeling, you know?"

"What is?" he asked.

"Getting it right. Helping someone find love."

"Yeah. It does feel good. What happened with Jennifer?"

Natalie sat on the couch and tugged off her heels. "She looked like she was having fun. She played at different tables and by the end of the night, she was having a drink with a guy one on one."

"You didn't stay to see how it worked out?"

Slouching back into his couch, making herself comfortable, she said, "Nah. She didn't need my support any more. Plus, Damian might've gotten the impression I was waiting around for him."

"Who?" His question was sharper than he'd intended, but he automatically went on alert when she mentioned another man.

"Damian. The camera guy. He wanted to buy me a drink."

"What?" Great. Now he was speaking in single syllables.

Natalie waved a hand. "He was flirting. Wanted a date." Then she reached over and stroked his jaw. "Don't worry, caveman. I told him I wasn't interested."

"He probably wouldn't have asked if we told people we're a couple."

She curled up in the corner of the couch. "Not necessarily. He's one of those guys who doesn't take a hint. He probably wouldn't think anything of asking out an unavailable woman."

"What do you mean he doesn't take a hint?"

She yawned wide. "He asked me out repeatedly. Even though I shot him down every time. He was pretty insistent. Thought I looked like fun. Said we'd look great on camera together."

Something about the situation nagged him. It wasn't that Natalie wasn't a beautiful woman, but something about the exchange seemed off. "Where did he ask you out?"

Her eyes were already fluttering closed. "Told you. At the bar."

"While Jennifer's date was going on?"

"If you could call it a date."

"So he had the camera rolling."

"That's his job," she mumbled. "Nothing to worry about, babe. I'm all yours. Let me take a nap, and I'll show you how much fun I can be."

Mac knew something wasn't right. He'd worked with plenty of people on the crew and all of them had always made a point of steering clear of the filming. Especially the cameramen.

Dread settled in his stomach and he drained his glass of whisky. He knew his mother was up to something again.

The following day, Mac rose early to go visit his mother. Natalie said she had job-hunting prospects, so she wouldn't be around until evening. They made plans to meet for dinner. He'd tossed and turned most of the night trying to figure out what his mother was up to. On the drive over to the office, he considered he might be overreacting. Some man asking Natalie out was bound to happen. It probably occurred more often than he'd like to think.

Maybe jealousy was getting the better of him.

He parked and went straight to his mother's office, knocking once before entering. She was on the phone and glared at him for entering without permission, but he didn't care. He needed to know.

Taking the chair in front of her desk, he waited patiently for her to end the call. Based on the volume and frequency of her laugh, she was speaking with a friend, not a client.

As soon as she set the phone in its cradle, she said, "What can I do for you today, Malcolm?"

"Please tell me you didn't put a cameraman up to asking Gem out last night."

She folded her hands on top of her desk, but didn't answer.

Fuck. Sometimes he hated when his gut was right. He reined in his anger. "I told you to leave her alone."

"Malcolm, really. You must stop being so melodramatic. I saw footage of what happened at the dinner party. She's good."

"I don't need you to cheat to help me win. I'll win or lose on my own. This was your idea. You wanted me to do this stupid show. Let me do it my way."

She tilted her head and the haughty look she gave made his blood boil. "You think I don't see what's going on here? You're smitten. Gem is not the kind of woman you need to be involved with. She's too much like Ariel."

Mac shot out of his chair. "Enough!" His muscles went rigid. No way was he going to listen to his mother tear down Natalie. "Gem is not who she is. That's a persona for the camera."

"Which proves my point."

With his palms flat on the desk he leaned forward. "If you even think about doing one more thing to interfere, I'll leave."

She leaned back in her chair. "Go where?"

"Far from you. I'll leave Everyday Love and open my own matchmaking company with the attention I garner from doing this show."

Her face paled. He didn't know if it was the thought of losing him or him starting his own company, but she was paying attention now.

"Malcolm—"

He pushed off the desk. "Stop. Stay away from Natalie."

As soon as he spoke Natalie's real name, he regretted it. His mother's face changed, emotion shifted.

"Oh my God. You have genuine feelings for her."

He straightened his shoulders. "Yes, I do. And because of that, I will fight you if you try to make her look bad or take anything from her."

Tears filled her eyes. "I had no idea. I thought she was playing you to win the competition, take our business." She stood and walked around the desk and stood in front of him. "Why didn't you tell me?"

At the softening of his mother, his anger died. "Why would I need to? You watched the footage."

"I saw flirtation, banter, sexual attraction. I wasn't aware you had taken the time to know her."

He huffed. "And of course you couldn't trust me to live my life."

She smiled. "I let you live your life when it came to Ariel, and look how that ended."

"Natalie isn't Ariel. And you didn't really let me live my life there either."

Gail patted his cheek. "And not once in the years you were with Ariel did you defend her to me like you did just now. You love this woman passionately."

"I do."

"Does she love you too?"

"She does."

Her eyebrow arched. "Then you'll have to bring her back around so I can get to know her better."

Mac rubbed his jaw. "Not yet. She doesn't want people to know we're a couple. She thinks it'll make her look bad for the show."

"Make her look bad, but not you?"

He shook his head. "You know what I mean."

"You mean people will assume she slept her way into the winner's circle." She raised a sharply pointed nail in his direction. "I raised you better than that."

"I don't think that. Natalie doesn't have a conniving bone in her body. But she's private and she doesn't want to be scrutinized."

Gail laughed. "I've seen her videos. She's not that private. And I think you're both underestimating her ability to hold her own." She walked back around the desk. "But have it your way. Keep your secrets and bring her to me when you're ready."

"And you'll stay out of it?"

"Of course, darling. When have I ever meddled in anyone's life?"

That caused a huge belly laugh to burst from him. "You are Queen Meddler."

"We all have our talents. Now go away. I have work to do."

Natalie spent hours driving around a small town about two hours outside of Chicago. She'd never thought of herself as a small town girl. When she'd applied for the job as librarian at the private school, she hadn't expected to even get called for an interview.

Being offered the job had never landed on her radar. As far as she was concerned, she was just doing her due diligence in trying to gain employment.

The interview had gone well and they offered her the position of school librarian. She told the principal she needed some time to think about it, but their current librarian was pregnant and would be going on maternity leave within a few weeks. They wanted Natalie to fill in for the rest of the year and then the position would be hers for the next school year.

She needed to make a decision within the next week or so. If she decided to take the job, she had to determine how that would impact her life.

Hence driving around a town that, as far as she could tell, had only two stoplights. Would she want to live here? Or would commuting be better? Could she live in a town with no mall or nightclub or big box store?

She drove back into Chicago to the unwelcome bumper-to-bumper traffic of the afternoon commute. Rolling her window down, she let in the cool spring breeze, which ended up being filled with exhaust from a passing truck.

The road ahead of her was under construction, causing the lanes to merge. It should've added to her frustration when all she wanted to do was get home and see Mac. But something about the sounds of the pounding jackhammers and whirring concrete saws made her smile. This was home.

The thought added to the already roiling conflict in her gut. She'd said repeatedly she would keep her options open when it came to a job and that she would consider moving, but she hadn't really given it thought. She didn't think she needed to. A job was vital. Her living in Chicago, not so much.

Until now.

She got off the expressway and drove home. By the time she reached her apartment, her nerves were completely frayed. Unlocking the front door, she called, "Jillian?"

She knew it was a long shot. It was only about six o'clock. Most days, Jillian didn't get home before dark.

It was an excellent surprise when her best friend called back, "In the kitchen."

Nat heard some banging around and the oven closing. Then Jillian met her in the living room.

"So? How'd it go?" Jillian asked as she wiped her hands on a towel.

Natalie opened her mouth and a flood of information poured out. "They offered me the job. It'll be a substitute position for the remainder of this year, but the current librarian isn't coming back. She's taking time off to be with her baby. It's a beautiful campus. Everything is new. The technology, the books, everything. I would be able to build the collection I want for the kids, and I'd work closely with teachers. I'd be a real resource."

"Wow," Jillian said as she sat on the arm of the couch. "I'm happy for you."

"You don't sound happy."

"It's far. If you're working there, what sense would it make for you to stay here? I'll lose my roomie and bestie."

"Don't start redecorating my room yet. I haven't decided to take the job." She stepped out of her heels, sat on the couch, and pulled Jillian down to sit beside her.

"From everything you just said, it seemed like you had."

"It's a big step. But you're right. It is far. I don't know that I'd want to live there."

"What's wrong with...where was it? Mayberry?"

"Ha. You're funny. Harvest Grove isn't quite that small.

But it is small enough that I think I'd be running into students everywhere. I don't know if I'd like to live like that. I enjoy my privacy." She inhaled deeply. "And then there's Mac. His whole life is here."

"It is," Jillian added with a nod.

"You're not helping here."

"What do you want me to say?"

"I'm nervous, Jilly. How do I tell this great guy I might be moving two hours away? Especially when I didn't even tell him about the interview." Nat rubbed her stomach as if that would somehow relieve the flight of butterflies taking over her system.

"Nervous about what? Mac loves you. You guys can make this work."

"All of it. I'd have to find somewhere else to live. I wouldn't be with you. It's a completely different job than I'm used to. And Mac." She didn't think she needed to explain anything else as far as he was concerned.

Jillian hugged her. "But you're excited about it. Your face lit up when you told me. Tell Mac the same way and you'll be fine. You guys can handle this."

Natalie blew out a breath. How could she explain why she was nervous? She wasn't even exactly sure. Her relationship with Mac was new and still felt fragile, like any new thing. But even though it was new, it was important to her. This was the first time in years that she had any kind of real connection with another person. Mac's opinion and input mattered. "You're right. I'll talk to him tonight."

With that decision made, her full smile returned. She *was* excited. For the first time in weeks, she felt optimistic, as if things were finally taking a turn in the right direction.

MAC ANSWERED HIS BELL WHILE STILL TRYING TO FIGURE OUT how to tell Natalie what his mother had done. When he swung the door wide, Natalie stood, wearing a huge smile and holding a bottle of wine to go with the dinner he'd ordered.

"Judging by the smile on your face, the news you have is good."

"Kind of." She stepped close, and her smile faltered. "We're gonna need this." She handed him the bottle.

He lowered his mouth to hers. When their lips met, the tension he'd been feeling since last night finally left. He pulled back and whispered, "Let's go eat so you can tell me your news."

She smiled before pulling him back for one more quick kiss. He only hoped his news wouldn't ruin whatever she had to say.

Holding his hand, she walked toward the table where he set up their dinner. He released her so he could open the wine. After filling their glasses, he held one up. "To what are we toasting?"

"I got a job."

"What? That's excellent." He set his glass down and pulled her into his embrace. Against the soft scent of her hair, he added, "I knew you'd get one soon. Tell me all about it."

Stepping back, he pulled a chair out for her to sit. Her face lit with excitement as she launched into details. "It's a small private school. Their current librarian will be going on maternity leave and not returning. I'd be the head librarian. The school has money to buy pretty much whatever the kids need. Their computer lab is state of the art, as far as schools go anyway. I'd be able to work with teachers to develop cool projects that would get kids into the library."

"Sounds great."

"It is. I'd have freedom to build a collection of books kids want to read. I toured the school and it was amazing to see kids actually engaged and doing stuff in the library, not just using computers to watch YouTube videos. The school grounds are beautiful and well cared for. The staff seemed friendly. The current librarian spoke about her job as a place she was really going to miss. She loves working there."

Mac held up his glass. "Congratulations. I'm happy for you."

She took a healthy drink of wine followed by a deep inhale. "Don't celebrate just yet. I haven't accepted the offer."

"Why not? Not enough money?"

"No. The money's good. It's the location that's a problem."

"Where is it?" His mind immediately thought if she had to work in a suburb, they could find a place to move to that would be a compromise for both of them. He wasn't so tied to his condo that he needed to stay here.

"Harvest Grove." She spoke the two words and then waited, staring at him.

"I've never heard it. Where is it?"

"Calling it a suburb of Chicago would be too generous. It's a small town about two hours outside of the city."

"Two hours?" He hadn't seen that coming. Two hours outside the city would mean a horribly long commute during rush hour. She'd told him she expanded her search. He hadn't thought she'd look for a job so far away.

"Yeah." She toyed with the silverware he'd set out. "It's a really small town. I've never lived anywhere but here."

That was her biggest concern? Living in a small town? Maybe he'd jumped the gun in telling his mom about them being in love, because right now, it felt like Natalie was letting him down easy.

He stared at her and waited for more. She sat silently moving her fork over and then back. "You want this job."

Her eyes finally met his. "A huge part of me does, yeah. I

hate being out of work. And there's so much to love about the school and the position."

"But?"

"But…" She licked her lips. "You're here."

And just like that, the vice squeezing his heart and lungs loosened. He wasn't an afterthought. She was still being cautious with her emotions. He reached across the table and held her hand. "Tell me what you're feeling."

"I feel like an idiot."

"Why?"

"Because we've been a couple for a few weeks. You shouldn't matter so much that I'm questioning what to do with my life." She tightened her fingers on his. "But you do. What you think matters to me. More than it should for such a new relationship."

He wanted to tell her to keep looking for a different job, one that wouldn't take her away from him. But he couldn't be that selfish. "I don't think the length of time matters as much as how you feel. I think we've both acknowledged what we have is serious. I love you, Natalie. If you want to make this work with me, we'll make it work."

Her eyes filled with tears and her smile returned. "I'm so glad you said that."

Her comment confused him. "What did you expect me to say? See ya later?"

"I half expected you to tell me not to take the job."

"No matter what, you need to do what's right for you. I'm not going to lie, the thought of asking you to turn down the job occurred to me. I don't want there to be any lies between us. I want you to be happy. If this job will do it, then take it."

"But?" she asked, the same way he had a few moments ago.

"But I want you here, with me all the time. I want us in the same house, in the same bed every night."

"What?" Her eyes widened.

He knew the suggestion was moving too fast for her, especially in light of her news and the decision she needed to make. "As soon as you mentioned the location was a problem, I began to think about where we could move that would be convenient for both of us to be able to get to and from work. In fact, while I was waiting for you last night, I was thinking about asking you to move in, but I knew you would freak out. I had a key made for you, though, so you can let yourself in whenever you want."

Her jaw slackened and her tongue darted out to wet her lips. With a shaky hand, she brought her wine to her mouth. Mac waited for her to gather her thoughts. He'd just thrown a curveball at her that she hadn't expected.

Natalie drained her glass and set it back on the table. "I don't know what to say."

Mac took her hand again, this time bringing it to his lips. He kissed her knuckles. "You don't have to say anything right now. I want you to know I'm here, unequivocally. Nothing you say is going to change that. So if you tell me you want this job, we'll start looking at places between here and there." He stroked her knuckles with his thumb.

She stood and took two steps until she was directly in front of him. He leaned back in his chair to look up at her. She straddled him and lowered herself onto his lap. Wrapping her arms around his neck, she said, "I can't begin to tell you how much it means to me that you're willing to do that. I'm not ready to move in together, especially since we still have the show to finish. I'm not sure about this job, but I'm definitely considering it. I was worried I'd have to make a choice between you and the job."

He reached up as she spoke and brushed her hair off her shoulders, allowing the silky strands to run through his fingers. "I would never do that to you."

"But I also don't want you to disrupt your entire life for me. You've done that before."

She stared into his eyes and her words sank in. He'd gone wherever Ariel wanted him to go, and Natalie didn't want to be the same way. He wished he could explain how he knew this was different. "I went to New York because I wanted to build a life with Ariel."

Natalie tilted her head and raised a brow. "Are you saying she didn't expect you to do that?"

"It was a decision we made together."

She didn't look like she believed him, but she let it drop.

He moved his hands to her hips and held her snug against his body. "Tell me all about the town. How small is small?"

"Fewer than five thousand people live there. No mall. No big box stores."

"Hmm…I bet they have an awesome diner where you can get great coffee."

Her thumbs stroked his jaw, against the whiskers of his beard. "What makes you say that?"

"Isn't it a requirement for every small town? A cranky diner owner who has the best coffee for miles around."

Natalie let loose a laugh. "I think if it's the only coffee for miles, it has to be the best by default."

She sighed and leaned forward to rest her head on his shoulder. "Thank you," she said quietly.

He rubbed her back. "For what?"

"For understanding everything. For knowing me well enough to know what I needed to hear. For making me laugh when I'm completely overwhelmed."

"No thanks are necessary. I'm glad you brought this to me to talk about."

After another sigh, she pushed off his lap and stood. "Let's eat before dinner is totally cold. You can tell me all about your day."

"Mine was nowhere near as eventful as yours."

She didn't need to hear about what Gail had done. Natalie had enough on her mind without having to worry about his mother, especially now that Gail had promised to back off.

CHAPTER 16

Mac sat in his living room, staring at his phone. Gem had uploaded another video. It was awful. Natalie stared into the screen with faux flirtation, but he'd seen the anger in her eyes. As he watched her rant about some guy who expected her to have sex because he'd bought her a drink, Mac's emotions ran hot.

First, there was anger. How could she go out to a club to pick up men as if they weren't a couple? He knocked that thought aside quickly enough when he remembered what his mother had put the cameraman up to the other night.

A sickening dread filled him as he considered that maybe Natalie hadn't told him the entire story about what happened.

Why wouldn't she tell him but then share it with her entire viewing audience? Did he mean that little to her? The key he'd had made for her stared at him from the coffee table.

When his doorbell buzzed, he moved without thought to let her up. He unlocked his front door, but instead of waiting for her in the doorway as he usually did, he returned to his seat on the couch. She swept through the door in a rush.

"So sorry I'm late. I hope you're not too hungry since I kept you waiting."

"Actually I'm not very hungry at all."

"Huh?" She set her bag on the chair and looked at him. "What's wrong?"

He turned his phone to face her.

"That?" She waved it off. "I told you I needed to continue to post videos."

"But this? Why didn't you tell me?"

"Tell you what?" She sat beside him, her face a mask of confusion.

"Why would you only give me a small detail about what happened? Did you think you'd come in here and make me jealous? Was I supposed to go start a fight with the guy?"

She laughed. Actually laughed. "I doubt you would even be able to find him."

"I don't think this is funny. Why would you keep this from me?"

Her face sobered. "I didn't keep anything from you. I very plainly told you I needed to post videos as Gem. I posted. I wasn't aware you expected me to inform you of the content of the video as well. Am I supposed to get your approval?"

Why the hell was she getting mad at him? He tossed his phone on the table and stood. Paced. "It's not about the damn video. I'm mad you didn't tell me the whole extent of what happened with the cameraman the other night. That kind of behavior"—He pointed at the phone—"should get him fired."

Natalie leaned forward, head cocked to the side, mouth slightly open. Suddenly, she sat straight with a smile. "Oh my God. You think the video was about Damian? No. God no. Why would you think that?"

"The alternative was worse."

"The alternative…" Her voice faded as she considered what the alternative was. Her jaw clenched and she stood, crossing her arms. "So let me get this straight. You figured I either lied to you about what happened with Damian, or I went out clubbing and picked up another man."

"What was I supposed to think?" he asked quietly, although hearing her speak like this now made him wish he'd considered other options.

"How about you give me the benefit of the doubt as someone who wouldn't lie to you or cheat? How about *that*? You could've called and asked me instead of sitting here, lying in wait to accuse me."

"I wasn't lying in wait—"

Her glare had him shutting his mouth. That's exactly how it appeared to her.

She stepped closer and pointed. "That video was old. I taped before we slept together. Before we were anything to each other. The afternoon Jillian came to the studio to watch me film, we went out after."

Mac's anger fizzled to remorse. "I didn't know."

"Obviously."

He stepped closer, reached up and brushed her hair off her shoulder, letting his touch linger. She didn't pull away. "I saw the video and it freaked me out. It felt like betrayal. The thought of you cheating went in and out of my mind in a blink, so I looked for another explanation. The one I came up with wasn't much better."

"I wouldn't do that," she whispered.

"I know."

She snorted her disbelief.

Cradling her jaw, he lifted her face to look into his eyes. "I do. The thought of another man putting his hands on you, trying to force you to do anything had me seeing red. I lashed out and it shouldn't have been at you. I'm sorry."

She sighed and leaned into him and his touch. "I think we might have to send you in for sensitivity training, Mr. Sterling. It seems you have an issue with putting your foot in your mouth, speaking without thought."

He threaded his fingers through her hair. "Only with you. You have a way of scrambling my brain so I can't think straight."

"I might buy that if we were lying in bed naked, but since it was a video that did this to you, I'm not believing it."

"We're in a relationship. The thought of you being with another man..." He paused to gather his thoughts so he wouldn't sound like a complete idiot again.

Natalie patted his chest. "I get it. If I saw you with another woman, I'd be pissed too. Let's just agree that we're exclusive."

"Easiest agreement I've ever made." He lowered his lips to hers. Against them he murmured, "I'll make this up to you after dinner."

Her lips curved. "You said you weren't hungry. I think make-up sex will stir your appetite."

"Hmm...I guess that was our first fight."

She tugged him toward his bedroom. "We fight all the time."

"That's for the cameras. This was real." He allowed her to lead him to his bedroom.

She released his hand to flick on the light and strip off her dress. Before she got completely naked, he pulled her back into his arms. "I'm so lucky to have you."

"You'll be happier in a few minutes if you let me get my underwear off."

"No. I mean, we just fought. And we were able to talk about it."

"You fought. You got stupid and I helped you see the light."

He chuckled. "I'm serious. There was no drama, no throwing things, no storming out. We were able to confront each other and talk so we could fix it. That's good shit."

"Is that official therapist-speak? Good shit?"

"Lord, do I love you. You make everything so much better."

"Yeah?" she asked, squirming from his grasp. She hopped on the bed. "Show me."

~

For the next few days, Natalie and Mac had spent almost all of their time together. Their clients had been going on dates with the men they chose and she and Mac sat together to view the raw footage of the dates.

One night while they sat on Mac's couch, she asked, "What exactly does Brad want us to do now? The women are dating. That's what he wanted. I don't see the purpose of us watching this."

Mac had his arm around her shoulder and he toyed with her hair while they watched Ashley on a date with Chef Antonio. "We're supposed to be watching to be able to give our clients some pointers when we check in with them."

She sat up and fully faced Mac. "So we can have like one more day of filming and we're done. Finished for good?"

He nodded. "Except for the finale. Brad has that slated for a couple weeks from now, I think."

"Wow. I can't believe it's over. It felt like it was going to take forever, but now, it's done."

"I know, you're going to miss all of those confined spaces where you had to fight to keep your hands off me," he joked.

"Oh, yeah, it was a real battle to keep my hands from strangling that smug smile off your face."

He narrowed his eyes at her, which just egged her on.

"You're the one who couldn't keep his hands off me. Every chance you got, you were pulling me off to be alone."

"Maybe if you weren't constantly teasing me, I would've behaved better."

She smiled. "I'm glad you didn't."

"So am I." He planted a kiss and then asked, "What did you decide about the job?"

They'd both talked about it a lot over the last few days. She'd made a pro-con list, which ultimately didn't help. Mac had been completely supportive. "I still haven't made up my mind."

"I doubt they'll wait forever. Maybe your lack of a decision is one."

"No." She shook her head. "I've actually been leaning toward taking it. But instead of moving, I'm going to try to commute. At least for now."

"Really?"

"Yeah. What if I don't like the job? Then I'd be stuck living somewhere I don't want to be and I'd be out of work again. It'll be hard, but it'll only be for a couple of months. Then the school year will be over and I'll have the summer to figure out where to live."

"When do you start?"

Her stomach jumped. She'd made a decision. The weight that had been pulling at her for days lifted. "I don't know. I'll call the principal in the morning."

"Will you move in with me then?"

"We talked about this."

"Yes, but that was before you decided to take the job. With that commute, you're going to lose four hours a day. I want every moment I can get with you, even if it's just while you're asleep."

Her heart went all mushy. This guy. He was too much. "I'll think about it."

He smiled. "That's as good as a yes."

"It's a maybe. And even if it's a yes, it won't happen until this stupid show is over." Her gut told her it was a yes. She wanted to be with Mac as much as he wanted to be with her. The idea of coming home to him everyday sounded wonderful.

"The first episode is going live next week. Brad said they're going to put the episodes up in two batches. Half one week, half a week later, then two days later, the live finale. He said something about wanting to appease those who like to binge while still trying to build buzz and draw an audience for the finale."

"Sounds complicated. But it also means only three weeks and we're done."

"Speaking of the premiere, my mother is hosting a party. She's inviting everyone she knows. She'd like you to come."

"*She* would?" Natalie teased as Ashley's date continued to drone on in the background, forgotten.

"It goes without saying I want you there."

"Why is your mother inviting the competition to her soiree?"

For the first time in a long time, Mac looked uncomfortable. Natalie's neck prickled. "What is it?"

"I told my mom about us."

"What do you mean?"

"I told her we're a couple. That we're in love. I know you wanted to keep it a secret, and my mother can respect that. She wants you there as my date to get to know you better."

"Oh, crap. But no pressure, right? I'm supposed to be introduced to your mother at a fancy party in front of all of her socialite friends. How the hell am I supposed to make a good impression there? Especially when they're all going to watch me on screen as Gem? I can't be Gem on screen but Natalie with your mom." Shit. Now she was back to talking about herself in third person as if she were two different people.

"Relax." He turned her back to face the TV and the date they were supposed to be watching. He tucked her in close to him. "Come to the party as whoever you want. I don't care how you're dressed as long as you're with me. My mother likes you."

"Your mother came to me to offer advice to set me up to look like an idiot in front of Brad."

"Well, I think she was actually hoping you would've plowed ahead with the bad ideas and filmed them. Making you look bad in front of Brad wouldn't have had a big enough effect."

"That doesn't help. She wanted me to look like a fool in front of the world."

"She only did that because she saw you as a threat."

"And now I'm supposed to smile and be polite and make her like me?"

"She does like you. Despite what she did, she likes the way you work. You scared her because everyone underestimated you." Mac began stroking her arm again. "Besides, she knows I love you. You don't have to do anything."

Ashley's date had ended and the next clip was Melissa's date with David, the man who Mac had set her up with. Natalie tried to focus so she could offer some good advice, but all she could think about was going back to meet Gail as Mac's girlfriend. She'd enjoyed being in their own little bubble where no one knew about them, and therefore couldn't interfere in their relationship.

~

ONCE NATALIE CALLED TO ACCEPT THE JOB OFFER, DR. Harding, principal of Wells Academy and Natalie's new boss, wanted her to come in. He was willing to pay her to come in and work with the current librarian to get the lay of the land. So she found herself waking at four thirty in the morning so she could be on the road by five thirty. With any luck it was early enough that she could escape rush hour.

She looked back where Mac lay in bed. He lifted one eyelid.

"It's not nice to stare." His rough morning voice teased her senses, making her want to crawl back under the covers.

"Go back to sleep." She went to the side of the bed and kissed his cheek. "I'll see you tonight."

"Good luck. Coffee's on in the kitchen." Then he rolled over and dozed off again.

As she walked into the hallway and sniffed, sure enough, she smelled coffee. The man was a saint. He must've set a timer for the machine. In the kitchen, she filled a travel mug, double checked her bag, and completed some deep breathing exercises.

The two-hour drive was the last bit of quiet she had for the day. Laura, the current librarian, who looked ready to pop a baby out any minute, was lively for a woman moving so slowly.

When Natalie sank into a chair across from Laura at lunchtime, she sighed. "I forgot how loud kids are."

Laura waved her hand. "You get used to it. I'd rather have them be loud in the library and using the space than not come in at all."

"Oh, I agree. It's a bit of culture shock. My last job was at a neighborhood library and most of the patrons were older. The place was always quiet."

"You won't have that problem here."

Natalie's phone buzzed with a text from Mac.

Hope your day is going well.

She smiled. It had been a while since she had anyone in

her life who would call just to check how her day was going. She was really starting to dig this relationship thing. Of course, the regular sex didn't hurt either. She sent a reply letting him know she was having a great time and then returned to her lunch.

Natalie and Laura ate their food and chatted about the town and Laura's experiences at the school. Then Laura trained her on the school's systems and showed her where they kept supplies, before handing her off to Human Resources to fill out paperwork. She signed everything and filled out tax forms and gladly accepted the faculty handbook, as well as a copy of the student handbook.

Before leaving, she went back to Dr. Harding's office and knocked.

"Come in, Natalie. How did today go?"

"It went well. I feel lucky to have had a chance to run through everything with Laura. She was very detailed and helpful."

"I'm glad." He sat back in his leather chair, his suit jacket tight on his broad shoulders. He removed his glasses and set them on the blotter covering his desk. "We do our best to make sure the students don't experience confusion when we have a change in staff. We do everything we can to make sure things continue to run smoothly."

"That makes sense. The one thing I'm not clear on is what I do now. Should I just wait for you to call when Laura goes on maternity leave?"

"Oh, no. I'm sorry. I thought I was clear. Laura will finish up today, and then the position is yours."

"Oh." She tried to keep the utter shock out of her voice. She'd thought she still had a week or two before starting.

"Is that a problem?"

"No. It's fine. I thought Laura planned to work until she had the baby."

"Like I said, we prefer a smooth transition." He stood and extended a hand. "I look forward to seeing you tomorrow. Don't hesitate to reach out if you have any questions or concerns. My door is always open."

Natalie stood and shook his hand. As she left the building with her bag loaded with copies of paperwork, her mind scrambled to come up with a plan. How was she supposed to finish up filming and work a full time job two hours away? She got into her car and pulled out of the lot in a daze.

The whole drive home, she mentally sketched a schedule. As soon as she got home, she'd call Brad and figure out when she needed to film. Then she'd create a plan for her days in the library. Laura had given her a copy of the schedule of classes already booked for the upcoming weeks, with a warning that she would be inundated with calls for help as the end of the semester neared and finals loomed.

By the time she parked in front of her apartment, she was worked into a frenzy again. By her estimation, she needed approximately three extra hours added to each day until the show was done. Crap. That didn't account for spending any time with Mac.

She was screwed.

Inside her apartment, she stepped out of her heels and leaned against the door to get her bearings and take a breath. A noise from the kitchen startled her because even with her long commute, she hadn't expected Jillian to be home. "Jill?" she called.

"No, it's me," Mac said as he came from the kitchen. "How was your day?"

He crossed the room and took her bag from her shoulder before offering her a sweet, gentle kiss on the lips.

"What are you doing here?"

"I called Jillian and asked if I could borrow her key to

surprise you. She was under the impression we'd already done the key swap thing."

Nat felt a little sheepish. "We did, kind of. I have your key. I didn't feel right about giving you a key because of Jillian. It wouldn't be fair to her for you to just show up unexpected."

"I didn't mean it as a jab. I don't need a key." He pulled her toward the couch. "Tell me about your day."

As soon as he sat beside her, she unloaded, and it helped relieve the crazed feeling that had been burdening her for the past two hours. Mac was an excellent listener.

"So you're starting tomorrow."

"I have to. I can't risk losing this job. It took so long to find one. But at the same time, I need to finish filming. Do you have any idea how much more Brad is looking for?"

Mac took her hand. "As far as I know, we only have to do one more session. Brad said he was happy with the footage of the women on dates, so he'd have us do one more commentary session."

The tightness in her chest loosened a little. "That's better than I was expecting."

"I'll have Brad schedule us to finish Saturday afternoon. That way, we can sleep late and you can get it done before going back to school next week."

Natalie turned toward him. "You're a smart, smart man. I'm lucky to have you." She stroked his jaw, still thrilled with the way his beard tickled her palm.

"And I haven't even fed you yet."

"You made dinner?"

He lifted a shoulder. "I ordered in. Does that count?"

She pressed her lips to his. "Anything that doesn't require me to cook counts. I think you might be a keeper."

"Best thing you've said yet. It's a good thing, too, since I have no intention of going anywhere."

He pulled her onto his lap and kissed her senseless.

Mac made it easy to get used to being treated well. The more time she spent with him, the more she wanted to have that happy ending she didn't think existed.

~

MAC SPENT THE NEXT WEEK STRUGGLING TO FIND BALANCE. He was thrilled his mother was happy about the show finally airing. Regardless of the outcome of the show, she was ready to treat him more like a partner in Everyday Love. Gail had already changed the web site to include his bio on the matchmaker page, which had previously only been about her.

The filming being over also meant he saw less of Natalie. Brad had decided they didn't need to meet with the clients again. He and Natalie each filmed a short message of encouragement and advice for the clients this past weekend. Natalie had been running ragged. Even when they did see each other, she was so exhausted she could barely keep her eyes open. He loved having her in his bed every night, and at this point, she wasn't fighting it anymore, but he wanted to spend time with her the way they had been.

Tonight, after the premier, he wanted to make it official. He wanted her to move her things into his place and he wanted to extend a job offer for her to join him at Everyday Love. Although his mother hadn't approved the position, they had talked about needing to expand. Natalie was a natural choice. Paul could publicize the hell out of the show and how he and Natalie were now working together.

He dressed in his tuxedo in the bedroom since Natalie had commandeered the master bath claiming she needed the time and space to make herself beautiful. When the door finally opened, he stared. The black dress she wore hugged every curve and shimmered as she walked toward him. Her hair was piled loosely on her head, with a few locks intentionally left out to draw his attention to her bare neck that begged to be kissed.

She nervously ran a hand over the dress. "Something wrong?" She looked carefully down at her own body.

"Not a damn thing," he whispered, his throat tight. "You're gorgeous."

When her eyes met his, they were wide and shone with happiness, instead of the exhaustion he'd grown used to over the last few days. "You're pretty hot yourself. That tux fits really well."

"It should, since it was custom tailored." He took two more steps.

"You own your tux? Fancy."

She hadn't yet stepped into her shoes, so when he moved to kiss her, he needed to lower his mouth. She tasted so good, all he wanted to do was scoop her up and take her to bed. And not to sleep. Not tonight. Her hands fisted in the lapels of his jacket as his tongue stroked hers.

When she moaned into his mouth, she suddenly let go and pulled away. "We need to stop or we won't make it to your mom's party."

"Fuck the party."

She smoothed her hands down his jacket, flattening the wrinkles she'd made. "You convinced me to go to this thing. And I'm all dressed up now. Plus, I doubt your mom will be very forgiving if the stars of the show blow off the premiere."

He shot her a look, knowing she was right, but not liking it. "Then you should avoid words like blow."

A smile burst on her face and she laughed loud. "I'm pretty sure you have enough restraint. Let me put my contacts in and we can go."

"You can leave your glasses on. You're still sexy."

She shook her head. "But Gem doesn't go anywhere

without her contacts and full makeup. Ten minutes and we can go."

He hated that she continued to use Gem. Of course he understood she needed to for the show. Realistically, Gail probably invited some local press to the premiere party, so Natalie would need to be Gem. He just wished they could celebrate this as themselves.

Natalie came out of the bathroom again fifteen minutes later, full face made up. He saw the armor in place and his irritation grew. "I can't wait until we're done with this and can go back to a normal life."

Grabbing her purse and stuffing it with lipstick, her cell phone, and wallet, she seemed oblivious to his shift in attitude. "When did you say Brad is releasing the episodes?"

"He has this master plan, which involves trying something new. He's streaming episode one tonight. Tomorrow—actually at midnight tonight—half the season will go up. Next week, the other half of the season. Then we'll do the finale live streamed so people can vote."

"And I can kick your fine ass."

He chuckled, some of his tension dissipating with her teasing. "Don't be too sure about that. You may have a lock on Ashley, but Melissa and Jennifer are both dating men I set them up with."

Looping her arm through his as they headed to the elevator, she said, "Correction. Melissa is dating the man you set her up with. Jennifer is dating both the guy she met at game night and the man you chose for her."

The elevator doors opened and they stepped in. "Have you spoken to her?"

"Jennifer? No." She shook her head.

Jennifer had become a wild card. He truly couldn't guess which way her vote would go. In truth, he didn't care, though. It didn't matter which of them won because it would be great for Everyday Love no matter what. His mother was more than happy with his performance.

The car his mother sent sat waiting at the curb. The driver opened the back door for them.

"Ooo," Natalie said. "Is there going to be a red carpet when we arrive too?"

"With my mother, you never know."

The entire ride to the hotel that his mother booked for the party, Mac wanted to ask Natalie about living and working with him. But he knew it would be too much for her to think about and process before being thrust into the limelight of one of Gail's famous parties. Not to mention having to be Gem for the next few hours.

They sat silently beside each other, doing nothing more than holding hands and looking into each other's eyes. A few weeks ago, Natalie had talked about how soul gazing was one of the pick-up artist tactics she'd learned early on. Staring deep into someone's eyes was a guaranteed way to make a connection.

Staring into her beautiful face, into those wide blue eyes, he couldn't believe doing this with a stranger would have the same effect. This was communication at a new level. The emotion was deep and real. This was the kind of love his parents had shared.

As the car pulled up to the curb, Mac lost all sense. In that moment, the recognition hit and he knew he'd spend the rest of his life with Natalie. She could talk about perfect penguins all she wanted, but this was more real than even he'd thought. The hell with moving in together. He began to think about what kind of ring best suited her.

She patted his leg. "Everything okay?"

He blinked, and she waved at the window. "We're here."

"Sorry. Lost in thought. You have that effect on me."

She smiled, but it was wobbly. He caressed her hand between his. "What's wrong?"

Shaking her head, she said, "Sudden case of nerves is all." She sucked in a deep breath through her mouth.

"Time to put on a smile and enjoy the party."

"Did you know the average person only smiles like twenty times a day? A really happy person smiles more than twice that. And our brains recognize the difference between a fake smile and a real one."

Even if she hadn't said she was nervous, her current bout of rambling random facts would've given it away. Instead of trying to tell her to calm down, he knew it was best to let it play out. "What's the difference?"

"You know when you read a book and the author says the smile didn't make it to the character's eyes? That's the difference. The fake smile only engages the corners of the mouth. A real smile uses the muscles around your eyes too." She took a slow inhale when she finished.

"I suppose if you know that, you can learn to fake it."

"Hmm…I don't know. I'll have to do some research." Her rate of speech had returned to normal.

"Ready?" She smiled—a real one, no doubt, and Mac turned to open the door.

From behind him she said, "Huh. No red carpet. I really thought I was going to play the famous starlet tonight."

On the curb, he held out a hand to help her from the car. "Don't worry. Everyone will see you as a star."

"That's what I'm afraid of," she said quietly as they walked into the hotel.

CHAPTER 17

Mac let go of her hand as soon as they stepped into the hotel. They were, after all, enemies on the screen. They'd agreed they needed to keep up appearances until the show was completely aired and the finale streamed. Well, she decided for them. Mac had been ready to scream their relationship status from the rooftops.

As far as Natalie was concerned, Gail Sterling knowing was bad enough. Just before they got to the ballroom, she turned to Mac and said, "Thank you for letting me ramble."

"Feel better?"

"You know I do."

"Well, the only other way I know to calm you is to kiss you, and you've made it clear that isn't happening as long as we're at this party, so I figured letting you spout facts would have to do. Plus, I always learn something new when you get nervous."

"Glad to help." She threw back her shoulders and called on the strength she'd built as Gem. Those muscles were weak from disuse. Gem had been closeted for a couple of weeks now, other than brief snippets during filming. And even then, if she was with Mac, she was able to be herself more than Gem. Tonight, though, she needed Gem.

Mac held open the ballroom door and Natalie tried to rein in her shock. Gail had filled the room. A giant screen was set up at the front of the room. Who the hell would want to see her that big? Natalie hadn't given it too much thought, but she hadn't expected any of this. She imagined a group of people socializing while the show played in the background. This was obviously making the show center stage.

A waiter walked by with a tray of champagne and Natalie snagged a glass.

Mac grabbed one as well and said, "I'm going to find my mother. Want to join me?"

She arched a brow at him. "I'll catch up later." Then with bravado she didn't feel, she added, "My adoring fans await."

Without waiting for him to comment, she waded into the sea of people standing at high top tables around the perimeter of the dance floor. Barely halfway across, three different people stepped in her path simultaneously.

"Gem," the first one said. "We were wondering if you were coming. Gail Sterling had said you were invited, but from the clips we've seen, it doesn't look like you and Malcolm Sterling have a friendly relationship."

Nat snickered. If they only knew. "I'm sorry, you are?"

Each of the three—one man and two women—introduced themselves a reporters. Keeping her smile in place regardless of the butterflies in her stomach or the tension creeping across her shoulders, she agreed to answer some questions. Such was the beginning of a long night. She laughed and joked, teasing at what happened on the show without revealing anything.

Soon her group of three grew to a small crowd, all

standing around her and throwing constant questions. She drank her entire glass of champagne and a second one and the questions hadn't yet stopped. At the edge of the dance floor, she saw Mac doing his own thing, chatting up a leggy brunette. His eyes met hers and she wanted nothing more than to scream, "Help me," but knew she couldn't.

A moment later, cool, slender fingers were wrapped around her elbow with a tug. "Excuse us, I need to borrow Gem for a few moments."

The group fell silent and Nat turned to see Gail holding her arm. The woman smiled at her. "TV show stuff." With a wave to the reporters and whoever else had joined in, she said, "She'll be back."

"Is Brad here? Does he need something?"

"Oh, no, dear," Gail said quietly from behind a smile she kept in place. She patted Nat's elbow. "I know a woman in crisis when I see one. You needed a rescue and from what Malcolm has told me, he couldn't be that rescue for you."

Natalie's heart fluttered. Even without being with her tonight, he asked his mother to run interference. If she didn't already love that man, she'd be falling for him tonight. He understood her in a way no one else had.

"Head toward the kitchen. My table is set back there. Grab something to eat. Relax for a bit. The show will be airing soon. I'm sure at that point, Brad will want to make a speech and show the two of you off. You might not get another break."

As Gail let go of her arm, Natalie stopped and said, "Thank you."

"Not a problem." Then the woman spun and moved back through the crowd.

Natalie had no idea what to expect from Mac's mother. Natalie liked her when they met at the beginning of this. She had a hard time reconciling the woman she'd met at Everyday Love with the woman who had intentionally tried to get her to screw up in front of the cameras. Then just now, although she had in fact offered a much-needed rescue, Gail remained aloof. Mac had said Gail wanted to spend time with her, get to know her, but tonight didn't seem to be the night for that to happen.

Ducking toward the kitchen, Natalie placed herself against the wall, so no one could ambush her with more questions. She was quickly running out of the talking points Brad had given them. Her stomach rumbled even though she wasn't hungry. She ate a stuffed mushroom to quell the tumbling.

From her quiet corner, she had a perfect angle to watch almost the entire room. Mac was in his element. Nothing slowed his pace. He talked and laughed with everyone who crossed his path. He was good at this. Natalie hoped Gail knew how lucky she was to not only have Mac in her corner, but also that he wanted to work with her to improve Everyday Love.

Natalie was able to hide in the shadows for twenty blissful minutes before a spotlight shone on the dance floor and Brad stepped into it. Natalie took another swig of champagne and edged closer, sure that Brad would introduce her and Mac to the attendees.

"When we first conceived the idea of *Love Match*, it had been different than what we ultimately developed. Like everything in the television business. In all honesty, we wanted to be different. We've all seen dating and match-making shows. We've cheered people through reality show competitions. That's when we struck on the idea of trying to find the best way to find love. There must be something better than dumb luck, right?"

The audience chuckled.

A warm hand landed on her hip. She didn't have to look to know it was Mac. "Kind of touchy-feely there, Mr. Sterling."

"We're in the dark right now, but Brad's gearing up to call us into the spotlight. I wanted to check to make sure you're okay."

She smirked. "I'm fine."

Then Brad introduced them, and although they walked toward the spotlight in sync, they weren't going as a couple. Mac gave her the wide berth she'd requested. How could she not love a man who respected her wishes?

Luckily, they weren't expected to make a speech; they simply had to wave at the audience. However, Brad said they'd be available for questions later.

With a final wave, Nat stepped back into the dark quiet off to the side of the room. She downed another glass of champagne and hoped no one noticed. When she took her next glass, she held it as a reinforcement as the show started.

The room fell silent. Mac came and stood at her table, close, but not too close. The opening played some catchy music and the video had descriptions overlaid on their images. Mac the respected matchmaker, Gem the Internet dating expert. Of course, then in parentheses below that, it said, "pick-up artist."

"Why didn't you get an explanation?" she whispered to Mac.

"Because everyone knows what a matchmaker is, even if they don't know what we do. A dating expert can mean a lot of things."

Nat licked her lips and watched her own face fill the screen. The scene playing out in front of her was her first meeting with the clients. The cameras had been rolling longer than she'd thought because they just played a clip of her talking about picking up lots of men. The line was totally taken out of context.

Mac chuckled beside her.

"That's not exactly what I meant. They took out the rest of the conversation."

"That's what they do during editing." He bumped her shoulder with his. "Don't worry. I'm sure they've done the same to me. It's what makes good TV."

Oh, God. They'd filmed her flirting with the intern. They were supposed to have been done already. Nat shook her head. When she saw Brad later, she was going to give him a piece of her mind about integrity.

The shot changed to Mac's meeting with the women, which felt formal, held in the conference room. They had a quick verbal exchange about what each woman wanted most in a partner and that was it. No embarrassing moments for him.

Nat swallowed back the anger. Jillian had warned her about this possibility when she'd signed on to do the show. Nat closed her eyes and envisioned all the times she stood in front of a camera and tried to convince herself Brad did this to draw in viewers but it would get better.

Unfortunately, the episode didn't. By the time the episode was half over, Natalie had had enough.

Her stomach was in knots, her shoulders tight with tension, and her throat narrowed. Without any preamble, she said to Mac, "I'm leaving."

MAC WATCHED THE DISASTROUS SHOW PLAY OUT ON SCREEN. He hadn't expected stellar television, but he also hadn't thought it would tear down the woman he loved.

"Wait. Don't run out."

"I'm not going to stay here and wait for people to ask me how it felt to be portrayed as an idiot on screen."

As the footage of Gem continued in front of them, Mac's first thought was that his mother orchestrated this. This was exactly what she'd been hoping for with the antics she'd pulled. "Give me a few minutes. I need to speak with my mother."

He squeezed Natalie's hand to reassure her, but her focus remained on the train wreck everyone else was watching. It only took him a few moments to find Gail. She was near the center of the room. Mac took her elbow as he lowered his mouth to speak in her ear. "I need to talk to you."

"Can't it wait?"

"No." The word was sharp enough that she didn't question, but allowed him to pull her out to the hall.

When the banquet door closed behind them, he said, "Did you do this?"

"Do what?"

Pointing back at the room they'd left, he said, "Make Natalie look like that, as if she can't control herself and doesn't have a brain."

"Why on Earth would you think I have any control?"

"Because you've been manipulating things from the beginning. You gave her awful advice that luckily went no further than Brad, but could've been a hell of a disaster if she'd used it on screen. Then there was the whole cameraman you used."

"What cameraman?" a small voice asked beside him.

Natalie stood there, eyes wide and expectant.

He sighed and shook his head. He hadn't wanted her to know. He definitely hadn't wanted her to find out like this. He didn't want to drive an even bigger wedge between Natalie and his mother.

"Oh my God. This entire thing was a setup."

The look in her eyes shifted and stopped him dead. Betrayal. He knew that look.

"Natalie—"

"Don't you dare use my name here. In fact, don't say it at all. Ever. I can't believe I trusted you." She choked on the last word and then backed away from them.

He reached for her as his brain slowly processed what she'd said. She thought he was in on this? "Gem. Stop."

"No, Mr. Sterling. I will not. Well played. Between you and Gail, you have quite the team. One charmer, one manipulator. Everything has been stacked in your favor from the beginning. I knew that going in. You didn't need to cheat." Tears filled her eyes. "You didn't have to make me look like a fool. I didn't care about winning."

She turned her back on them and took off. Mac moved to go after her. He'd forgotten how damn fast she could move in heels. But his mother grabbed his arm.

"Let her go, Malcolm."

"Hell no."

Her grip tightened. "If you go after her now, there will be pictures or worse. You don't want an argument like that out on the Internet." She paused. "Neither would she."

She had a point, but Mac couldn't bear the thought that Natalie believed he had anything to do with how the show aired.

He pinched the bridge of his nose. He needed the truth; he had to know. "Did you do this?"

"Absolutely not. I'll admit to a slight bit of sabotage when I thought you might be floundering, but what I did had nothing to do with how they edited the show. Anyone with half a brain can tell they spliced together scenes that didn't belong."

"It doesn't matter what you know or can tell. The audience is in there—hell all over the world—laughing at her."

Gail smoothed her hand down his arm. "Once you told me how you felt about her, really felt, I did nothing. Your happiness means more to me than anything. Everyday Love has been in business for thirty years without being on television or winning any awards. We'll keep going regardless of the outcome."

He wanted to believe her. He'd never known his mother to be as manipulative as she'd been during filming. It wasn't like her. "Then why did you do it at all?"

"I wanted to light a fire under you. One way or the other. If she fell apart during the filming, she wouldn't be strong enough for you. You need someone strong enough to challenge you. And if I know anything about you, the easiest way for you to grow a pair is to threaten your sense of right and wrong."

Mac's head was spinning. "So you tried to sabotage her to prove her worthiness?"

Gail flicked her fingers. "A little. After I saw the rough cuts that showed something was happening between you. I thought she was manipulating you, using her sexual prowess to make you lower your guard. I wanted you to pay attention, get your head in the game. And you did."

"You should've stayed out of it."

"Even if I had, it wouldn't have changed the outcome of tonight."

"She wouldn't have run away from me."

"Are you sure? No matter what, Brad made her look foolish and you like a star."

"What am I supposed to do?"

"A conversation with your producer is in order. But first we have to make it through tonight." She walked back toward the door. "Coming?"

He nodded. "I need to make a call first."

"Tell her I'm sorry. We'll do what we can to fix this." She opened the door and walked back into her party.

As the door slowly swooshed closed, he heard the sounds of the audience's laughter and he cringed. Pulling his phone from his pocket, he pressed the button beside Natalie's beautiful face. It rang, but she didn't answer. "I know you're upset. I didn't have anything to do with this. Neither did my mother. We'll get it straightened out. Don't block me out. I love you."

Just as he disconnected, the door behind him opened again and Brad said, "Come on, man. The episode is almost over. People want to talk. Where's Gem?"

Mac's jaw turned to stone. "She left."

"Damn. Well, come on."

"We need to have a conversation about this premiere before anything else airs."

"All talk will keep until tomorrow. Right now, we need to focus on riding the wave attention we're getting. They love it." Brad patted his shoulder and they went back into the banquet room.

The show neared the end, and the audience was whistling and cheering. Snippets of upcoming episodes flashed on the screen and Mac felt sick. He had no idea how he was going to convince Brad he needed to re-edit all of the episodes.

NATALIE HAILED A CAB WITHOUT CONCERN FOR WHAT IT would cost her to get home. She just needed to get out of there. During the ride to her apartment, she cycled through emotions that filled her eyes from hurt and anger. Nothing about this evening had gone the way she'd expected.

Tossing money at the driver when they arrived, she flung the door open and stomped into her apartment. Jillian was sitting on the couch, wine glass in hand. With wide eyes, she held the glass up to Natalie. "I think you need this more than I do."

"Crap. You watched." She dropped her purse on the table and sank onto the cushion next to her best friend.

"Of course I watched. What kind of friend would I be if I hadn't?"

"At least if you hadn't, you could reassure me with platitudes. You know, *it couldn't be that bad* or *I'm sure you're overreacting*." She took a gulp of Jillian's wine and waited.

Her friend said nothing. Not a good sign.

"How did it end? Did it get worse?" She almost didn't want to know.

Jillian angled her head in thought. "No...not worse, but not better either. The clips they showed of upcoming episodes look entertaining though."

"Entertaining at my expense?"

"Not that I could tell, but that doesn't mean anything. What did Mac say?"

Natalie drained the glass and refilled it. "Not much. As it turns out, his mother might've been behind all of this." Waving her hand at the TV, she said, "Making me look ridiculous so her precious son could win."

"Oh." Jillian leaned forward and grabbed the wine bottle. She handed it to Nat. "You might as well just take the whole bottle. How did you find out?"

Nat shook her head at the bottle. Getting drunk wouldn't help this. "I overhead Mac accusing her. The bad advice she gave me? Not the only sabotage attempt. That night when the cameraman hit on me? She put him up to it."

"Wow."

"Not such a leap to think she had a hand in all of it. The worst part is Mac knew."

"Are you sure? He never struck me as someone to play

games. Certainly not with your emotions. He's into you, babe."

Natalie set the glass on the table. "I don't know what I can believe right now. He always talked about how honesty is so important to him, but he lied, Jill."

"Wait. You think he put her up to this?"

Nat shrugged. She didn't want to believe it, but the producers made him look like a friggin' savior to her court jester antics.

"Fucker." Jillian took a swig of the wine. "You want to go egg his car?"

The suggestion was so crazy Natalie laughed. She laughed so hard that the tears she'd been holding back finally fell. Jillian hugged her and it helped, but not nearly enough.

"Is there anything I can do about the show?" she asked.

"Not really. You signed a contract. You have no control over how they edit the film."

"That's what I was afraid of." Nat ran a hand over her face and sighed. In her purse, her phone began a string of vibrations. She groaned as she reached for it.

"Mac?"

"I don't know when I'll be ready to talk to him." Looking at her phone, she saw it wasn't a text from Mac. She was getting notifications from her blog. Hundreds of comments were flooding her inbox. "Holy crap."

She got up and grabbed her laptop from the dining room table. With her legs stretched out on the coffee table, she booted up the computer. Her email and blog had comments from hundreds of people. Most were not good.

Scrolling through the messages, she was even more discouraged.

"What is it?" Jillian asked.

"Mostly trolls talking shit. Telling me what a bimbo I am. Even more offering to show me a good time." Never before had she been so happy that she kept the blog under a pseudonym.

"Ignore them."

"I know. It's not like I've never gotten stupid comments before. I didn't expect so much to happen so quickly. The damn show just ended. I can't face this every time there are more episodes."

Her phone shook again. Mac. She pushed it to voicemail. He didn't leave one.

Closing the laptop, she said, "I'm going to bed. I can't face this anymore tonight."

"What about Mac?"

"What about him?"

"Honey, do you really think that man isn't on his way over here?"

"Why would he?"

"Because he loves you."

"Funny way of showing it."

"He might not have known anything about this."

"It was his mother."

Jillian sighed. "Get some sleep. Tomorrow will be better."

As she rose to go to her room, the doorbell rang. "Are you kidding me? Are you psychic?"

Jillian smiled and let Mac in. She gave Mac a stern look that conveyed a good amount of displeasure. Then she squeezed Natalie's hand before hurrying from the room.

Natalie stayed standing and crossed her arms. "Why are you here?"

"We need to talk."

"About what?"

"I tried to talk to Brad, get him to fix the editing and how he portrayed you. The first half of the episodes goes live at midnight. He wouldn't listen to anything."

Nat glanced at the clock on the wall. An hour. One hour

until there were ten hours of her looking foolish. "Well, I guess you and your mother will be thrilled."

"My mother didn't have anything to do with this."

Nat snorted.

Mac stepped closer, but didn't touch her. "She swears she hasn't done anything."

"She gave me shitty advice while pretending to keep an even playing field. When that didn't work, she tried to get me in bed with someone from the crew!"

"She didn't know."

"Know what?"

"About us."

"That shouldn't matter. What's more, you did know. You knew what she did, and you didn't tell me. So much for the importance of honesty. A little warning would've been nice."

He scrubbed a hand over his face. "I didn't tell you because she promised me she'd stop."

"First, why the hell would anyone believe her? Second, you still should've told me." She waved her arms as she yelled at him. For such a smart guy, he was being so dumb right now.

"You're right. I should have. But I thought it was over. My mother tried to sabotage you because she thought I was going to let you win. She didn't know I fell in love with you." He moved closer still and touched her hand.

She pulled away. "Regardless. I deserved to know."

"What difference would it have made?"

She thought for a moment. Would it have made a difference?

"You would've been even more pissed off at my mother. I didn't want you to start a relationship with her like that."

"Too late for all those good intentions."

"Why are you so angry? I get it. I should've told you."

"I'm just mad, Mac. Can't you understand? I worked my

ass off for weeks with our clients. They did everything they could to make me look like a brainless twit."

He pulled her into his embrace. "It's not that bad."

She melted against him a little. He felt so damn good. "Yes, it is. The comments are already pouring in online all over my blog. I'm sure the comments on my videos will be at least as bad. The trolls are out in force telling me what a bimbo I am."

Mac chuckled, his chest vibrating beneath her cheek.

She stepped out of his arms. "This isn't funny."

"It shouldn't be, but it is. You're not a bimbo. I know it and you know it, but your viewers? You kind of set yourself up for that, don't you think?"

Her blood began to boil once again. "What? Because I'm a woman who's comfortable with my sexuality, that means I'm asking for them to treat me like crap?"

"That's not what I said."

"No. What you said was worse."

"Come on. Are you going to tell me no one has ever said this? When you're Gem, with the hair and the lips and the boobs..." He pointed at her chest, which, yes, showed quite a bit of cleavage. "Gem uses her body to make a statement. How others interpret that statement isn't surprising."

His comments speared through her chest. Was that what he really thought of her? "Get out."

"Natalie—"

"No. I'm done talking to you. Just leave."

Without waiting for him to respond, she turned and left the room. The one person she should've been able to count on right now was him. While she didn't truly needed to be defended, he should've been the first in line to do so.

She locked herself in her bedroom. Mac would get the hint. No way was she listening to that garbage any more. A minute later, she heard the front door close. She eased back into the living room. Sure enough, Mac was gone. Standing in the same spot where he'd said those awful things, she became angry all over.

Instead of focusing her anger on Mac, she turned to her laptop. Gem hadn't done a video in a while and even though Jillian had always warned her not to film while angry, tonight was the perfect night to talk to her viewers.

CHAPTER 18

Mac had given Natalie time to cool off. Then he tried calling. She didn't answer.

His mother called him into her office and pointed at the chair in front of her. He stared at his phone, willing Natalie to return his call when Gail snapped her fingers. He looked up.

"What did you do, Malcolm?" She spun her computer monitor to face him.

Natalie's face filled the screen. His mother pressed play.

"Hello, friendly viewers," Natalie began, looking like Gem. "Many of you have been looking forward to the premier of the reality show I'm in. Well, it aired tonight. If you haven't already run off to watch, hear me out."

She leaned closer to the camera. Gone was the flirty girl who kissed at the camera and winked at her audience. She was pissed. "I've gotten quite a bit of flak about how I dress since I started this video series. People are judgmental like that. But you know my attitude—surround yourself with people who lift you up. Tonight, I needed a boost." Her eyes went glassy and she looked up at the ceiling. "But instead of feeling supported by the person I've come to rely on, my foundation was chiseled away. This person, someone I've respected, acted as though how I dress and how much makeup I wear should dictate how others treat me. As if my outer appearance determines my self-worth. After watching how the producers portrayed my involvement in *Love Match*, I'm sure you can understand my reaction."

She leaned away from the camera and slowly licked her lips. "So today's dating gem is that you need to be cautious in your words. Be sure you say what you mean. And most importantly, look beyond the image."

The screen went black. Mac was stunned. Of course he knew she'd been angry with him. He hadn't meant to put her down. He wouldn't do that to her.

His mother turned the screen back. "Well?"

"Well what? I went to see her after the premier. I obviously fucked that up too. Everything she said there? Dead on. I should've been there to comfort her and I ended up insulting her. Of course I didn't mean to, but that matters little now, doesn't it?"

"The more important question here, Malcolm, is what are you going to do about it?"

Mac rose from the chair. He needed to see Natalie, talk to her. He could explain himself if she would give him the chance.

That evening, he went to her apartment, but she wasn't home. Jillian gave him a sympathetic look, but wouldn't tell him where Natalie was. The following morning, she finally contacted him. By email.

He read the note and tried to keep his temper.

Dear Mac,

Please stop contacting me. I need space. The pilot episode was bad enough, but when the first half of the season went live, my life —my online life—became a mess. I've decided to move to Harvest

Grove for the remainder of the school year. I can't deal with the fallout of the damn show. Brad has continued to make you look like a winner while I look like an idiot. I can't do this. Not telling me what your mother did was bad enough, but the way you spoke to me after the premier...I don't know how to forgive that. And in all honesty, I can't even think about it without getting upset all over again. Gem is part of who I am. For you to act as though she's a bimbo and it's acceptable to think that way means that's what you think of me. How can I be with someone who thinks that? I know I've taken the coward's way out by emailing you, but I knew if I called, I wouldn't get to say this. And I needed to say it.

Goodbye

Natalie

Mac stared at the screen. He read the words over and they weren't any better the second time. She was breaking up with him. In an email. He replayed everything they had said that night, everything that had happened with his mother, but nothing seemed fatal. This should've been nothing more than a fight. A big one, sure. But definitely something they could overcome.

He grabbed his phone and called Natalie. It rang and rang and went to voicemail. Disconnecting, he looked at the clock. School was over for the day. She should be in her car on her way back to Chicago. Instead she was living somewhere in Harvest Grove. He dialed again. This time, he left a message.

"I got your email. I can't believe you broke up with me in an email. Hell, I can't believe you broke up with me at all. I love you, Natalie. You don't walk away from each other because of a fight. I fucked up. I'm sorry I didn't tell you what my mother did. It was selfish and I regret not telling you. But what I said about you—about Gem—it's not true. My words came out wrong. I don't think you're anything less than a truly amazing woman. And I'm not giving you up without a fight. I refuse to stop contacting you. I can't believe you really mean that. I love you and I know you love me." He disconnected again, hoping his words would be enough to sway her.

But just in case, he had something else in mind. There was still the second half of the season that would air next week, before they filmed the finale. He'd already been working with Brad to fix the way Natalie was portrayed. He refused to let her go.

NATALIE HAD CLOSED ALL COMMENTS ON THE BLOG AND HER videos. She hoped that since people loved to binge shows, they would devour the ten episodes Brad released and the fervor would die. Of course, she had no such luck. All over the Internet, people were discussing the show. Brad got everything he'd hoped for: a show people were drawn to and couldn't stop talking about as they waited for the next installment of episodes.

The only thing that had kept her from crying nonstop was the message from Mac. He sounded as crappy as she felt, but his words made her feel better. She still wasn't ready to call him, let alone think about making up with him, but his voice brought her comfort.

She paced in her small motel room snacking on a bag of pretzels from the vending machine. She couldn't remember the last time she ate such a crappy breakfast. Sad pretzels as a meal. Not having to drive four hours a day should have made her more well rested, given her more time to have a real meal, but for the past two nights, she struggled to sleep. Then she overslept, so now she shoved pretzels in her mouth as she packed her bag for school.

The signs were there. She loved Mac. She knew that, which was why she emailed him instead of calling. But after being in a marriage with a man who thought she was boring, she didn't think she could be with a man who thought she was slut.

No, Mac hadn't said it, not in so many words, but the laugh, the dismissive attitude, it spoke volumes. Volumes that hurt. He said he was sorry, but she didn't know what she could believe at this point. She knew he was sorry about the way she reacted, but not so much for having the thought.

Crumpling the empty bag, she aimed and tossed it in the trashcan. Just as she was about the slip her phone into her pocket, it bleeped with an email. Pulling her bag onto her shoulder, she opened the email program. It was from Dr. Harding, who requested she come to his office as soon as she arrived at school.

She hurried from the motel to get to school. She'd planned to spend her morning prepping for the Sophomore English class she had coming in to work on research papers, but a meeting with Dr. Harding took precedence, so she needed to get every minute in she could. When she got to school, she stopped in the library and set her bag by her desk. Then she went to Dr. Harding's office. The halls were quiet because most students didn't arrive this early. The cafeteria had a few small groups chatting and eating breakfast.

Natalie had the thought then that she should ask Dr. Harding about expanding the library's hours to include before school, especially with finals coming up in a few weeks. She wanted the students to utilize the library as much as possible. When she arrived at Dr. Harding's office, his secretary smiled and told her to go on back.

Dr. Harding sat behind his desk and gestured for her to take the seat across from him. Today, his suit jacket hung on the back of his chair and he had his sleeves rolled to his elbows. His thick forearms looked like they belonged to a football player. The round glasses perched on his nose were on the geeky side of things. Natalie still hadn't quite figured him out.

"How are you, Dr. Harding?"

"In truth, I've been better. We have a problem."

Nat's heart crashed against her ribs. Her mind raced across everything she'd done since she'd been hired, every conversation she'd had, every student she'd interacted with. Nothing rang out as a problem. "What is it?"

He turned his computer monitor to face her. Staring back at her was the first episode of *Love Match*. Her throat closed and she began to fear she'd pass out.

"This is you, isn't it?"

She nodded and swallowed hard to try to clear her throat.

Dr. Harding sighed. "I knew, of course, but part of me hoped you had a doppelganger out there somewhere."

"I'm sorry," she finally said. "I didn't tell you because I didn't think it was relevant. I did the show under a pseudonym. In fact, the only way I would sign the contract was if they agreed to not use my legal name. I was out of work and they made a great offer. Unfortunately, I had no idea how they would make me look."

"I understand. And in general, I believe you have the right to privacy."

A horrible feeling filled her gut. There was a giant but coming next.

"However, being a small private school, we have to answer to our board, and in turn, our parents. This was sent to me by three different parents."

"You're firing me, aren't you?" Her voice wobbled. Her life could not possibly get any worse.

Another heavy sigh. "The board has requested your resignation. They're offering a small severance package."

"And if I don't resign?"

He turned the monitor away and leaned back in his chair.

"Then they will probably move forward with firing you. The contract you signed has a morality clause."

"I've done nothing immoral."

"Not immoral, per se, but this show reflects poorly on you and you then reflect poorly on the school. I'm not saying it's right. I don't even know if the board thinks it's right. But they're feeling pressured by parents and rather than a long drawn out contentious battle, they want to keep it quiet."

Sure, quiet. Natalie excelled at that. Except when she was Gem and look where that had gotten her. Natalie nodded. "Should I even bother working today? Or do you just want me gone?"

"You can go back home. We'll get a substitute in until we resume our search for a permanent librarian."

She nodded again, which made her feel like a bobblehead.

He stood and extended a hand to her. "I'm sorry it didn't work out."

Natalie shook his hand but didn't say anything. She had no words. Just as everything else in her life was falling apart, she had been counting on this job to keep her sane. Now she had nothing. She didn't speak to any of the students or teachers as she walked back to the library for her bag.

She trudged through the doors and to her car, her bag of unused ideas and plans weighed heavy on her shoulder. She drove back to her motel room and flopped on the bed. What did she do now?

She'd left Chicago because she didn't want to face Mac or Brad or any of the mess from the show. But now she had no reason to stay here. Rolling over, she pulled her phone from her pocket and texted Jillian. Although her friend would be at work, she'd answer the text.

I just got fired.

Typing the words was almost as painful as thinking them.

Curling up on top of the blanket, she cradled her phone. It vibrated in her hand.

"Oh my God. What happened?" Jillian said when Nat answered.

"My principal asked me to come in this morning. Three different parents sent him the links for the show. The board asked me to quietly resign and they'll give me a severance package."

"They can't fire you for what you do on your time. And you did it under Gem's name."

"They can. There's a morality clause in my contract. My actions reflect poorly on the school."

"You can fight this."

"Even if I could, why would I want to? They don't want me working there. Think about how bad the gossip and comments will be once word gets out."

"Fuck, Nat. I'm so sorry."

Having her friend's support helped, but not enough to remove the truck sitting on her chest.

"Wait. Where are you then if you're not in school?"

"I'm lying on the bed in my motel room."

"Check out and come home."

"This is supposed to be my new home." The thought caused a fresh wave of tears. Tears for what should've been as well as tears for what it actually was—a crappy motel room.

"Your home is in Chicago. Leave now. You'll be home by lunch. I'll take a half day and meet you there."

"You don't need to do that."

"What's that? Oh. I think I feel a migraine coming on. I don't see how I can be expected to read through all of the briefs they dumped on my desk right now. Especially since I left my meds at home. I bet I can get all of this done tonight after the meds kick in."

Jillian's fake drama brought a brief smile to Natalie's mouth. "One of these days, you're going to get fired too."

"One can only hope."

"You're terrible."

"I'll see you in a couple of hours and we can commiserate. Maybe I'll stop and buy material for making voodoo dolls. What do you think?"

Nat's smile broadened. Calling Jillian to talk had been a good choice. "I'll see you for lunch."

She disconnected and pushed off the bed so she could pack her things and go home.

FOR THE WHOLE WEEK BEFORE THE SECOND HALF OF THE SHOW was supposed to air, Mac worked nearly around the clock with the film editing crew. Brad loved Mac's idea, but it required a lot of work. Brad hadn't apologized for the way the first episodes aired. His position was that his job required he deliver entertainment. If it came at someone's expense, so be it.

Knowing he had no room to fight, Mac offered him something better: a behind-the-scenes love story. At first, Brad thought Mac was making it up, but after paying attention to a lot of the footage that had been edited out, Brad was fully on board. The marketing department ran new advertising spots promising a unique twist.

Gail had called Mac daily to tell him how much business was improving based on the show. Everything she'd been hoping the show would bring was happening. When Mac had told her Natalie left him and moved away, she didn't believe it. She even tried to call Natalie.

He powered through the editing with little sleep because he still hadn't gotten any response from Natalie. He continued to text her a few times every day, telling her the second half of the show would be better. That he missed her. That he thought about her constantly. That he missed her laugh. That he missed her random facts spoken at weird moments. That he loved her.

But he got nothing in return. He wouldn't allow himself to believe he'd lost her for good. Because he saw the proof every day as he worked through the footage. She loved him every bit as much as he loved her.

He was exhausted, so he brewed a whole pot of coffee to drink before he went to the studio. He glanced at the clock. By now, Natalie would be at school. He'd thought about just driving to Harvest Grove and waiting for her outside Wells Academy, but beyond that being on the stalkerish side, he couldn't afford the time away from the studio if he wanted to pull this off.

So instead, he Googled the school and got the phone number. At least she'd have to answer, even if it meant she hung up on him. He'd have the chance to try to convince her to talk to him.

"Good morning, Wells Academy. How may I direct your call?"

"Good morning. Could you please transfer me to Natalie Hale?"

"I'm sorry. Ms. Hale no longer works here. May I transfer you to the library?"

"No. Thank you." Mac disconnected and absently poured his coffee. What the hell happened?

He didn't know what to do. He dialed her number again. As he listened to the ringing, he considered other ways to reach her. Jillian wouldn't give him information, but he had no doubt she was in touch with Natalie.

"Hello." Her voice was cold and distant and it completely startled him since he was so used to her not answering.

"Hi. I'm so glad you answered."

"What do you want, Mac?"

God, she sounded so sad. "I've been calling and texting."

"I'm aware."

"But since you haven't answered, I called Wells Academy to reach you. What happened?"

"Parents were not happy with my involvement with the show. They complained to the principal and the board, who then requested my resignation."

"Oh, babe. I'm so sorry." He began to pace the kitchen. There had to be something they could do. "Isn't there a way to fight it?"

"It wouldn't be worth the time and energy. And in all honesty, I can't handle the spotlight any more."

She sighed heavily, and all he wanted to do was pull her into his arms. "What can I do?"

"Stop calling me. I just—I need to figure out my life. I took the show on as a way to pay the bills, and it has taken over my quiet, unassuming life. I have to figure this out."

"Don't shut me out."

"It's a little late, don't you think?"

"I'm fixing it, Nat. Trust me. The show is going to be better."

She released a mirthless laugh and it broke his heart.

"I know you think you can fix everything, Mac. But not this. I have to do this on my own."

"Come to work for Everyday Love."

Silence lingered.

"Natalie?"

"You really don't listen, do you? I told you I need to figure this out. It's my life. I don't need you swooping in to rescue me. You can't fix how Brad made me look to the entire world. You can't give me a job because I'm feeling the repercussions of the choices I made."

If she were yelling at him, he could take it. In fact, he would revel in it because it would mean she was still his Natalie. But she sounded resigned, almost hopeless.

"I appreciate your effort," she continued, "I know you mean well. But I have to get my life back on track."

He didn't know what to say to fix this. "I'm not going anywhere, Natalie. If you need space, take some time. But I love you and I'll be waiting when you want to come back to me."

"Goodbye, Mac."

He continued to hold the phone to his ear long after she disconnected, as if he'd be able to hear some echo of her sweet voice. Her words circled through his head. Of course, he wanted to fix this mess. Although he hadn't caused it, he was certainly benefitting from it, whereas she was suffering because of it.

He had to have faith that the effort and work he'd put in would change her mind. She hadn't said she was done with him, just that she needed to sort out her life. He would remind her how well they worked together, even if she didn't join him at Everyday Love.

Natalie's days and nights began to blur. She stayed up late watching silly romcoms to avoid life and then she slept most of the day. So much for figuring out her life. If what happened at Wells Academy was any hint at what she had in store, she didn't see the point in even applying for another job. At least not until people lost interest in *Love Match*.

She had no interest in anything lately. Lying on the couch in her PJs was the perfect way to live. All she needed to do was find someone who would pay her for it. Her blog and vlog lay dormant since she was afraid to reopen them to comments and interactions. She had no inspiration for creating a video. No desire to go out and pick up a man.

She missed Mac. She loved Mac. But she refused to try to fix her relationship with him until she knew what she was doing with her life. What if she found a job in a different state? They couldn't do long distance. For the one week she had that horrible commute, she'd begun to doubt her ability to do that long term.

It had nothing to do with him—it was all her. She needed to be with the man she loved.

But she couldn't explain that to him without it sounding like the trite *It's not you it's me* speech, which was horrible because it really *was* her.

Her email bleeped at her. She clicked the message to see it was from Brad. A quick reminder that the new episodes would be airing tonight and that she was expected to be in the studio for their live finale in two days.

Two days.

Two measly days until this nightmare would end. Maybe. What was the likelihood the viewers who had been drawn in would inhale those last episodes as quickly? Some shows hit streaming services and then had a long life because people wouldn't stop talking about them.

Two days until she would have to face Mac. That was the scariest part. Even after their conversation and his reassurance that he would wait for her to unfuck her life, she still wasn't sure she could be in the same room with him. It would be too easy to fall into his arms and let him take care of her. Let him fix her problems.

The front door opened and the light from the hallway nearly blinded Natalie. Through her squinty eyes, she stared at Jillian.

"Come on, now. This is pitiful. I know your life sucks, but lying on the couch all day won't fix anything." Jillian set her briefcase on the floor near the couch. "Whew. When was the last time you showered, girl? Come on. Don't you remember the old mantra *fake it till you make it?* Time for you to start pretending."

"I don't wanna." Her whine sounded like a petulant toddler even to her own ears.

"Well, you can't sponge off me. You need to do something."

Jillian's jab was harmless. Natalie hadn't fallen behind on any bills yet thanks to her severance and the money from the show. But eventually, she would run out of money. "I think you mean parasite. A sponge, while boring, does serve a function. It filters water. A parasite, on the other hand, lives off its host without necessarily giving anything in return. Like head lice."

"Eww. Only you could turn an insult into a disgusting lecture. Get up and go shower."

Natalie pushed up to a sitting position. She caught a whiff of herself. She was pretty ripe. "Fine."

Jillian stood in front of her with her arms crossed, waiting.

Guess she means now. Nat heaved up from the couch. "You're kind of bossy. I don't know if I like it."

"But you love me. And I'm being bossy for your own good. Have you eaten anything other than a package of cookies?" She pointed at the crumbs and wrinkled wrapper on the table.

Guilt swiped at Natalie. "No. I hoped they would make me feel better, but they didn't."

"Take your shower. I'm ordering dinner. Then we're going to come up with a plan for you. You've moped enough. Pity party is over." With that, she went to the living room window and threw it open. "It's a beautiful spring day. You haven't enjoyed anything in almost two weeks. Time to get back in the game."

Natalie shuffled toward the bathroom. "What have you done with my roommate? She would never talk nature to me." But even as she moved, she couldn't deny the scent of warmth and spring lifted her spirits.

AFTER HER MUCH-NEEDED SHOWER AND A DINNER CONSISTING of real food, Natalie felt like a new person. She and Jillian sat on the couch with the TV murmuring in the background. Nat held a notebook on her lap with a pen swirling doodles while they talked.

"I think you should consider a different type of job. At least for a while," Jillian said.

"Like what? All I've ever wanted was to be a librarian."

"But you have a degree in English. You can write. You can edit. Maybe consider freelancing. There are other places to put your skills to work other than a library." She took a sip of wine. "If nothing else, you can get a job at a bookstore. The pay wouldn't be great, but chances are, no one would pay attention to who you are."

"As you so aptly pointed out, I need to pay rent. I can't imagine that even if I got a job at one of the few bookstores left in the city I would make enough to carry my half of the bills. Which means I'd have to supplement with something."

She tossed the notebook on the table. The thought of Mac's pity job offer circled her mind.

"What are you thinking?" Jillian asked.

"Mac offered me a job at Everyday Love."

"What? He did? When?"

"He first brought it up a while ago. I thought he was joking, but when I spoke to him the other day, he offered again. It feels like a pity offer. Like he needs to take care of me."

"What's so bad about that?"

"Nothing in general. But I like to be able to take care of myself."

Jillian shrugged. "It would be a good way to stay busy while you look for a better job."

"But I don't know how to be a matchmaker. And I'd have to work for Gail. I don't know if I could even be in the same room with that woman. Even if she had nothing to do with the editing of the show, she did try to sabotage me two other times." Nat sipped her wine and considered her options.

"You'd get to work with Mac, though. That would be a huge plus in the pro column."

Nat sank deeper in the couch. "Is it? I don't even know exactly where we stand right now. I told him I needed space while I figure out my life."

"How did he take it?"

Natalie grumbled. "He was supportive. And nice. And understanding."

Jillian's hand flew to her chest. "Oh no. What an asshole! What did you ever see in him?"

Natalie flopped over until she was practically hanging off the couch. "I know, right? What is wrong with me? He said some stupid shit. Really insulting, stupid shit, but I think he was suffering from foot in mouth."

"So he hurt your feelings. Did he apologize?"

"Yeah."

"What more do you want? Wait. That came out sounding bitchy. I just meant that you're wallowing in self-pity when there's a guy you love who wants to be with you."

Jillian's words hit hard. She was right. "My life is so messy right now, Jill. I don't want our relationship to start with him trying to fix my brokenness. I want to come to him with a plan so we can be on equal footing."

"Now that's something I can understand. Have you explained that to him?"

"I'll talk to him after the finale. I have to build up my resistance to everything."

"Oh, yeah. The rest of the episodes air tonight."

"Don't remind me."

"You're not going to watch?"

"Hell no." Natalie levered herself off the couch. "You go ahead and watch. I can't stomach any more of it." She scooped up her notebook and her wine glass. "I'm going to bed early tonight so I can spend tomorrow looking at other job options."

"Party pooper. I'm going to make some popcorn and I'll let you know how it is."

"No, please don't. I don't need the stress."

As she set her wineglass on the kitchen counter, her phone bleeped with a text from Mac.

Watching tonight?

She shook her head. This was his idea of giving her space? *Nope.*

You should. It might be worth it.

Doubtful. Then she went to her bedroom. Before turning off her phone, she added another text. *I miss you too. We'll talk after the finale.*

I look forward to it.

She felt a little lighter and was glad she sent the text. She wanted Mac. That hadn't changed. Having someone by her side while she figured out life wouldn't be a bad thing.

CHAPTER 19

*N*atalie woke early the next morning, determined to go at the job search with fresh eyes. Jillian was already gone to work, but she'd left a note stuck to Nat's bedroom door.

You HAVE to watch the show!

She crumpled the paper and carried it to the kitchen to toss in the trash. Another note was stuck to the coffee maker.

No joke. You have to see it. It's good.

She threw that one away too. After starting the coffee maker, she went to the living room with her notebook. She began with the notes she and Jillian made the previous night. She had a list of skills and qualifications that would take her beyond a library.

Opening her laptop so she could revise her résumé, she found yet another note.

Go watch now!!

Natalie sighed as she removed the sticky note. Ignoring Jillian's notes, she opened her résumé and began copying and pasting the sections that would be good for other jobs. By the time the coffee finished brewing, she had the beginnings of three different résumés. After finishing her first cup, they were ready to print.

For the first time since being fired from Wells Academy, she felt focused. She had a mission. Scrolling to various job boards, she began the tedious process of searching and applying. Three hours later, her phone bleeped with a text.

I know you're not watching because you haven't called. STOP whatever you're doing and watch the damn show.

Jillian was persistent; Nat would give her that. She considered watching, but she was in a groove for job hunting and didn't want to lose her momentum. The show wasn't going anywhere.

Late in the afternoon, her brain was fried. She'd applied for twenty jobs. Her back ached, and her fingers were numb from all the typing.

She stood and stretched. Needing a break, she figured now was as good a time as any to see what Jillian was fussing about. She'd turn the show on, see how horrible it was, and then Jillian would leave her alone.

After refilling her coffee, she curled up on the couch with the remote in her hand. She stared at the black TV screen, hesitant to push the button. "God, Natalie, stop being a wimp. It's just a stupid show."

She clicked the remote and cradled her coffee. The show opened with scenes from previous episodes. Thankfully, none of the clips were of her acting like an idiot. Then the new episode began with a voiceover. Mac narrated.

What the hell? No one asked her to do any voiceovers. Yet another way the cards had been stacked against her. As her anger began to bubble, she focused on what Mac was saying.

"As we embarked on this journey to help three women find love, as competitors, Gem and I had a rough beginning."

The scene opened with their first argument about the clients in the studio's hallway. Then it showed Mac's first meet-and-greet when Nat had snuck in and they argued. She'd forgotten about that footage. That's when Brad said he'd wanted them to fight more.

Mac's voice continued, "However, no one expected us to foster a relationship."

The scene shifted to the night at the bar when she taught Jennifer how to pick up a man. Nat saw the spark between them, even though they were talking across the table. Then Mac leaned in and said something. Nat saw the blush creep up her cheeks. She remembered Mac talking about how correcting her wouldn't get him off.

An odd kind of flirtation they'd had back then. Nat smiled. They were both so obviously fighting the attraction. She had no idea they'd gotten them on film. The cameras were supposed to be following the clients.

The show went on to show the clients going on their first dates. Jillian and Mac had been right; the show was much better than it had been last week. She relaxed a little as she watched. It felt weird watching the women on dates as if she hadn't been there witnessing the whole thing.

Mac's voice began another voiceover. "The more time we spent together, the more we realized we shared more than contention. There was attraction."

The camera shot showed a dark hallway. Oh crap. It was the night Ashley met Chef Antonio. That was the hallway where she and Mac kissed briefly thinking no one would see. Damn. Those cameramen were good.

Natalie began to wonder if Brad had suspected she and Mac had begun dating. Why else would the cameramen have followed them?

Although they were nothing more than silhouettes in the dark hall, the moment they shared was pretty freaking hot.

Their bodies close, brushing slowly. A brief kiss before Nat pressed a hand to his chest, not really pushing him away. His body leaning in, touching everywhere as they whispered. Nat didn't think it was her memory washing over her. Objectively, she watched the couple on screen and it was hot.

Her heartbeat picked up. The whole world knew she and Mac had a fling. How did he think this would make things better for her? Now instead of people just thinking she was incompetent, they thought she was incompetent and slept with her co-worker.

She was pissed that he'd opened their personal business to the world. This was private. It was just supposed to be between them.

Her phone vibrated. Another text from Jillian.

Well? What do you think?

Nat glanced around the room. She was beginning to think Jillian had cameras posted so she could spy.

I think I'm going to kill him.

Why?

He let the world know we were dating.

How many episodes have you watched?

The first just finished.

Keep going. It only gets better. I couldn't stop. Best all-nighter I've ever pulled.

Nat couldn't believe Jillian had given up a night of sleep for this. She texted back. *Your love life is in a sadder state than mine if this was the best way to spend a night without sleep.*

Just wait. She responded.

The next episode began automatically. Nat's coffee grew cold on the table as she fell into following a story she already knew the ending to. The clients went on dates and had sessions with her and Mac. She heard herself giving them advice and knew she'd done right by her clients. She knew what she was doing even though she hadn't grown up in a matchmaking business.

Gail had been right; she did like to help people.

Woven between the stories of Jennifer, Ashley, and Melissa was the story of her and Mac. While she wanted to be angry with him for exposing everything she'd specifically said she wanted to keep private, as a viewer, she was falling in love.

Although the clients' dates and sessions were shown in chronological order, the snippets and scenes of her and Mac were mixed up. Not that it mattered. Whoever pieced this together was a master storyteller.

After the fourth episode, she called Mac. It had barely rung twice when he answered, almost as if he'd been sitting there waiting on her call.

"Hi."

"How could you tell Brad about us? You had them use every private moment they could find to show our relationship to the world."

"I wanted to show the world the real you. You didn't deserve the mess Brad made in the first half of the season."

"So instead I look like the trampy girl who slept with her co-worker."

"No, you don't. No one sees you like that."

"How would you know?"

"Because the episodes aired last night and the reviews are pouring in. Brad is thrilled."

"Good for fucking Brad. That doesn't change the fact that you knew I wanted to keep this private and you ignored what I wanted. Again."

He let out a sigh. "Have you watched all the episodes?"

"More than half."

"Keep watching. If you're still mad at the end, you can punch me on camera tomorrow."

"You might lose your man card if a girl knocks you on your ass."

"If it fixes us, it would be well worth it."

She smiled in spite of herself.

"It's really good, Natalie. I don't regret it. I want the world to know how much I love you. There's no reason to keep it a secret."

Her throat tightened. She wanted to be mad, but she was tired of being mad at him. He knew what to say to make her feel better. And she missed him.

When she didn't say anything and they were just listening to each other breathe, he finally said, "Finish the show. We'll talk tomorrow."

She disconnected and realized that she'd missed the opening of the next episode. She let it run while she grabbed her laptop. Closing out all her open job-related windows, she navigated to her browser and searched for reviews. While Melissa and Jennifer went on dates on her TV, Natalie read the reviews about the new batch of episodes. Everyone was raving. They loved the backdrop of the behind-the-scenes love story.

Many commented on how poorly the first episodes portrayed her. They clamored for the live finale. People wanted to see her and Mac back together.

Back together? Had he also revealed she left him after the premier?

She closed the laptop and returned her attention to the TV. Jillian came in at some point and sat beside her, saying nothing. As the last episode wrapped up, she once again felt like a fool. Mac stared into the camera and spoke. She felt like it was a personal message to her.

"Regardless of how this competition turns out, I have no regrets. This journey taught me about my work and myself. And I have Gem to thank. She turned my life upside down in the best possible ways. While I spent weeks trying to help my clients find the person they want to spend the rest of their lives with, I accidentally found mine."

In that moment, she knew how badly she'd screwed up. She kept pushing him away, when what she needed was to go to him, to work together to build what they'd started. Now she just needed to make it up to him.

～

MAC PACED THROUGH THE STUDIO. HE'D BEEN WATCHING FOR Natalie, but she hadn't arrived yet. After her call last night, he thought for sure he would've heard from her before the show. Melissa, Jennifer, and Ashley were all on stage. The men they'd been dating sat nearby until they were asked to join the women.

Brad and Mike were huddled together in quiet discussion, so Mac interrupted. "Have you from Gem?"

Brad didn't even look up from the clipboard Mike was showing him. "She's in hair and makeup now. We start in five. Get in position."

"I need to talk to her."

Now Brad met his eyes. "She specifically asked to be left alone until we're ready to start."

Shit. "Did she seem upset?"

Mike chuckled. Another bad sign.

Brad answered, "Yeah, she's pissy. Laid into me about how the first half of the season looks. Let me know the only reason she was here today was to fulfill her contractual obligation."

Mike chuckled again. "Then she pretty much said we could all go fuck ourselves."

Brad shook his head, as if he didn't want that tidbit shared.

Mac didn't know how to interpret that. Was she just angry with Brad? Was she ready to make up with him? If so, why not call him?

Mike ushered him toward the stage. They had chairs set up for him and Natalie to sit in until they needed to go on stage. Brad hired a host to conduct the interviews. Tyler was going to spend the bulk of the time with the clients talking about and dissecting their experiences before asking them to choose who was the better matchmaker.

The filming started and Natalie still hadn't emerged from the dressing room. Dread filled him. He pulled his phone out and texted her. *Everything all right?*

Definitely. Just explaining to the hair and makeup people that they don't get to decide how I look.

Hmmm…She didn't sound upset at all. *Do I need to brace for a punch?*

No.

Nothing else. No further comment. No sign telling him she was happy with what she'd seen last night. It was killing him. On stage, Tyler went down the line and asked the women what they enjoyed about the experience and if they had any regrets. He brought Ashley's and Melissa's boyfriends out to talk about being part of the show. They were all happy about the outcome. They felt like it had been a worthy experience.

He had no doubt Ashley would vote for Natalie to win and he was pretty confident Melissa was firmly in his corner. Jennifer was a wild card. Mac briefly wondered if Brad had put her up to that. She had continued to date both David and the man she met during the game night Natalie had taken her to. The woman hadn't hinted she was ready to move forward with either man.

And when he considered the online audience, he had no way to guess where the votes would fall. Winning didn't matter any more. His mother had accepted his involvement in Everyday Love. She loved what he'd accomplished on the show.

At least if Natalie won, the prize money would give her some breathing room and they could hopefully get back on track.

Finally Natalie strode across the studio. He glanced over his shoulder and was struck by how much he'd missed her. His next thought was that she looked like Natalie, not Gem. He looked her up and down and raised his eyebrows. She offered him a soft smile as she slid onto the chair beside him.

He opened his mouth to whisper to her, but Tyler introduced them. Mac knew she planned it like this. She didn't want to be alone with him. That couldn't be good. As they walked to the stage, his mind raced to think of ways to convince her they needed to be together. He didn't know how else to tell her he loved her.

Why couldn't that be enough?

"Gem, Malcolm, how are you?" Tyler asked.

"Good," Natalie said.

Mac nodded.

Tyler pointed at Natalie. "Gem, this is certainly a new look for you."

Natalie smoothed a hand over her skirt. "Actually, this is a normal look for me. Gem, my alter ego has a slightly different style." She paused with a smile that would stun any man in a fifty-foot radius.

Tyler's eyes locked on Natalie's and Mac struggled not to say anything.

Their host continued, "I know I'm supposed to ask about your journey and what you think about your clients' choices when it came to dating, but I'm going to ask what the audience really wants to know." He leaned an elbow on the armrest of his chair and leaned closer to Natalie. "Give us the scoop on the two of you."

She cocked and eyebrow and asked, "What do you want to know?"

"When and how did it start?"

She slowly licked her lower lip and then smiled. "Hmm…" She turned her face slightly toward Mac. "That's a tough one, don't you think? It kind of evolved slowly."

Mac smiled back at her. "If I remember correctly, you flirted with me the first time we met."

She huffed. "We hadn't met yet. You were just some guy standing in the lobby. Once I actually met you…well, you weren't quite as appealing."

Everyone on stage snickered. She was toying with him and he let her.

Tyler cut in. "You're opinion must've been swayed again at some point."

Natalie nodded and her face softened. "He's actually a nice guy. Like genuinely thoughtful. For example, when I had gotten sick early on in filming, he brought me soup."

"And?"

She blinked, pretending not to know Tyler was digging for details. "The soup helped me feel better."

Mac touched her bare leg, which got her attention. "I think Tyler is asking the details of when we moved from being colleagues and friends to more." He let his hand linger on her leg, just above her knee, nothing inappropriate, but he needed that simple contact. "I'm pretty sure it was when I kissed you in the producer's office."

"That sounds interesting. Tell us about it, Gem," Tyler was eating this up.

Natalie patted Mac's hand. For the first time, she looked directly into his eyes. "I think that was moments after I accused you of being too afraid to make a move."

"Yes, yes it was." He didn't want to look away. In one glance he wanted to convey his love for her.

"You certainly proved me wrong that day."

The entire studio was silent. Natalie inhaled deeply, smiled at Mac, and then turned back to Tyler. "It's been a heck of a journey for me too. I wasn't looking for love. I just needed the paycheck. Hell, I signed on for this not even quite sure if I believed in true love forever. Mac's good. He made a believer out of me."

The clients all sighed with a collective "aww."

"I fought the reality of our relationship. I played it like Mac was nothing more than a fling, a guy I could pick up and toss aside. But from the beginning, I was lying to myself." She took his hand. Something hard pressed into his palm, but she held tight. Looking toward their clients, she said, "I'm happy for you and I hope I was able to teach you or help you in some way, but it doesn't really matter to me how this competition turns out. I'm the real winner here."

Tyler took over again, but Mac couldn't hear a word the man said. Mac couldn't take his attention away from Natalie. If he understood everything she'd just said, they were okay. She was coming back to him.

Mac's heart lifted and when Tyler announced how people could vote and when the results would be posted, Mike called it a wrap.

Mac pulled Natalie to stand because he couldn't bear the thought of not having her in his arms again. He tugged at their connected hands. "What is this?"

When she released his hand, he was left with a little rock. That explained the painful dig in his palm. He looked at Natalie for an explanation.

"It's the most perfect pebble I could find. I'm hoping you'll accept it."

Here she was, the beautiful, brilliant woman—his woman

— in front of an audience, telling him she was in this with him forever. "I love you." He dropped the stone in his pocket.

"I love you too."

Without waiting for an invitation, he pulled her flush against his body and kissed her. Cheers erupted behind them, but they didn't lift their heads. He'd missed her too much. This was the first of many, many kisses.

A month later, Natalie strode down the hallway of Everyday Love on her way to Mac's office. Most of the fervor of the show had died, but business was still booming for the matchmakers. She tapped on the office door, but didn't wait for a response before swinging it open.

"Really," Gail huffed. "What is it with the two of you rushing into a room before being invited?"

"Good morning to you, too, Gail," Natalie responded with a smile. Normally, she would've waited for Mac to invite her in, but she knew Gail was in his office. She also knew simply walking in would bother Gail.

She plopped on the chair beside Gail, across from Mac's desk. Mac looked up from his computer screen and smiled.

"So what's with the pow-wow?" Nat asked. She'd been working for Everyday Love for the past few weeks. Her job search was on hold because the popularity of the show skyrocketed after the second half of the season aired along with the finale. People couldn't seem to get enough of her and Mac.

So in lieu of searching for a new job, she agreed to help

out at Everyday Love as a consultant. And she was enjoying herself more than she thought possible. She spent her days researching places for clients to go on dates. She researched and cross-referenced client data.

Mac and Gail did their thing, she did hers. And every night, she went home with Mac. They'd moved in together into his condo, but they'd talked about buying their own place.

"I asked to speak with the you and Malcolm together."

Natalie smiled. She understood why Mac had been so bothered by her not using his nickname earlier. The only person who called him Malcolm was Gail. Nat folded her hands in her lap and waited patiently.

"As you're both aware, I've been considering cutting back my hours and work schedule to ease into retirement."

"Mom, you don't have to ease into anything. I have this handled. Go enjoy your life."

Gail shook her head. "I do enjoy my life, Malcolm. I'm just getting old enough that I move a bit slower. I love every minute I spend here. But it's time to move on."

Nat leaned forward. "This sounds like a conversation you should be having with Mac. This is your business and your family."

Gail turned to look at her, one eyebrow arched regally as if to ask how dare Nat interrupt. But Natalie knew better. She had in fact, gotten a few martinis in Gail one night when the woman apologized for trying to sabotage Natalie on *Love Match*. Gail loved two things dearly and would fight to the death for either of them: Malcolm and Everyday Love.

"You are part of this family now. Regardless of whether my son gets off his keester and makes an honest woman out of you."

"Mom," Mac said at the same time Nat said, "Gail."

Gail waved a hand. "Hush, now. This is my moment." She

sat straighter and looked back and forth between Nat and Mac. "I want the two of you to take over full-time operations of Everyday Love."

"What?" Nat asked quietly.

If Gail heard her, she made no mention. She continued to speak. "You can bring the company into the twenty-first century. You understand people more than I give you credit for, Malcolm. And Natalie." She shifted her body to fully face Nat. "The ideas you bring to the table are amazing. And it's no small matter that you keep him in check. You call him out when he's being an ass."

Natalie couldn't hold back the laugh this time. Gail reached over and patted Nat's hand. "I had to do the same with his father. The man was brilliant in so many ways, but sometimes, the most obvious thing would fly right past him."

"I appreciate the offer, Gail, but this is your company. I'm working here temporarily. I don't know what I'll be doing in a month or a year from now. This is your legacy and it belongs to Mac."

"No one knows what the future holds, dear. But you can make a commitment. I'm asking you to join us permanently."

Nat's heart picked up. She hadn't thought about this being permanent. Mac had avoided all conversation regarding her leaving and looking for a different job. She knew he liked having her there. But it was a Sterling family company. It wasn't hers.

Mac stood and came from around his desk. "Can we have a few minutes alone, Mom? I think Natalie and I need to talk."

Gail left without a word, the door clicking closed quietly behind her. Mac took the seat his mother had vacated.

"I don't know what she's thinking, Mac. This should be your company. I didn't belong here for this."

"You belong here all the time."

His words carried a lot meaning. He wasn't just talking about this meeting with his mother, and Nat knew it.

"As usual, my mother is meddling in my life. She can't help herself."

Natalie smiled. "I kind of like that about her. Except, of course, when she's working against me."

"I don't think you have to worry about that ever again." He shifted forward and took her hand in his. "That meeting was her way of nudging me along."

"Nudging you for what? You've done everything she's asked for in regard to this company. You shouldn't have to keep proving yourself."

Mac's smile filled his face. "I love that you'll defend me even when it's unnecessary."

"That's what we do for each other, right?"

"Definitely." He took a deep breath. "My mother was pushing me to do this now."

He slid from his chair and knelt in front of her, holding out a jewelry box. Natalie's eyes filled with tears.

"I've been carrying this damn ring around with me for weeks. I planned to propose during the finale, but my mother warned that you would hate having such a private moment shared with the world."

Natalie choked out a laugh. "You're mom is really smart."

"It took all my strength not to slip the ring on your finger as soon as you gave me the pebble." He reached into his pocket and produced the rock she'd given him.

"You didn't have to keep it, you know. It was symbolic."

"This will always be with me. This means more than any ring. This is your promise to me." He took the diamond ring from its case. Pushing it on her finger, he said, "And this is my promise to you."

Natalie blinked to try to stem the flow of tears. "Hey,

you're jumping the gun there. Aren't you supposed to ask before you do that?"

Taking her face in his hands, wiping away the tears that had fallen, Mac looked into her eyes. "Natalie Hale, will you please do me the honor of being my perfect penguin and wife?"

Natalie jumped from the chair and into his arms, kissing his whole face. "Of course I will. I love you."

"I love you too." He kissed her in the way that told her she was the only one for him. Then he brought them to their feet and called out, "You can come back in now."

The door eased open and Gail popped her head through the opening. "She said yes?"

Natalie laughed again. "Was there a doubt?"

Gail smirked. "With him, you never know." She came into the office with a bottle of champagne. They spent the rest of the afternoon talking about love.

The forever kind.

IT TAKES A THIEF

EXCERPT

*D*ecember

Jared waved at the doorman as he made his way to the elevator. He spent enough time here that no one expected him to sign in. When Mia first moved in, they stopped him every time, worried that he was an overbearing lover. The thought still made him cringe. Explaining that they were cousins gave him a pass to go up to her apartment without question.

When the door swung open, Mia looked surprised to see him. "What are you doing here?"

"Happy birthday." He bent and kissed her cheek. "Did you think I would let you spend your thirtieth alone?"

"Who says I plan to be alone?"

He glanced around the empty room, taking note of the open bottle of wine on the table and single glass beside it, and raised an eyebrow. The woman had lived barely above hermit status for years. She worked, spent time with her mother, and came home to a tastefully and artfully decorated condo. Alone. She'd been gun-shy ever since her engagement ended in a very public humiliation. Her face was free of makeup and she had her thick black hair tied back. She wouldn't let a new man see her bedtime routine, even though she still looked regal. Mia was like her mother in that way.

She huffed. "Fine. So I'm alone. I have things to do. Plans to make."

He took off his coat and hung it on the rack. Then he turned and handed Mia a wrapped gift.

"You know you didn't have to get me anything."

"Until you find some guy that will spoil you, I reserve the right. Everyone should have a gift on their birthday."

She tugged at the ribbon and slid her finger under the tape.

"Hey, you know you don't have to save the paper, right?"

"Leave me alone."

It was the same exchange they had every year, at her birthday and at Christmas. Mia was meticulous in her approach to everything. Jared preferred to dive in.

Moments later, she held up the thin diamond bracelet. "It's beautiful. Thank you."

She placed it back in the box and went to the liquor cabinet. After she handed him a glass, they settled on the couch in front of the marble fireplace where a fire burned.

He picked up the open bottle and poured himself some white wine. "Are you slumming today? Since when you do you drink regular wine? No vintage Dom for your birthday?"

"There is nothing regular about Domaine Leflaive, thank you very much."

"So what has you so busy you're not celebrating with a party?"

She sniffed. "As if. That's the last thing I would do."

He set his glass on the table without drinking any. "I thought things had gotten better for you. You've been making the society circuit again."

Their fathers' crimes had taken a toll on Mia and he

wished he could do something to repair the damage done. Both her mother and his felt like pariahs in the society they'd been a part of long before they'd gotten married. In his personal life, he hadn't taken a hit, mostly because he was a man. Professionally, however, his dreams had been crushed.

"I've been to functions and other than the occasional whisper by the same catty trolls I've dealt with my whole life, it has been better. But no big celebrations with me in the spotlight."

"Other than sitting around in your pajamas and drinking alone, what are you doing?" He picked up his glass and drank the wine, even though he'd prefer whiskey.

She reached across the table and flipped open a file folder. He knew immediately what it was. The faces of men they'd grown up around, men who were their fathers' confidants and friends. "You're really doing this?"

Years ago Mia had come to him with a plan to get back at the men who'd gotten rich with their fathers by bilking innocent people out of their life savings. She couldn't go after her own father or his because they'd fled the country. But she wanted to do something proactive.

"Did you think I was kidding? You should know better."

"I do. Part of me hoped it was a whim you'd plan out and never act on."

She laughed. "I would never waste my time. And now that I'm thirty, I have the funds to put everything in play."

Their mothers were smart women. They'd made their husbands sign prenups, which protected the Washington family fortune. Mia's and Jared's inheritances were safe from the federal government. Their mothers also made sure the money wouldn't be wasted on immature whims, so they had to wait until their thirtieth birthdays to access the money.

"Let me help."

"It's dangerous. If I get caught, I don't want you going down with me."

That had always been her argument every time they discussed this. "Then we won't get caught. Wait until my birthday. I'll be able to foot half the bill for the plan."

"I've already waited five years."

"Then six more months won't matter." He was well aware of how long it had been. He'd just graduated law school and all of his plans and dreams had been sucked into the black hole of his father's dirty deeds. Who the hell would hire the spawn of a criminal? "It'll give us time to find the right people to carry this out."

She sipped her wine and studied him. His offer intrigued her, but Mia was not someone who liked to give up control.

"I can be very useful. I have connections you'll need and have no idea how to get." Once his law career had gone down the drain, he'd taken all the tools his father had instilled in him, and he'd learned to play in all the gray areas of the world. And he was damn good at it.

He'd embraced their fathers' teachings about business and people. While Mia had bucked against the lessons in manipulation, he'd made a career from it.

"I don't want to use people who know us, who we are. Word will spread and our anonymity will be lost."

"You should know better," he said, throwing her own words back at her. "The players I know on the dark web never reveal their identities. It's a given that we all use aliases."

She sipped more wine. "All right, then. Let's talk about who we'll need. A thief, obviously."

"A hacker, someone who can get past security systems." Immediately he thought of Data. He'd used her services many times over the last few years. Efficient and relatively cheap. "I have someone I can reach out to when the time is right."

Mia crossed the room and returned with a small notebook and pen. She made a few notes. "I've been looking for a forger, but I haven't found anyone I like."

It figured she would start with the forger. Art was her area of comfort.

He chuckled. "You don't have to like them."

"I'm aware. I meant I don't like the quality of their work in conjunction with their attitudes. It's as if making a forgery isn't enough. They want to make it better."

"I'll put some feelers out for a thief while you continue to hunt for a forger." He leaned back on the couch and drank the rest of his wine.

She paused in taking notes, tapping her pen on the pad. "What about selling the artwork once we have it?"

"I can definitely find buyers."

Her jaw muscle pulsed. It was a small twitch, but he knew his cousin. He leaned forward, resting his elbows on his knees. "Is there a problem?"

"It suddenly feels like you're taking over. I've spent years gathering information and planning this, and now you walk in and want to handle all of the active pieces."

He sighed and shook his head slightly. "We each have a skill set. You've utilized yours masterminding this plan. Let me use mine to help you carry it out."

She didn't seem convinced. He reached over and laid a hand over hers. "This is my legacy, too."

Sometimes it seemed like she forgot he shared the same guilt she felt.

"Fine. But I make all final decisions. This is what I have so far." Spreading the images from the folder across the coffee table, she ticked off the list of twelve—men who not only aided and abetted their fathers, but who also got rich off the same scheme.

"How do you see this working?" he asked.

"I'm still developing the list of artwork they have. We'll only get one shot, so I want to choose the piece from each of them that will hurt. I'll commission a forgery. Then the thief goes in, swaps the forgery for the original and we sell the original."

"And then?"

"We use the money to make some reparations for what they did. We might not be able to repay every family, but we can make a difference."

He smiled. That was the cousin he knew—all cold steel on the outside but a soft, mushy center. "And how do you decide who gets the money?"

"I haven't figured that piece out yet. I have a list of names, people who came forward and publicly criticized our fathers for what they did. That is one way you can help. They can't know it's coming from us and you can dig around and see who needs the most help. Prioritize who needs what."

Jared nodded and considered who he could have do background checks on the victims. He picked up Mia's notebook and saw a list on the inside cover. It took a minute, but he recognized the lessons. Their fathers had said these mantras as if they were motivational quotes:

1. Spending money to get the best is worth it 99% of the time.

2. Endearing yourself to others makes it easier to manipulate them.

3. Loyalty to the right people is vital to success.

He'd assumed that Mia had never paid attention to the rules for business. She'd been an art history major, after all. She preferred the pretty things in life over the gritty side of making money.

He pointed at the list. "Why have this here?"

"Because I plan to use their life lessons against them." She splayed her hands across the photos. "I'm going to teach all of them—including our fathers—Mama's lesson: actions carry consequences."

Karma might be a bitch, but it had nothing on Mia. This summer was going to be interesting.

*

Green: I know it's the holidays, but are you available?

Data: I'm always available for you.

As soon as she hit send, she cringed.

Green: Interesting. I hadn't realized we'd arrived at that point in our relationship.

Data: I'm available for WORK. You know what I meant.

Green: Hmm…I think it might've been a Freudian slip.

Data: And I think your ego is too big. What kind of job?

Green: I'll send you photos. I need you to dig up some dirt.

Data: Oooo…Blackmail. Intriguing.

Green: I said nothing about blackmail.

Data: It was in the subtext. I read between the lines.

Green: It's all right for you to read between the lines but I'm not allowed?

Data: Glad we're clear. :-)

She waited for the link to pop up and scanned the information he sent.

Data: What's your timeline?

Green: Soon. But given the holidays, I can wait the week.

Data: Got it. I'll let you know when I have info.

Audrey closed her laptop with a smile. Things usually quieted down for her over the holidays. She was grateful to have anything pop up, and the fact that Mr. Green had a job was all the better. The man always paid well, and at this point, she needed every penny she could get. After shoving her computer in her bag, she bundled up against the cold for her walk to the bus stop.

Before leaving the apartment, she glanced at her bedroom door. She'd been living here with Misty for almost three months, but over the last couple of weeks, she'd had the feeling that her room wasn't secure. Misty said she hadn't stepped foot in the room since Audrey moved in, but her roommate often had guests. The sleazy kind she brought home from her job at the strip club.

Her equipment was all she had of value and most of Misty's "dates" wouldn't have a clue what to do with any of it; she just didn't want creepy guys touching her stuff, so until she came up with a better lock, she carried her laptop with her. She patted her pocket to double-check that her present for Gram was still there. This was their first Christmas apart. Not really apart, but not living together. Three months ago she'd made the painful decision to sell everything she had and pour every penny into getting Gram the care she needed.

Audrey couldn't take care of her anymore.

The assisted living facility cost more than Audrey made, but Gram deserved the best care possible. So here she was on Christmas Eve trekking on the bus in twenty-degree weather to share Christmas with Gram. The dark sky made it feel closer to midnight than dinnertime.

Horizons looked like any other residence on the outside. Kind of stately but bland. Inside, they at least put in some effort to be festive. They had a Christmas tree in the corner of the lobby as well as a menorah on the reception desk. Audrey signed in without chatting with the receptionist and went straight to Gram's room.

Room. That was funny. Gram actually had more of an apartment than she did. Gram's place had a small kitchen as well as a living room–bedroom combo. Gram answered the door.

"Audrey? What are you doing here?"

"Hi, Gram. How are you? I thought we'd spend Christmas Eve together like we do every year."

"I don't know that I'm done being mad at you for sticking me here," Gram said as she walked away from the door.

Audrey took it as an invitation. She unwrapped her scarf and laid her jacket and bag on a side table near the door. Pulling the gift out, she said, "I brought you a gift."

"Pfft. Hope you weren't counting on anything. I'm like a prisoner here. I couldn't go shopping." She settled in her recliner facing the TV.

"They told me they do trips to the mall." In all likelihood, Gram had probably forgotten. That had been happening more and more. "Here."

She accepted the small package and peeled at the paper. It wasn't much, but Audrey had chosen a box of Gram's favorite chocolates, ones Gram typically only indulged in for special occasions. The doctor had said that small reminders might help prompt her memory.

"What's this?" She studied the box for a minute and then practically threw it at the table beside her. "I hate chocolate. Makes me sick."

"No, it doesn't, Gram. Remember? These are the ones filled with booze. They're your favorite."

She sniffed, a look of irritation on her face. "I never drink."

Audrey sighed and sat on the edge of the loveseat. So much for holidays with family. They fell into silence, except for the blaring of the TV showing reruns of General Hospital. Audrey longed to talk with Gram like they used to do.

Gram suddenly turned and looked at her. "Tina? What the hell are you doing here? I told you to stay away."

"Gram, it's me, Audrey."

Gram rose and jabbed a finger at her. "Don't you lie to me. Get out!"

Audrey's throat closed. This was why she'd been forced to bring Gram here. There had been more days of confusion than reality. Audrey missed Gram.

"Have a good Christmas," she said quietly as she picked up her jacket and bag and left.

On the bus ride back home, she swallowed tears. She'd believed she'd have more time with Gram. Being alone had never really bothered Audrey, but losing Gram was unfathomable.

She let herself into the apartment and stepped over three pairs of sky-high heels that Misty typically tossed when she walked through the door. A smudged mirror sat on the coffee table, alerting her to the fact that partying had been happening in her absence. Misty must've celebrated the holiday before going in to work.

She went straight to her bedroom. Burying herself in work was just the antidote for her abysmal thoughts. Mr. Green had given her a job, so that was where she would focus her energy. Spending the night digging into someone else's misery made her feel better about her own circumstances.

It didn't take long at all. Seven hours later, she had a dossier of dirt for her client. With it being almost three in the morning, she debated whether she should send it now or wait. It was officially Christmas, so would it be rude to interrupt his holiday? No, he was the kind of guy who worked around the clock. She didn't know how she knew that, but she did.

Data: I have a Christmas present for you.

She immediately rethought the message because the dude might not even be Christian. If he was Jewish would he be offended that she'd made the assumption? She sent the link to the file and set her laptop on the bed next to her with the intention of logging off for the night. But a message immediately bleeped at her.

Green: You work fast. I appreciate that.

Data: Don't you sleep?

Green: Of course. Do you?

Data: Sometimes

Green: Alone?

Audrey snickered. Where the hell did this guy get off asking if she slept alone?

Data: Sometimes. You?

Green: Sleeping? Always.

Hmm…Mr. Green was letting her know he was a player. She shouldn't care, but this was the most personal they'd ever gotten.

Data: Kind of a sad comment on your life. Not only do you always sleep alone but you're working on Christmas Eve.

Green: The same can be said of you.

Data: I'm just fulfilling the stereotypical image of a hacker sitting alone in a dark room playing with my gadgets.

Green: Oh, to be one of those gadgets.

She burst out laughing and she couldn't stop.

Misty suddenly pounded on her door but didn't wait for a response before swinging it open. "Are you okay?"

Audrey gulped air and swiped at the tears on her cheeks. "I'm fine."

"Damn, girl. You're always so quiet that when I heard the noise, I thought you were having a seizure." Misty placed a hand over her heart as if to calm it. She must've just gotten home from work. Although the baby pink hoodie and sweatpants might appear to be workout clothes, Audrey knew that was Misty's to-and-from-work outfit.

"I'm fine. Just laughing over something that probably shouldn't even be that funny."

"Okay." She turned, her overly teased and sprayed red hair looking like a cloud around her head.

"Thanks for checking on me." It's good to know that if I die in this crappy room someone would notice. Her computer bleeped again.

Green: I'm sorry. Did I offend you?

Data: Not at all. I was laughing so hard my roommate felt the need to check on me.

Green: That's good then. Have an excellent evening.

Data: It's closer to morning.

Green: Not for people like us.

A few minutes later, she received notification of payment. If Mr. Green kept her busy like this, paying for Gram's care wouldn't be too bad. She opened the payment email. Mr. Green included a note in the memo.

Get yourself a nice new gadget and think of me.

While there was no new gadget in her budget, thoughts of him would be hard to ignore.

To keep up to date with the Counterfeit Capers, sign up for Sloane's newsletter: https://www.subscribepage.com/sloanesteele

Or visit her web site: www.SloaneSteele.com

ACKNOWLEDGMENTS

Every book is a labor of love. Although I spend hours sitting in front of my computer creating the stories, I doubt I ever would've published if not for the support of the members of Chicago-North RWA and my friends at the Sunday night Panera supper club. You guys rock!

And to all of the bloggers and reviewers and the readers out there who continue to read my words, Thank You!

ABOUT THE AUTHOR

Shannyn Schroeder is the author of the O'Leary series and the For Your Love Series - contemporary romances centered around large Irish-American families in Chicago. She also authors the Hot & Nerdy series about nerdy friends finding love. Look for her new series in 2021, Counterfeit Capers, where she will be writing under the name Sloane Steele.

www.ShannynSchroeder.com

<u>**Counterfeit Capers**</u>

It Takes a Thief

Between Two Thieves

To Catch a Thief

www.ingramcontent.com/pod-product-compliance
Lightning Source LLC
Chambersburg PA
CBHW011148190726
48288CB00010B/3231